Caught in the
Line of Fire

Enjoy,

A A Benton

Also by Art Burton

For Hire, Messenger of God
a murder mystery

Hobos I Have Known
a collection of short stories

Check out: users.eastlink.ca/~artburton

Caught in the Line of Fire

By Art Burton

Cover Photo by Flame

Order this book online at **www.trafford.com**
or email orders@trafford.com

Most Trafford titles are also available at major online book retailers.

Printed in the United States of America.

ISBN: 978-1-4269-7136-5 (sc)
ISBN: 978-1-4269-7137-2 (hc)
ISBN: 978-1-4269-7135-8 (e)

Library of Congress Control Number: 2011909982

Trafford rev. 06/14/2011

 www.trafford.com

North America & International
toll-free: 1 888 232 4444 (USA & Canada)
phone: 250 383 6864 ♦ fax: 812 355 4082

For Flame

ACKNOWLEDGEMENTS

WE LEARN FROM our mistakes, at least we are supposed to. The second most common thing I heard about my first book, *For Hire, Messenger of God*, was here is a list of the mistakes I found. That came after people told me how much they enjoyed the story. They eased into it. I thank you for pointing out these errors. Those of you who read that book know what I'm talking about. It was good and there were typos.

This time things will be different.

Jim Ettinger did the initial proofreading. He made some good catches and offered interesting suggestions about choices of hunting rifles and ammunition. Thanks, Jim.

I followed up on Jim's recommendations and then submitted the final product to an editor.

That can only be described as a humbling experience.

Several of you commented on the Canadian location for the last book. You will be pleased to note that this time around we have also gone with Canadian spelling throughout.

By we, I mean my editor, Bev Dauphinee and myself. Bev was a blessing. She raised the bar. She had me doing a lot of things differently, and by differently, I mean properly. It was fun. Let me know what you think.

Thanks to my wife, Flame, for her continued support, suggestions and for allowing me to drag her through the forest taking hundreds of pictures to find that perfect one for the cover.

Finally, I thank all of you who bought the last book and then encouraged me to release this one. Enjoy.

CHAPTER 1

CLIFFORD LAWRENCE SHIFTED his position, trying to find a little comfort. The small, canvas seat had been designed for someone with a smaller backside than the one attached to his 230 pound body. Despite the manufacturer's advertising claims that he could wait in ease for that trophy deer to appear, he was suffering from a severe case of numb bum. The chair registered its objections with a mournful creak every time he moved. From his perch ten feet above the edge of the chopping, he could see about two hundred yards to his left, his right and directly in front. He had been in this position for almost an hour and the only signs of wildlife to appear were three squirrels with their incessant chattering.

Surrounding the chopping were the blazing colours of an autumn Nova Scotia forest: vibrant scarlets of the red maples, shimmering yellows from the birches and the brilliant oranges of the sugar maples. Interspersed among these were the more subdued greens of a few rogue pines and spruces that had found a home in this hardwood grove. This should have been the ideal spot to find game. The undergrowth, denied by the forest canopy of the life-sustaining force of the sun, was virtually nonexistent. Any animal walking here would be clearly visible.

As Cliff adjusted his seating position, his eyes fell on his knapsack hanging on the branch beside him. Must be time for something to eat, he thought. He opened the front pouch and fished out a toasted, fried egg sandwich wrapped in Saran Wrap. He took off his shooting glove, struggled to find an edge and then freed this tasty treat. With his other hand, he pulled down the opening of the balaclava that was keeping the wind off his face. The overnight temperature had taken a late fall plunge. Kevin had assured him this downturn was a good thing. It would have the game moving about. With the wind blowing across the chopping towards him, his scent would not be picked up by the animals. Cliff was practically guaranteed a successful morning.

Kevin Barnhill owned the nearby hunting lodge. This particular tree stand was usually reserved for Kevin, himself. The previous night while they were sitting around the lodge, shooting the bull, Kevin detected that Cliff was getting a little discouraged by his string of unsuccessful hunts. He took it upon himself to change his friend's luck. Cliff's current location reflected Kevin's sacrifice.

Cliff noticed the gusting wind had died down to practically nothing. He debated with himself about removing the face covering but decided to wait a little while longer. This might just be a lull. A stiff breeze could resume at any moment. Being uncomfortable was bad enough; being cold as well would challenge his desire to continue this blood sport. He wasn't that dedicated to it.

Half of the sandwich disappeared into his mouth. Three chews and he swallowed. The second half vanished equally as quickly. He fumbled with the buttons of his jacket and pulled a whisky flask from inside. He looked at it wistfully wondering why he had let Kevin talk him into filling it with coffee instead of its normal alcoholic contents. Cautiously he took a swallow of the hot sugar-laden liquid. The warmth spread throughout his insides. It felt good. He left his jacket undone and replaced the flask. Then he stuffed the sandwich wrapper into a side pocket and scanned the clearing for some sign of game.

Now that the wind had finally died, he wouldn't have to worry about adjusting his aim to allow for any variations this quirk of nature would cause. He chuckled to himself: as if he had any idea about making adjustments for wind. All he did was point and shoot. His lack of success attested to his technique.

After a few minutes, his attention started to wander from the chopping to his knapsack. He knew another sandwich lurked there, calling to him. He resisted the urge. At this rate of activity, it was going to be a long morning. In the periphery of his vision, he saw something move.

His eyes snapped to the left. He strained to peer deeper into the distant forest. His .30-06 Remington rifle was half way to his shoulder, ready to spark into action. He could feel his heart rate increase and struggled to control his excitement. After holding this pose for a full minute, he relaxed and lowered the rifle to lie across his thighs again.

He raised Kevin's binoculars from around his neck up to his eyes. Instantly his vision was in among the distant trees. Slowly, he adjusted the magnification control until each individual leaf stood out like a pimple on prom night. He scanned the gently sloping perimeter for any signs of life. Nothing. He lowered the glasses to get his bearings again. The magnification was so great that he couldn't be sure he was looking in the right area. Satisfied as to where he should be searching, he brought the glasses back up.

"Jesus Christ," he yelled as he staggered back in his seat. He readjusted the binoculars. Staring back at him was what appeared to be the front of a huge telescope emerging from the dried yellow and brown leaves. Directly below that was the bore of a rifle. Seen through the field glasses, the black hole of the barrel appeared to be right in his face. An orange dot danced across the front of his shirt through the open blaze orange jacket and settled over his heart.

The shock was still registering in Cliff's mind when the barrel opening blossomed into a red flare. Everything slowed down for Cliff. He imagined he could see the projectile expanding in size as it came right at him. The bullet's journey was a mere half second. To Cliff, it was an eternity. Again, he leaned back in his seat as if this would allow him to slip under this incoming missile. The binoculars dropped from his face.

Before the glasses had reached his nose in their downward descent, an excruciating pain hammered him in the chest. He was lifted clear of the seat and tumbled backwards among the tree branches behind him. His arms windmilled as he floated to the ground, reaching for something to hold him up; finding nothing. With a heavy thud, life returned to normal speed. He slammed into the layer of humus and felt all the air from his lungs expelling through his open mouth. His binoculars, still fastened around his neck, jerked down and cracked across the bridge of his nose before ending up askew across his chest covering the hole where his life blood was seeping into his shirt. His jacket lay open on the ground around him. His rifle landed at his feet but did not go off from the force of the fall. Cliff was a cautious man. The safety was still on.

He tried to lift his head but movement was impossible. *I can't be dying,* he told himself, *my life is not flashing before my eyes.* He was wrong. There was no final life-reviewing video, simply blackness and then nothing. He hadn't even heard the killing shot.

A half-mile away his hunting companions, Victor Boyd and Kevin Barnhill, did hear the rifle report. "Hey, did you hear that? Sounds like Cliff got lucky," Victor said. "Only one shot."

Kevin laughed. "Must have. If the deer was still running, he'd still be shooting. He said this was his year." Inwardly, he felt a sense of pleasure. He loved it when a plan came together.

"He's been saying that for the entire time we've been hunting together," Victor scoffed. "I'll believe it when I see the deer hanging from a tree outside the lodge."

"True, but this year I gave him the best spot. Sounds like the son of a bitch came through. That clearing is where I always hunt when I come up here. Lot easier than plodding up and down these old woods roads."

Kevin lowered the butt of his rifle to the ground and leaned on the barrel. Despite the chill in the air, a sheen of perspiration shone on his forehead. "Now I know why I always opted for the comfort of the tree stand. This is like work. Usually I at least see some game from up there. Managing to shoot it is sometimes more of a challenge."

Victor nodded his understanding. He had yet to have his first kill. "I guess we should go and give him a hand."

"Hell, no. He's got his. Let's get ours."

Victor looked back towards the direction of the shot and shrugged. "You're right. If he gets one and we get skunked, we'll never hear the end of it." His words didn't carry much conviction.

He pulled a pack of cigarettes from his hunting jacket pocket and laughed. "Want a smoke?" he offered.

"Not while we're hunting." The suggestion was an affront to everything Kevin had read about hunting protocols. Then he looked over at the crumpled package in Victor's hand and smiled. "Bought those when you bought the jacket, didn't you?"

"Only get out once a year. Someone told me cigarette smoke would keep the bugs away. Remember how warm it was last year?"

Kevin grunted. "Everyone said it was global warming. We sure paid for it in January and February. Worst winter I can remember since back in the '60s."

The two men proceeded up the logging road, heads down, looking for fresh tracks. Their hope was that some game would walk out in front of them and surrender. Neither man felt confident enough in his abilities to risk leaving the rutted dirt road and getting lost. They had no delusions about their expertise in the great outdoors. Up ahead, a six-point buck stood in the ditch watching the approaching hunters. After a few seconds, it turned and bounded safely off into the forest, unseen.

Victor was the first to break the silence. "This is one heck of a setup you have here. Cliff tells me you won it in a poker game."

Kevin gave him a sideways glance. "I don't really like to talk about it."

Victor stopped. "That's not what Cliff says. He says I'm the only person he knows who hasn't heard the story at least once. He claims you stop people in the street to tell them about it."

Kevin laughed. "Cliff exaggerates. That's what makes him such a great salesman. We've been in business together for over ten years. I had a dream about building affordable houses that really met the needs of the buyers. Cliff brought in most of our initial investors to turn that dream into reality."

"You've succeeded. The houses practically sell themselves."

"They seem to, but we both know that's not true. Cliff tells me you're the best realtor in his company. Four years in a row in the million-dollar club? No wonder he brought you up here with him when he took a few days off. He's afraid you'll take over the company while he's gone."

"I've learned at the knee of a master. And let me tell you, I enjoy this break. It's like Cliff has given me permission to relax for a few days. No phones, no closing deadline hassles, no indecisive customers." Victor made a sweeping gesture with his arm. "And look at all this. You can't buy this kind of beauty. Let's face it, we can all afford to travel anywhere in the world, but why would we want to when we have this in our backyards."

He turned back to Kevin. He had heard the barebones version of how Kevin had acquired the cottage. Now, he wanted the intimate details. He wanted to be part of the in-crowd. "And you own this little piece of paradise," he said. "Tell me about the poker game."

Kevin was still looking around. His face showed the tranquility found in a Buddhist monk.

"It was a fluke really. The card game simply got out of control. We never played for these kinds of stakes, not even close.

" I think it was the hand that I had earlier in the evening that set it all up, two or three before the big one. I had a seven high."

Victor looked confused.

"You don't play poker, do you?"

Victor shook his head. "A little bit, but nothing for money. Cribbage, forty-fives, that's my limit. We used to play poker for matchsticks when I was a kid. I had a sheet of paper with the value of the hands on it. Every time I consulted it, everyone would fold." He laughed.

"You missed some great opportunities to bluff." Kevin made a dismissive gesture. Victor wasn't the kind to bluff. "Seven high is the worst poker hand you can have. It's like striking out every time at bat when you're playing baseball. Fumbling in your own end zone in football."

Victor's expression remained unchanged. "Failing to close the sale on a million-dollar house."

Victor's eyes finally lit up.

Kevin continued, slowly, as if talking to a child. "We always played dealers choice. That way no one could complain that their favourite game was overlooked. Alfred Putnum was dealing. His game of choice was five-stud. First card down, four up. He referred to it as real men's poker.

"My hand had the potential to build into a straight. Each card one up from the previous one." He looked at Victor for some acknowledgment. "Five in a row. Beats a pair, two pair, three of a kind. A fantastic hand in five-card-stud, but I never got the final card I needed to fill it in. Instead I ended up with a 2, 3, 4, 5 and 7, all of different suits. The seven was my hole card; the deuce, my final up card. The worst hand possible.

"I kept betting, hoping to fill in the straight. By the fifth card, there was myself, Derrick Watts and Alfred left betting. Alfred had a pair of aces showing. I had been winning throughout the night so I had a good size pile of money in front of me. I figured what the hell and made a pot sized bet. Derrick looked at Alfred's aces and then folded. We all expected Alfred to either raise or at least call. A pair of aces is a good hand in this game. He folded.

"I couldn't help myself. I flipped over my hole card. 'Seven high,' I yelled, 'world's worst hand' and maybe I did a little dance around the table. I don't remember."

Victor stated the obvious. "You won with the worst hand."

"Yes, Victor. Anyone who had stayed in would have beaten me. Some of the others laughed at the folly of the whole thing. Derrick Watts didn't. He looked at me and barked 'Deal.'"

Kevin turned serious. "Two or three hands later, the game had changed to seven-card stud. First two down, two up, one down and final two up. We bet on every card except the first two. I had a pair of eights in the hole with my first two cards. Derrick's first two up cards were aces. I had an eight and nine of hearts showing. My third hole card was the last eight. I had four-of-a-kind in the first five cards.

"I bet. Derrick raised. I re-raised. My sixth card was the six of hearts. Derrick got a king. The wild betting continued with everyone else dropping out after the third down card. My last card was a five of hearts. I don't remember what Derrick had. I looked like I could have a straight flush. That's the best hand possible. I knew that Jonathan Putnam had folded the seven of hearts. I was sure Derrick knew it too. I also knew that Alfred had folded an ace.

"I might have a straight or a flush but I was betting like I had the straight flush. Derrick was sure I was bluffing again. It looked like a replay of the previous hand. Me trying to fill a straight; him with aces showing. The betting got crazy. It was like we had both suddenly lost our rational minds. The next thing I knew there was a huge disarray of paper currency and coins in the centre of the table and perched on the top of it all were two sets of keys reflecting in the overhead lights.

"One set would fire up my brand new Jeep Commander parked outside the lodge. The other set unlocked the front door to the lodge itself. The game took place right up here. The room was so quiet you could hear the foam evaporating on your beer.

"The final bet, lodge against Jeep, was Derrick's idea but I was quick to go along. Too quick maybe. It was a stupid bet even though I knew I had the best hand. We just didn't play poker at that level. Up to then, fifty dollars was an extreme raise, a hundred and people thought you were crazy."

"What did he have?" Victor asked. Victor made more than a million dollars a year in commissions but even he understood that this had become about more than money.

"He goaded me a little before showing his cards. He looked over at Jonathan and said: 'Didn't I see you scrub the seven of hearts earlier?' Then he looked back at me and laughed. 'Nice bluff but a mere flush isn't going to cut it this time.' He flipped over his cards and displayed a full house–three aces over two kings. It was a pretty hand. His smile made the overhead lights look dim.

"I sat there for a few seconds without saying a word. I was letting him savor his moment in the sun. Some of the others were giving me sympathetic smiles. Then he screwed himself. He said 'I think I'll sell the Jeep. I already have a better vehicle.'"

"Up 'til then, I was debating with myself about actually taking ownership of the lodge. The idea seemed ludicrous at the time. That statement did it. I flipped over my three eights all at once. Derrick was slow to recognize what I had. I reached forward and slowly slid the fourth eight from the up cards back into line with its mates."

Kevin screwed up his face at the memory. "Then, I may not have been a good winner. I grabbed both sets of keys and jangled them together like cymbals. I let out a few war whoops and waved them in Derrick's face. Derrick said nothing. He kicked back his chair and stormed out of the room. We haven't been friends since."

Kevin took another look through the trees to see if any deer were lurking around. None jumped out and waved at him. He took on a philosophical look. "The calibre of both hands could have easily made them winners in a seven-card stud, nothing wild, game. Only one was. That's the way poker works. Like life, it's not always fair. Sometimes being good just isn't enough. That's why I cover all the angles in everything I do."

The two men lowered their heads again and searched for more tracks in the roadway.

A fourth companion, Josh Daniels, became a bit too intimate with his distant cousin, Jack, the night before. He was still snoring away in his bunk when the others left at the crack of dawn in the search for big game. Frying pans rattling, fridge doors slamming, coffee perking, none of these things had roused him from his deep slumber. Everyone had to take responsibility for their own actions. Drink too much, tough shit. Despite everyone's lack of concern, Josh slept through the breakfast preparations like a baby.

Only the big, rough hands hanging outside his blankets belied that image. Josh started out his working career as a carpenter. He spent more time with computers and calculators now, but hammers and saws were still his tools of choice. He was the contractor who built the houses that Kevin financed and that Cliff and Victor sold. He, too, hauled in his share of the big money.

He heard the door rattle and forced his eyes open to check his watch. The red digital numbers read 11:30. His eyelids resealed themselves. He couldn't remember the last time he had slept the morning away. He worked seven days a week during the building season. His day started at dawn and ended sometime shortly before the sun came back again. He had a full-time staff of about sixty men from all trades plus a contingent of day labourers as needed. It was his responsibility to make sure the electricians were there ahead of the drywallers, the plumbers ahead of the floorers and every task was completed before the keys were handed over to Kevin. By November, he both needed and deserved a break.

His headache was down to a dull thud. Somewhere around nine, he had crawled out to the kitchen and downed a handful of Aspirins and two bottles of spring water. He vaguely remembered burning some toast and eating a couple of bites of it. He didn't recall returning to bed. He must have sat down on the edge to put on his boots and just toppled back in. His mother had told him the body knew when it needed to rest. As always, she was right.

"Are you still in the sack you lazy son of a bitch?" Kevin's thundering voice penetrated his head and removed any idea of pretending to be asleep. "You've missed a great morning for hunting. The sun's bright; the temperature's perfect for walking; there's not a bug to be seen anywhere."

Josh rolled over and squinted into the sunlight coming in around the two men in the doorway. "Yeah, where's your deer?"

Kevin laughed his big booming laugh. "Still lurking in the woods growing bigger," he said without hesitation. He looked around. "Was Cliff back? We heard him shoot at something. Thought a buck would be hanging outside when we got here."

"Never saw him," Josh said as he swung his feet onto the floor.

"Someone had some breakfast," Victor said. He pointed to the plate of toast on the table. He had washed the others' morning dishes before leaving. "Maybe he didn't want to wake you."

Josh shook his head. "I think I did that. I remember getting up awhile ago. Don't know how I ended up back in bed."

"Probably staggered back," Kevin said. He picked up an empty whisky bottle from the side shelf. "You killed this soldier all by yourself."

"Don't remind me. I think I got up to take some seasick pills. The room was spinning in circles."

Victor looked at his watch. "It was three or four hours ago that we heard Cliff shooting." He looked back at the cabin door. "I wonder if he needs our help."

Kevin again laughed a deep belly laugh. "Maybe he does. Has he ever gutted an animal before? Not as easy as it looks the first time. Knowing Cliff, he probably has his BlackBerry out with a video showing him how to do it."

Victor did not return the smile. "In that case, let's go look for him. If he only wounded the deer and then started to track it, he may be lost." He started out the door. "Come on guys. This adventure is supposed to be about having fun. Being lost is not fun, especially for a city boy." His voice carried the authority of experience.

"Wait just a second," Kevin said, the smile gone. "Let's not go rushing off blindly." He looked at Josh. "You coming with us?"

"Of course, that's what I'm here for." He wiped some white goo from the corners of his mouth. "But first I've got to clean the shit from my teeth. The Fifth Cavalry has ridden through my mouth and stopped along the way to relieve the horses." He gave his head a shake to emphasize the point. "My first guess would be that Cliff probably missed and was too excited to jack another shell into the chamber for a second shot.

"Give me a minute and I'll be ready."

"That's a possibility, too," Kevin said. "While you're doing your morning ablutions, we'll make some sandwiches and refill our thermos with coffee. No sense roaming through the woods all afternoon on an empty stomach." He patted his rotund belly as he said this. "A couple of more minutes won't make any difference on this end. If he really is tracking a deer, we may have a few miles to walk."

Like Cliff, Kevin's lunch was gone long before the morning sun had risen high in the sky.

Victor hesitated.

Kevin scowled at him. "Get in here. Get the butter out of the fridge. This won't take long." He took several slices of whole grain bread from a bag on the table and spread them out ready to be slathered with filling.

CHAPTER 2

"THE CLEARING IS down this road." Kevin pointed to a rutted opening in the trees. Deep tire tracks from a skidder scarred the landscape. "Looks like they dragged the trees out too early in the spring. The road must have been nothing but a quagmire."

Josh stepped up on the hump between the tire tracks. "The almighty dollar always trumps the environment. How long ago did you say this area was cut over?"

"It was freshly cut when I acquired the camp. That would be about four years ago. The young maple shoots are great feed for the deer. Did I tell you I took one from here last year?"

Josh and Victor groaned.

"I guess I did. Derrick Watts got one the year before. In fact, he tipped me off to this clearing. He's the one who built the tree stand." Kevin snickered aloud. "I'm talking about the previous owner. Tried to buy the place back but I told him no deal. Told him he could call me anytime he wanted to come hunting here and I would see if I could work him in. That pissed him off big time. Last year he didn't come back and I haven't heard from him yet this year. When he was leaving the last time, I was changing the name over the door from Derrick's Hideaway to Four Eights."

Josh had heard the story before. Kevin never tired of retelling it.

"There's a rumour that Derrick found God. Doesn't play poker any more. Doesn't hunt. His lawyer calls me a couple of times a year to remind me the offer is still standing. If the rumours are true, I don't know why he still wants to buy the place." Kevin shrugged his shoulders. "Doesn't matter anyway. I'll never sell. As Victor said earlier this morning, this is like owning a piece of paradise."

Victor surveyed the splendor around him drinking in the beauty one more time. "It is a great place to recharge your batteries. How much did Derrick offer?" The realtor in him couldn't be held down. To him, that question was the natural extension of the conversation.

"Too much. The price shows his desperation to reclaim all his hard work. The lodge, as he calls it, is totally winterized, has a propane fridge, stove and furnace along with the quietest propane generator I've ever heard. Somehow or other he dragged a proper septic tank up here and buried it. Sits on six acres with a guaranteed right–of-way. I love it. My wife, on the other hand, hates it. Says it's in the middle of nowhere and that I spend too much time up here. If she knew how much money I'd turned down from Watts, she'd have given me the John the Baptist treatment."

Victor and Josh looked at him questioningly.

"You know, had my head served on a platter."

Both men laughed. They knew Kevin's wife wanted him to get rid of the place. She had even asked Victor if he knew anyone interesed in buying it. He hadn't taken her seriously, but good salesman that he was, he kept an ear open for any interest.

"The pastor of my church, Pastor Dave, mentioned that we might be acquiring a place like this as a retreat," Victor said. "I wonder if Derrick Watts is a member of our congregation."

Kevin put out his hand to stay their progress. "Cliff should be just over this rise. We'd better announce we're coming or he might shoot us. If Josh is right and Cliff didn't get a deer earlier this morning, he'll be getting pretty anxious by now. Ready to shoot anything that moves." He put his hand up to his mouth. "Cliff, don't shoot. It's us. We have food."

Victor laughed. "That will get his attention. I bet he ate his lunch before eight o'clock."

Kevin gave him a semi-smile. "Cliff. Cliff, we're coming into the clearing. Don't shoot." He waited for a response. When none came, he shouted again. "Cliff, answer me."

"Let's get up there," Josh said. "Just exercise a little caution when you step into the clearing."

They hurried to the top of the rise and stopped to study the surroundings. Kevin knew exactly where the hunting perch was mounted. He immediately spotted the fluorescent orange jacket. Even among the blazing glory of God's autumn colours, man's testament to paranoia stood out like a lighthouse beacon. The material was designed to be seen at a distance of three miles. From 125 feet, it slapped them in the face. "Over there, on the ground."

Josh turned to the direction indicated. "Christ almighty. He must have fallen out of the tree." He sprinted towards the orange lump on the ground. The tangled dead falls grabbed at his ankles. He stumbled forward. By sheer force of will he regained his balance before falling and resumed his headlong dash. The other two men followed him cautiously picking their way across the rough, uneven terrain. Josh got to the sprawling body a few steps ahead of the others. He stopped short when he spotted the red scar in the centre of Cliff's chest. All the colour drained from his face and his legs started to tremble. "Oh my Jesus," he said. "Cliff's been shot."

Josh lowered himself to the ground, covered his face with his hands and took three long, deep breaths. By then Kevin had drawn up beside him. His eyes captured the sight of the blood on Cliff's chest.

"Oh, shit," he said. Slowly, he covered the remaining few steps to where Cliff lay. He leaned forward and slid two fingers under Cliff's head covering to check for a carotid pulse. The flesh at the open neck was already cool to the touch. He moved his fingers to another spot and tried again before looking back at the others and shaking his head. He detected no blood surging from the heart to the brain.

Kevin backed away to where Josh and Victor were now standing. His face was ashen. "He's been dead for awhile. He feels cold." Kevin's eyes swept the clearing. He came up empty. "I guess we've got to contact the police, somehow. Cell phones don't work up here."

The colour had returned to Josh's face. He followed Kevin's gaze around the clearing. "What time did you say you heard the shot?"

Victor looked at his watch. "Somewhere around eight. We thought he had gotten lucky."

"You were wrong there. Whoever did this would be long gone by now. That was four hours ago." Josh looked back at Cliff. "Looks like the shot went right through his heart. Probably was dead before he hit the ground. What do you think? Has to be an accident."

Suddenly, without warning, he could feel the contents of his stomach churning. An acidic taste hit the back of his throat. He turned from the others just in time and vomited over the ground. The stench of stale alcohol permeated the fresh forest air causing the others to screw up their noses. A sheen of perspiration popped out across Josh's forehead. He wiped his mouth with the back of his coat sleeve.

"Sorry," he said, "last night's whisky is catching up to me."

Victor looked squeamish, as well. "I don't think so," he managed to get out before he too deposited a matted gob of his lunchtime sandwiches into the bushes. "And all I had to drink last night was orange juice."

Josh stepped away from Kevin. "Care to join us?" he asked. He tried to force a smile. It didn't come.

Kevin shook his head. "Not this time." He looked around the clearing. "Has to have been an accident. Who would want to shoot Cliff, especially way out here?'

"True, but it's a hell of a shot. Right through the heart."

Kevin looked down at his friend. He shook his head. "A fluke shot could hit you anywhere."

He looked back into the clearing, trying to make a decision. "One of us has to stay here while somebody drives down to the village. Any volunteers?"

"I'll stay," Josh said. "I'm all right now. You're more familiar with that track you call a road. You'll make better time."

Kevin nodded. He looked at Victor. "Coming or staying?"

Victor looked from Kevin to Josh to Cliff and then back to Kevin. Before he could answer, Josh interrupted. "You go with Kevin. I've got this covered."

A look of relief passed over Victor's face. "If you're sure?"

"I'm sure. Now get moving."

CHAPTER 3

DETECTIVE-SERGEANT JIM MCDONALD stepped down from the white RCMP Explorer. "Thanks for the lift," he said to the uniformed officer before turning to take in the crime scene. Yellow tape circled one area at the top of the hill. Several men milled around. Some were taking pictures, some were dressed in the white coveralls of the forensic team and some were just looking.

The sergeant studied the group looking for any familiar faces. He was a long way from his usual territory. As a member of the major crimes unit, robbery and homicide, most of his work centered around the city and immediate surrounding area. Being chauffeured in a four-wheel drive vehicle for a half-hour through the woods was a definite change of scenery for him. The last time he could recall this type of location was an apparent fishing accident that developed into a murder case. Today's case was suspected to be a hunting accident, for now. Only time and some investigation would tell.

A uniformed corporal looked up from the knot of people near the body. "Sergeant Mcdonald," he said, "over here."

Jim looked towards the sound of the familiar voice and smiled. "Hi, Scott, what have we got?" He waited while Corporal Scott Bowen stepped away from the others. The two men had successfully teamed up on previous cases that brought Jim outside his comfort zone in the urban area. Scott had spent many years patrolling the highways and byways of rural Nova Scotia. They had a comfortable working relationship.

"Looks like an accidental shooting at this point." Scott flipped open his notebook. "Clifford Lawrence. Shot once in the chest. No exit wound." He looked up from his notes to the sergeant's face.

"No exit wound? That's not consistent with a high-powered hunting rifle." Jim looked around Scott to the body still lying on the ground.

"Exactly what I was thinking when I called for you." Scott pointed to three men sitting on a log off to one side. They looked like abandoned puppy dogs. "Those three are his hunting companions. The blond claims to have still been in bed at the time of the shooting. He says he didn't even hear the shot. The other two were further up the road hunting together. They did hear the shot. Said it sounded like a rifle to them." Scott went back to his notes. "Kevin Barnhill, he's the heavy one in glasses, owns the hunting lodge, said he shot his first deer here last year. The other man, Victor Boyd, has never shot a deer in his life. That's the calibre of hunter we're working with.

"They get out once a year for a couple of days. I gather it's more of a social occasion than anything else although they do roam around the woods with loaded weapons. I'm not sure either of them would be able to distinguish between a rifle and a pistol shot. They said for sure it wasn't a .22. They both know the thwit sound of the smaller calibre weapon."

The two policemen started walking towards Cliff's body. Jim kneeled down and looked at the hole in his shirt. "Well, if the bullet's still in there, we'll know soon enough what killed him." He looked up at the hunter's chair in the tree above him. "Real sportsmen. Did they have apples out to attract the deer to this spot?"

"No," Scott said. "They're not that sophisticated. They don't hunt enough to know any of the tricks of the trade. I doubt that their barbecues ever see anything but beef."

"Does one of them look good for the shooting? Could they be covering up their own incompetence?"

Scott shook his head. "I don't get that impression, but it's still too early to tell. We've collected their rifles for comparison purposes when we extract the bullet. They're bagged and tagged in the van out by the road."

He pointed to a broken branch hanging from the tree near the seat. "See that? That looks like a fresh scarring. Possibly slowed the bullet en route."

Jim adjusted his stance so that he was directly under the chair. His eyes created a path from the broken branch to the far side of the clearing. Scott followed Jim's stare.

"We've got the dog master on his way. We're keeping that area clear of people until he gets here. No sense in contaminating the scene."

Jim nodded. "The way the hill slopes away, a man could have been shooting at a deer standing down there near the other edge and easily hit someone up here in a tree. I'd like a closer look at the area." He looked down at the binoculars resting on Cliff's chest.

"Guess they are still part of the crime scene. I'd better not disturb them. Are there any other binoculars that I can use."

"There sure are," Scott said. His face was beaming. "Somewhere they have some new high-tech wonders. Wait until you see them."

"Great. New toys," Jim said. "I just want to have a look from up there in the seat. I want to see what Cliff Lawrence saw just before he got hit. I don't want to be overwhelmed by technology while I'm clinging to that tree branch. Are the teckies finished up there?"

"I think so. They were up there with the cameras and swabs. I'll check and get you their glasses." Scott went over to talk to the forensic man in charge, Robin West.

Jim went over to talk to Kevin and the others. He introduced himself as the lead detective and explained that all deaths were considered suspicious until a definitive ruling was made by the coroners office. He warned them to stick around. He would want to talk to them later.

"I can't believe this is happening," Kevin said. His lowered head slowly shook back and forth. He looked up at the policeman. "We should've come right over when we heard the shot. Things might have turned out differently." He stifled a sob. "It's all fun and games until you actually shoot something. Then the work begins. This was Cliff's first deer. We wanted him to have the full experience. You know, clean and gut it himself. If only we'd known."

Tears were welling in the corners of Kevin's eyes. Jim put a hand on his shoulder. "From the way things look, you could have been standing right beside him when he was shot and there'd have been nothing you could have done. Did you notice any other hunters in the area?"

All three men shook their heads in unison. This was not the first time that question had been asked of them. It wouldn't be the last.

"Know anyone who had a grudge against Mr. Lawrence?" Jim asked. "Anyone who might want to kill him?"

All three quickly answered. "No one."

"Take your time and think about that. I'll talk to you later." Jim made his way to the base of the tree where Scott waited for him. "Just planted the idea in their mind that this may be a homicide investigation," he said. "If they're involved, let's get them on edge. I'm not sure I buy the grieving friend routine. They're taking it too hard."

Scott looked back at the three men now deep in discussion. There was a lot of head shaking. "You're such a cynic, Sergeant. You've got them talking, anyway. Do you suppose they're cooking up a cover story?"

"You've interviewed them already. We'll see what happens when we separate them. If they're all singing from exactly the same page, we'll dig deeper." He reached out for the binoculars in Scott's hand. "They look simple enough."

Scott held on to them for a second and started pointing out some of the features. "This button creates a laser beam. Put it on some object, push this button and it will give you a distance reading, yards or metres." He passed Jim another small, black plastic object attached by cord to the main body of the binoculars. It looked like a door opener for your car. "With this you can paint an area in the distance. When you look through the binoculars, it will fluoresce for about 20 seconds. That way you know you are searching in the right area. Press this button and you have a photograph of your target."

"I'm impressed," Jim said. He put the strap around his neck. "What if I want to order pizza while I'm surveying a scene?"

Scott never missed a beat. "Red button on the side."

"I guess it goes without saying that if I drop them, I may as well just fall out of the tree on top of them."

"That would be best. You probably wouldn't be able to afford to replace them on a cop's salary."

They turned and looked at the trunk of the tree. Scott pointed out the smooth stubs of branches a foot or so apart forming a natural ladder. It was obvious that Cliff had followed a well-worn course to his final seat. Jim climbed to the host branch. He thumped his bum along the limb to where the hunting chair was anchored.

He held the "door lock opener" chest high and aimed it past the scarred branch. He triggered the paint switch and then scoured the landscape to see if anything had changed. Nothing had. He brought the glasses to his eyes and looked along the suspected line of flight of the bullet. After a couple of corrections in direction, a small area of the forest took on a green fluorescent hue.

"Neat," he murmured.

The natural curve of the hill made a straight line to his location. His view was only interrupted by a scattering of leaves for a long distance through the trees. A couple of undulations created a few blind spots in the landscape. The shooter may not have even been aware of

Cliff's presence. No one is looking up in the trees when they are deer hunting.

He touched the distance button and looked at the results. Two hundred and seventy-five yards. That was a long shot by anyone's standards if you were aiming. On the other hand, a fluke shot knew no limits. He looked down from his perch to the body below. Cliff hauntingly stared back. I guess your friends were wrong, Jim thought, this was not your lucky day.

CHAPTER 4

MUCH OF THE activity had moved from the top of the hill to the valley beyond the chopping. The tracking dog came barking on the scene and in no time at all had located blood droplets from a wounded deer. Robin West, the forensic chief, was not committing himself, but he allowed that the deer probably had been shot earlier that morning. More tests would be needed. To every one else it looked like a clear case of accidental shooting.

The bullet had passed through the deer, up the hill and into Cliff. The hunter's attention would have been fully on the deer before he shot and his eyes would be definitely tracking the wounded animal after the shot. Clifford Lawrence would not even have been in that man's universe.

"Any idea where the shot was fired from?" Jim asked. Now that he was on the actual scene, everything looked the same. He couldn't pick out the area he had spotted from the tree stand. The trees that had looked covered in layers of brilliantly coloured leaves were half naked. Their gray skeletons all looked the same.

"Blood trail starts right over there near the clearing edge." Robin West pointed to a section of forest leading up the hill. "Dog should be able to find the spent casing. I don't know of too many hunters who pick up their brass, especially after scoring a hit."

Jim looked in the direction indicated.

"Looks like the animal may have been lying down. The leaves are compacted at this spot."

Jim leaned in for a closer look and then looked up the hill to the killing site. "Deer would have to have been standing up when it was fired at." He made a line with his hand to indicate the bullet's flight. "Otherwise the slug would have buried itself into the side of the hill if it passed through the deer."

Robin nodded in agreement. "These overturned leaves indicated the deer had probably gotten to its feet," the man continued. "First we have to figure out how far away the shooter was when he took his shot. Probably no more than 70 or 80 yards through these trees. Maybe less. And then the bullet's path may have been deflected when it hit the animal. Without a carcass, we won't be able to determine that." He paused and looked Jim in the face. "Think you'll be able to get that for us before it's cut up?"

Jim didn't respond. Instead he studied the trail of blood leading down the side of the hill. "Doesn't seem to be a lot of bleeding. Do you think the shot was fatal?" He realized what he asked and quickly added: "for the deer."

"Depends on whether anything vital was hit. The shot may have just passed through the fleshy part of the neck. In that case, it may eventually clot and as long as there's no major infection, the deer could survive to be shot another day. We took the dog off the deer's path and sent him to look for the spent shell casing. Finding that will give us the location of the shooter when the shot was fired. We'll have the dog resume tracking the deer and presumably the hunter after that."

The two men took several more steps through the woods. Here and there, small drops of dark red popped into their sight. By now they were about 80 yards along the track. There was less and less blood. "I wonder why the hunter didn't fire a second shot?" Jim asked.

"Depends on where he was standing. There are lanes here where you think you can see forever. Get a few degrees left or right of those and all you can see are trees. If the deer took off at a right angle to the line of fire, you wouldn't be able to get a clear second shot."

Jim nodded. "To have a shot pass through an animal and then shoot a man out of a tree is a one-in-a-million shot. I don't buy lottery tickets because I don't like those odds. I guess I'm a little skeptical."

Robin laughed. "6-49 odds are thirteen million to one, but we still have winners on a regular basis."

Jim looked around him. The traces of blood had virtually disappeared. "Looks like that deer probably got away. The blood trail has evaporated. Can you have the dog track the man instead of the deer? It's been almost seven hours. The best-case scenario is for the dog to lead us back to the road where the man was parked. We can try to locate any tire marks he may have left or find somebody who may have seen the vehicle."

Robin nodded his head. "The dog will follow the freshest track. If the hunter is going slow and circling looking for the blood trail, that will be him. Finding where he parked his vehicle is the easy part. From there, well, you may have your work cut out for you. We'll check for tire tracks and the like." Robin stamped his foot on the ground. "Road's not frozen yet, but the ground is going to be pretty solid. It's been a couple of weeks since it rained around here.

"Maybe find some cigarette butts. They're not as prevalent as they once were. It's a pretty isolated area. This could be a lot of expense just to ruin some hunter's day. If this is accidental, the man didn't really do anything wrong. If there was a deflection, the chances are pretty good the hunter never even saw the victim."

Jim was silent for a moment. "I take it you're a hunter?"

"I am and accidentally killing another human being would be my worst nightmare." Robin looked back up the hill to where Cliff was being loaded into a body bag. The two groups of men could not see each other. "Before ever firing a shot I check the line of sight behind the animal, but it could happen so damn easily. Powerful weapons and people randomly roaming around the forest are a deadly combination. Throw someone up a tree and who is going to even think to look for a man up there? But, we both know that accidents do happen.

"I've got some tests to run on the clothing and on the bullet when we get it. I'll let you know what I find out. In my line of work, we don't jump to conclusions no matter how obvious things look."

"I'll wait for your results but in the meantime, I'm going to do everything I can to find the shooter. Then we'll decide if we want to ruin his day. It's no good coming back here next week and trying to put the pieces together."

"Detective, over here," someone called out.

Jim looked towards the voice. The man held up a portable radio and walked towards Jim.

"They think they've found the spent casing," he said.

Jim took the radio and pushed the talk button. "Sergeant Mcdonald."

"Look to your left Sergeant." It was Scott Bowen's voice. "See me waving."

Jim turned left and about one hundred yards away could barely make out the yellow stripe of a pair of Mountie pants through the trees. He waved.

The radio crackled again. "Looks like the dog found the casing. Thirty calibre carbine."

"Thirty calibre," Jim said. "That's an unusual choice for deer hunting. Didn't the U.S. military phase them out back in the '60s?"

Scott laughed. "Hey man, I'm not that old. I was a kindergarten kid in the '60s and you weren't even born then."

"Yes, I was. Just barely. And I remember they were using the M1 rifle in the early days in Vietnam. It was replaced by the M16. The M1 took a 30 calibre cartridge. Only had an effective range of about 300 yards. I made this shot at about 275 with the binoculars, add another 50 or so to where you are and we have about 325 yards That would explain the lack of an exit wound. It's hard to believe it penetrated the body of the deer and kept on going that far."

"Sure you remember all that," Scott said. "Even people who lived in the '60's don't remember the '60s. I've seen all those books in your office on various types of weapons. I've also heard that studying the various instruments of death and killing around the world is one of your morbid hobbies."

"Okay, maybe I don't actually remember the army using this rifle but everything else is true. I'll be right over." He handed the radio back to the other policeman and set off towards where the shot had been fired.

When he got there, he looked up the hill towards the location of the shooting. He could see glimpses of the people up there through the leaves. He picked up a four-foot stick from the ground, broke off about a foot and aimed it like a rifle. Cliff's tree was directly in his line of fire through the branches. He passed the stick to Scott. " This is about the size of an M1 . Check it out," he said.

"Already have," Scott said. "That's my gun you're using." He indicated the stick and laughed. "I used the version with the longer barrel."

Jim smiled back. "That would make sense but it would only add about two inches to the overall length." He held the stick up to his eye again and sighted along its length. "Only one problem with this theory: the arc of the path of delivery. The deer would have to have been at least six, maybe seven feet tall for a bullet fired here to hit a man up there." He carved the air with his hand to indicate the required arc.

Scott nodded his head, then drew an arc of his own. "What if he fired at and hit the deer..." He indicated a short arc. "...then the bullet deflected up again to make a second arc." This time his hand made a longer path.

"That would work," Jim said, "but now I would have to question if it still had enough power to go, let's say, another 260, 270 yards and kill a man. That's assuming the deer was about 50 yards from here."

Scott held up the spent cartridge. "What's the standard load in these things?"

Jim reached out and took the shell. "One hundred and ten grains is the norm. You think he might have been using a heavier load?"

"Some hunters do. They think they're hunting elephants with the fire power they use. A 30 calibre is a light load to start with. It makes sense that someone might beef it up."

"That's true. And let's face it, if this was an intentional murder, it would have made more sense to use a rifle that fired a .30-06 shell. You would be much less conspicuous if you ran into someone else. No one would question carrying a rifle like that during hunting season. Just about everyone does. But a carbine, people would notice and remember that.

"We'll have to wait for the coroner and forensics but I won't argue with a finding of accidental. A deliberate shot from this range would be one hell of a shot for an M1. To hit someone in the heart would be a fluke. Too bad they can't all be this easy."

Scott's head slowly and involuntarily bobbed up and down in agreement. "Do you still want to interview the hunting companions? I have their statements."

Jim thought about it for a few seconds. "We'll still treat it as a suspicious death until the experts tell us differently. As alibis go, from what you've told me, none of them would be in the clear. One was alone and the other two can only rely on each other. Somebody shot the victim. I want to find out if they've seen any other hunters or know who comes here on a regular basis. Most people hunt in the same place year after year.

"As I said, a carbine is a unique looking rifle, much shorter than the norm. They may have seen someone carrying such a weapon. Even with their lack of knowledge, it should have stood out. That information could save us a lot of time if we have to find the shooter. They may be able to take all the guess work out of it and simply supply us a name."

Scott nodded and the two men started up the hill and across the chopping. Both were thinking the same thing. Cliff Lawrence was one unlucky son of a bitch.

CHAPTER 5

"IT WAS KEVIN'S idea that we not go help Cliff," Victor Boyd was telling Detective-Sergeant Mcdonald. "He thought making Cliff gut his first deer all alone was a big joke. I was all for helping him."

Jim looked over at fellow officer, Corporal Scott Bowen. The two men were reinterviewing the hunting companions back at Kevin's lodge. They had talked to them briefly as a group while they were still at the scene of the fatal shooting. Now they were doing individual interviews.

"So, you tried to talk him into going back to the clearing?"

Victor didn't answer. He looked down at his clasped hands in his lap. Then he slowly looked up. "No, but I would have gone back. I've never shot a deer in my life. I know I would want someone to help me with the first one. I didn't think it was that funny."

"So what Kevin Barnhill says pretty much goes?"

Victor looked like he had been slapped. "No, but it is his hunting lodge. You have to defer to some of his wishes."

Jim made an entry in his notebook. "When the crime scene techs checked your hands and clothes for gun powder residue, they found you had fired your weapon. What did you shoot at if not a deer?"

Victor held his hands out in front of him and turned them over back to front. He studied them looking for whatever the cop was talking about. "We sighted in our rifles when we first got here yesterday. It was Kevin's idea."

Scott shook his head in disbelief. "How many rounds did you fire?"

"I don't know. Five or six each."

"Twenty or twenty-five rounds. It must have sounded like a war zone. I can't believe there were any deer still around this morning to shoot at. No wonder you never get any game."

"Josh Daniels was in the cabin asleep?" Jim jumped back into the questioning.

"Huh?" The change of direction unsettled Victor a little more. "He was when we got back, but he had been up. There were dirty dishes on the table."

Scott gave Jim a significant look. "And he knew where Cliff was hunting?" he asked.

Victor looked from one policeman to the other. "I don't know. I don't think so. You'll have to ask him." There was an edge in his voice. "Why all the questions, anyway? You don't think someone shot Cliff on purpose. That's stupid. Hell, he sells houses for a living. The business is not that cutthroat. It sure as hell wasn't one of us. We were all friends. They've known each other for years."

"And you haven't?"

"I know them. This is my first hunting trip. We're all friends."

"Someone shot him," Jim said. "That's an undeniable fact."

"But not on purpose. It was an accident."

"That is yet to be determined." Jim made this declaration as if homicide was a definite possibility in his mind. He too, had come to that same conclusion. "Have you thought of any enemies who might want to harm Cliff? Someone who might want him dead."

Victor didn't even hesitate. "No. Everybody likes Cliff. He was one of those easy going Mr. Nice Guys."

Scott rolled his eyes. "Why is it always the nice guys that get killed?" he asked Jim.

"I know," Victor said, "it's just not fair." Victor had missed the irony in the statement.

"Tell us again everything that happened from the time you got here until you discovered the body." Jim flipped his notebook back a few pages. He studied them as if the cure for cancer had been written there. He looked up at Victor. He was waiting for discrepancies in his story. None appeared.

This scenario played out again with Kevin and then Josh. The resulting information was pretty much the same in each case. Cliff was alone. No one saw anything or anybody. No one believed Cliff had any enemies who would shoot him. Kevin was not familiar with many other hunters who frequented the area. He passed along the name of Derrick Watts.

He simply referred to Derrick as the previous owner. He passed on the opportunity to tell the poker game story to this new audience. Derrick might be able to give them more information about other hunters, but to the best of Kevin's knowledge Derrick and Cliff were not even acquainted with each other. They came from two different and non-intersecting areas of Kevin's world.

After finishing their interview with Josh, the two policemen headed back to Scott's SUV. "What do you think?" Scott asked. "Are they telling us the truth?"

Jim shrugged. "As far as it goes, I'd say they have but as Otto von Bismark once said 'People never lie so much as before an election, during a war, or after a hunt.' What we have to determine is what they didn't tell us. Lies by omission are still lies."

Scott thought about that for a few seconds. "Unlike most hunters, they weren't trying to impress us with their prowess in the woods. That in itself is unusual. On the other hand, they may just be that bad."

The men's stories were similar but didn't sound rehearsed. They only reinforced the idea in Jim's mind that this was just an exercise in police procedure. Clifford Lawrence was probably another victim of being in the wrong place at the wrong time. He would speed up the forensic and coroner's reports so that he could file this case away and move on to searching for real criminals.

CHAPTER 6

JIM SNUGGLED DOWN into his jacket collar. The temperature hovered a few degrees above freezing. A looney-sized moon cast a pale yellow light above the horizon to the left of the city. Behind him, he could hear his Canadian flag snapping in the wind. He crowded closer to the barbecue as he flipped the steaks, smeared a generous portion of a garlic flavored steak sauce on the meat and lowered the lid.

Stella Martin poked her head through the patio door. "Just about finished?" she asked. "I've got everything ready on my end. Veggies are cooked. Table is set. Wine is breathing. Bring on the meat, big boy."

"Three more minutes. I'm searing the sauce on as we speak."

Stella shivered, slid the door shut and returned to the table. She adjusted the silverware so that it formed a perfect 90 degree angle with the table edge. Dropped three ice cubes in each glass and added some water. She threw her apron across the back of a chair in the kitchen and took her place at one end of the table.

Jim eased through the patio door, being careful to prevent the blowing curtains from coming in contact with the platter carrying the two cooked-to-perfection steaks. His eyes took in the elabourately laid out table. "Wow, what's the occasion?"

Stella smiled. "You wrapped another case today. Doesn't that rate a little celebration?"

A deep laugh rippled from Jim. "I'm always ready to celebrate, but this case wrapped itself up. Turns out there was no crime." He placed the larger slab of meat on his plate, slid the other on to Stella's, deposited the platter in the kitchen sink and dropped into his own chair. "Okay, let's eat."

Stella cut the tubular sweet potato in half, revealing its steaming orange flesh. She passed a portion to Jim. She removed the cover from the broccoli, allowing the steam to float up to the ceiling. Both added some of the shiny green trees to their plate. With a slotted spoon, she served some yellow corn from the hot water it still simmered in. She studied her plate. "Orange, green, yellow and brown – a virtual palette of colours. This should please the dietitians."

Jim picked up his glass of wine and raised it. "Let's not forget the red. To good food."

"To a couple of days off," Stella answered. "And to eating more healthy meals like this."

"Are you implying a Big Mac and black coffee aren't healthy? Tomato, lettuce, pickle on a sesame seed bun."

Stella stared across the table into his eyes. "In a word, no." She reached out with her knife for some butter and slathered it over her vegetables.

"Oops," Jim said. "There goes all the healthy goodness. The fat meter just peaked." Then he did the same.

They ate quietly for a few minutes, enjoying the diverse flavors. "It does outdo fast food," Jim said. "I should have you prepare supper for me every night."

Stella's eyes sparkled. "All you have to do is ask. My suitcase with all my worldly possessions is in my car."

Jim instantly regretted his comment. He loved Stella but having her move in was not in the cards for him at this point. His hours were too erratic, his moods fluctuated with how his cases were going at any given time, but, most importantly, he had seen the havoc rendered on the marriages of his work mates. Police work was not conducive to a successful long-term relationship. Living separately and dating as often as possible was the better choice. Stell did not agree. She knew she could cope with the police lifestyle and had often told him so. The look on Jim's face displayed his feeling.

Stella's eyes turned back to a flat brown. She didn't pursue the subject. This was not the time. She wasn't seeking a commitment, just some validation, an indication that somewhere down the line there was a future together. "Tell me why your homicide disintegrated into a mere accident," she said, instead.

"Forensics finally made their report. Definitely an accidental shooting." Jim was relieved by the change in subject.

"Didn't you suspect that all along?"

"I did, but until you hear from them, you've got to keep working as if it might be suspicious. Hunting accidents are an easy way to get rid of somebody."

Stella thought about that statement for a minute and sipped the last of her wine. "I can see that. What makes this one a definite accident?"

Jim refilled her glass and topped up his own. "A number of things. For a start, we just couldn't find anyone who wanted to get rid of Cliff Lawrence. He was liked by everyone who met him. Then there was the forensics. When they extracted the bullet from the victim," he paused. "Are you sure this is a subject for the supper table?"

She shrugged. "I don't mind if you don't mind. I am an operating room nurse. Talking about blood doesn't bother me."

Jim nodded. They both had occupations that came in contact with death on a regular basis. He preferred to think his attitude was one of acceptance and not one of indifference. "As I was saying, the bullet was a 30 calibre soft point. They found minute traces of deer hair imbedded in the twisted metal. It had sliced a small branch just in front of the tree stand. A closer examination of the scar showed animal blood."

"Did they do a DNA test to see if it was from the right deer?"

He started to respond and then realized she was joking.

"No, but in the trees on the other side of the clearing we found traces of blood where an animal had been wounded. It was a long distance from where the man was sitting in the tree. One hell of a shot, but I guess when your number is up..."

Stella wagged a finger at him. "Don't give me that line. I know you're no fatalist."

"Okay, when you're having a bad day. The range was such that it would have taken a remarkable marksman to hit someone from that distance. Also the wound had an elliptical shape to it. The bullet was tumbling when it penetrated the body. There were also microscopic traces of animal blood and hair fiber on his shirt where the bullet hit him. All in all, accidental is a pretty safe bet. It's not as if I don't have enough open cases to work on that I need the aggravation of this one with a crime scene miles back in the woods."

He raised his glass again. "You're right, this is something to celebrate."

He would remember those words later with a cynical laugh.

CHAPTER 7

BRIAN COSH TOOK one last look around his milking parlor before flipping off the power switch. Outside he could make out the images of his black and white Holsteins gathered in the dim first light of the false dawn. He took two steps into the main part of his barn when he felt the skin on his hip start to tingle. He reached down and shut off the pager and checked the readout. 9-1-1. There was a medical emergency. The alternate message would read 3819. Viewed upside down and with a little imagination, it was as close as they could come to spelling the word fire.

Brian's countenance changed from dairy farmer to fire chief. His face became grimmer, his step quicker as he hustled outside to his truck. Lives were at stake; he was in charge. Once in his Ford 150, he flipped on the two-way radio. Christine Seaton, the volunteer dispatcher, was passing on the information she had received from the 9-1-1 operator. A male in his late 60s was suffering from an apparent heart attack. She gave the address in her official dispatcher voice and then added with her rural twang: "Hurry boys, that's Gerald Booth. Mable must be beside herself with worry."

Brian fought back a smile. No matter how many times he preached to Christine about proper radio procedure on this official emergency channel, he could not curtail her personal editorial comments. Christine was right. Mable would be worried. Gerald was crowding seventy and despite Elizabeth's description of a man in his late 60s, Brian wasn't convinced on which side of the 70 mark Gerald lived. He had been farming in Raymond's River as long as Brian had lived there and showed no signs of slowing down anytime soon. His only concession was that for the last ten years, his nephew Ralph Foley shared the farming chores. Most people in the community viewed this more of Gerald giving Ralph a job than an admission that Gerald needed help. From his teen years, Ralph had worked in the local mill. Ten years ago it had closed down, leaving several men out of work. Most ended up leaving the community to find new jobs. Ralph was one of the lucky ones. His uncle happened to be hiring.

Brian jammed the accelerator pedal to the floor, covering the less than half-mile to the small, concrete block fire station in less than a minute. The building housed their three trucks: a bright yellow pumper, a similarly coloured tank truck and their nearly new, state-of-the-art, white and red rescue vehicle.

The latter still wore the colours of its previous owners who had been absorbed in a multi-town amalgamation. This merging of municipal units made this vehicle redundant to their needs. The people of Raymond's River had worked hard to barely raise enough money to purchase the fully stocked truck. The additional cost of repainting it was out of the question at this time. The chief could directly attribute three lives saved to this piece of equipment. He silently prayed number four was now in the works.

Two men were already waiting at the station when he pulled in. Both, like himself, were farmers who were well into their day's work when the alarm had been raised. They had been driving near the fire station when their pagers went off. One of them had the rescue truck out of the station and idling on the apron. He saw Brian's rapidly approaching headlights and waited the extra couple of seconds for the chief to arrive.

Brian keyed his mike. "Rescue 3 on route to Booth farm with three men aboard. Others meet us at location." With that he jumped from his truck and swung into the passenger seat of the emergency vehicle. "Let's roll," he said. In mere minutes from receiving the 9-1-1 call, help was racing through the darkness towards the downed man.

Mable Booth knelt beside her husband stroking his head. Gerald lay about five steps from his cow barn bathed in the illumination of the overhead motion-activated lights. Mable had ripped a table cloth from the breakfast table and covered Gerald as best she could. That was the extent of her first aid knowledge. Keep the patient warm. Across the fields, she spotted the flashing red lights approaching along the roadway. A wave of relief passed over her. "Hang on, you old fool," she whispered into Gerald's ear. "Hang on."

Gerald never moved. His face had a faint smile but there was no rise and fall of his chest. Mable chose to ignore this fact and instead prayed for a miracle. She silently chastised herself for having never learned CPR. Her tear-filled eyes urged the lights to come faster. "Hurry boys. Hurry."

A half-ton truck pulled into the yard from the opposite direction of the fire truck. A man jumped from the cab wearing the canvas turnout gear of the local volunteers. An iridescent stripe running around his upper arms and chest blinked at Mable. He carried a red helmet in his hands which he tossed on the ground beside Gerald. He put his ear down to Gerald's mouth and listened while his fingers sought a pulse. He avoided the pleading look in Mable's eyes and blew two quick puffs of air into Gerald's lungs before proceeding to thrust the heel of his hand into Gerald's chest.

"One, two, three four..." he rapidly counted aloud as he forced the heart to pump life-saving blood into the brain. Before he finished the first two-minute cycle, the rescue truck pulled in beside him followed by two other trucks. Chief Cosh was out the door before the vehicle came to a complete stop. The other man jumped from the back carrying a suitcase with an automated defibrillator in it.

The first man on the scene kept administering CPR but he looked into the chief's eyes and gave his head a nearly indiscernible shake. By now the leads from the defibrillator were connected to Gerald's chest and the others stood back, helpless to do anything until the machine made its report.

"No shock advised, if necessary continue CPR," the computer-generated voice said.

Now two of the fire fighters teamed up to do the life saving rescue breathing. One of the men blew two more puffs of air into Gerald's lungs. The second resumed pushing on his chest. "One, two, three, four, five ..."

"How long has he been down?" Chief Cosh asked Mable. Concern was evident in his voice. The machine's first message, combined with the look from his first responder, told him CPR was probably a waste of time. Gerald Booth was dead. The chief moved a black cap from under his knee. STIHL, the chain saw logo, blazed across the front in bright orange letters. Gerald's.

"I don't know," Mable said. "When he didn't come in for breakfast, I went looking for him and found him lying here like this in the dark. You've got to help him."

The fire chief watched his man going through the motions. He looked up at the brightly burning motion sensor lights. Most of the farms had similar devices on timers. If Mable found Gerald in the dark, the lights had completed their cycle. How long were they set to stay on: five minutes, ten, fifteen?

It didn't matter. Too much time had passed even if they were successful in restarting the heart. The magic-four minute mark of depriving the brain of oxygen had long passed. They were struggling to save what would amount to a vegetable.

"Checking casualty. Please stand clear. Do not touch the patient." The automated voice of the machine cut into his thoughts again with new instructions. Lights blinked indicating its progress and then it said: "No shock advised. If necessary, continue CPR."

The fireman doing the CPR looked at the chief for directions. The chief gave a slight shrug but indicated the man should keep trying. Miracles did happen. This continued for a few more cycles when another set of flashing lights appeared in the driveway. A white van with the letters EHS in large letters on the side wended its way through the parked vehicles and pulled up close to where the men were working to bring Gerald back from the dead.

Two paramedics jumped out. "What have we got?" one asked. He was looking down at Gerald's inert form and reaching for the stethoscope around his neck at the same time.

The chief slowly shook his head. "It doesn't look like we made it on time," he said. "Even with new technology, we can't win them all." He gave up his spot beside Gerald and let the paramedic move in. "He's been down for at least fifteen minutes, probably more."

The firemen had ceased their efforts while the paramedic checked the heart. "Fifteen minutes, eh?"

"Probably more." The chief looked at Mable for confirmation. She didn't respond.

The paramedic shook his head. "I'm sorry." He looked at Mable. "Your husband is dead. Let's not abuse his body any more."

"No-o-o-o-o-o." Her scream tore through the hearts of all the men present.

A new voice bellowed out. "For God's sake, man. Give him a shock. Don't give up." This instruction came from a neighbour, Chris Ritchey. Ritchey saw the red, flashing lights from his farm next door and came running over to see what was happening. His voice changed to a pleading quality. "Do something."

He pushed passed the chief and thumbed the big, red button on the defibrillator that had 'Deliver shock' written above it. Nothing happened. He jabbed at the button again. The chief pulled him back landing him on his backside.

"Hands off the equipment, Chris. The man is dead. The machine won't deliver a shock to a dead person." The neighbour was surprised at the chief's reaction but said nothing more. The glare from the chief left no room for argument. The chief glanced over at Mable and started to get up.

"I'm sorry to be so blunt, Mable, but we were too late." The chief reached for her hand. She pulled it away, tears now running freely down her wrinkle-lined face. Ten years of aging had been added in the last ten minutes. She leaned over her husband and hugged him, kissing him gently on the face. "Oh, Gerald, Gerald, what have you done?" The firemen shuffled their feet and looked away, embarrassed at their intrusion into Mable's grief.

"You can't just let him die," Chris said in a barely audible voice. He still sat where the chief had dumped him. "You can't."

"What do you think this was?" asked the paramedic. "Heart attack? The age looks right." He started to do a secondary survey of the body. He checked the muscled arms, legs, torso. Nothing seemed out of order except for the lack of breathing. Even the face looked peaceful. Not a stroke. He checked the neck and ran his hands up over the head.

"What's this?" He held his latex covered hand out to examine it a little more closely. "Is that blood?" He rubbed his fingers together. The substance smeared around.

"Looks like blood to me," the chief said. "Must have bumped his head when he fell."

The paramedic spread the strands of iron gray hair apart. A small round black spot could be seen with a little liquid seeping from it. "Holy shit," he said. "That's a bullet hole."

"What?" Everyone crowded closer.

"A bullet hole?" Mable said. "Nobody would want to shoot Gerald. That's stupid."

"Let's not be jumping to conclusions," Chief Cosh said. He made a calming motion to his firefighters. He looked back at the paramedic. "Are you sure?"

The man nodded. "Positive."

The chief's gaze shifted to the man with the red helmet, one of his lieutenants. "Robert, call the police. Everyone else get back. This is a crime scene now. We've got to protect it." He had learned that from watching television, not from any personal experience or training.

CHAPTER 8

SCOTT BOWEN SQUINTED into the rising sun as he sped along the twisty, country road. Pot holes leaped out at him jarring his car with abrupt jolts. Scott slowed down. It was more important to get there than to get there fast. A blown tire was no way to start the morning shift.

"We need another election," Scott said to the empty car. "That will at least get a shovelful of asphalt dumped into the deeper holes."

To his right, he noticed the carcass of a dead coyote on the far bank of the ditch.

Raymond's River was off the beaten track between Kennetcook and Maitland and only infrequently included as part of his normal patrol duties. A report of a man being shot didn't jibe with this peaceful farm country. At 6:45 in the morning, with the sun just waking up, an accidental shooting seemed highly unlikely. Scott had already alerted headquarters and put in a call for a detective. This would be the second shooting in as many months. The other death had been ruled a hunting accident. Now here he was again.

He rounded a sharp corner in the road and spotted the flashing red lights of emergency vehicles beside a big red barn. He pulled into the driveway and joined a handful of men and one distraught looking woman.

"Morning, Chief," Scott said as he approached the man with the white helmet and the identifying word in red letters across the front. He knelt down beside Gerald's body. Scott recognized that he had met the fire chief at community events. Meeting under these circumstances was a new experience for both men. "What do we know?"

"Got the call around 6:15 for a man not breathing. When we got here, we gave it our best shot but it was too late." He pointed to the uniformed medical person with his thumb. "Paramedics found the bullet hole."

Scott's glance shifted to the paramedic who joined him beside the body. The medic gently parted Gerald's hair exposing the small round entrance wound.

"Looks like a .22 to me," he said.

The cop was surprised by the statement. "You've had lots of experience with this sort of thing?"

"Yeah, too much. I served in the Gulf with the army for a stint. Saw people killed with every weapon imaginable. Never thought I'd see it out here though."

Scott lifted the head a little higher. "No exit wound?"

"No, a .22 wouldn't have the power to penetrate the skull and go right through. Killed him instantly, I'd say. No bleeding. There was barely enough seepage for me to detect the wound. At his age, this could have been written off as a heart attack. No autopsy and we'd have never known the difference."

Scott picked up the black cap lying on the ground. After some searching, a small, frayed hole could be found in the crown.

"And here's the corresponding hole in his hat. I guess that's a .22 hole as well."

Scott looked around the barnyard. In his mind he tried to visualize how Gerald would have been standing at the moment he was shot and where the bullet would have come from. "You think he was exiting the barn when he was shot?"

The chief nodded. He pointed to the cows gathered near the fence, curiously looking over at the crowd of men. "Cows have been milked. Morning chores were finished."

Scott noted the location of the wound and put his finger on his own head in a similar spot, then stood in the doorway of the barn. The barn reduced the view plane to 180 degrees. The house cut more than a quarter from the centre of the frontal view. That left one of two directions for the shooter to be standing, a small arc to the left of the house or a larger one to the right. The position of the wound near the front of the head suggested the shot had come from the right.

"If he was shot as he walked out, the bullet would have come from that direction over there. Who owns that farm?" Scott pointed to a house across the road.

Chief Cosh looked in the direction indicated. "That's the Ritchey farm. Chris is here somewhere." He looked around but didn't see the neighbour.

"I saw Chris leaving earlier," a fireman said. "Probably has to finish his own chores. He told me his wife, Linda, is sick, too, as if he cares. I hear they're not getting along too well lately. Chris has found God. He'll be over there praying for Gerald's salvation. Linda thinks he's gone nuts." Some of the other firemen gave him a questioning look. "Linda and my wife are sisters," he added as way of explanation.

The chief looked around the crowd. "Anyone seen Ralph?"

Everyone looked at each other shaking their heads.

"Who is Ralph?" Scott asked.

"Ralph Foley. Gerald's nephew. He works here as a hired hand. He should have been here helping with the milking. God, I hope he's not lying around someplace dead."

The others started to look in the shadows around the yard.

"No," Mable said. "Ralph is home sick today."

"Home, sick," Scott said. "How convenient."

Mable scowled at the implication. "Poor Ralph has the flu. He threw up all over the barn yesterday and I assure you he wasn't faking it. He is home sick."

"Sorry," Scott said, "but we will have to talk to him."

Scott took one more sweeping look around the yard. "Any of you men hear any shots?"

As one, the firemen shook their heads in the negative. The first man to arrive on the scene stepped forward. "I only live a little ways down the road and have been up since 5 o'clock. Was in the barn most of that time. What with the compressor going for the milking machine and moving the animals in and out, I never heard nothing. Twenty-two don't make much noise."

Chief Cosh shook his head. "The thing is, it's not that uncommon to hear .22's being fired around here. People shoot varmints: skunks, porcupines, rats, the like. You've heard the old cliché about the fox in the hen house? To people in this area it's not a cliché. They are a troublesome part of our existence and we shoot them. So, what I'm saying is, we are less likely to notice the sound of a .22 shot than someone in the city might."

Scott nodded his head in agreement. He checked his notepad. "So, Chris Ritchey lives across the road? I'll have to talk to him." He looked at the outbuildings near the two-storey farm house. "Looks like he's a dairy farmer, too. You say it's noisy in the barns while you're milking?"

"Can't say that I've ever noticed," Chief Cosh answered, "but I guess the machinery does drown out the outside noises. Suppose it's important to know what time the shot was fired."

"When and from where," Scott said. He looked over at Mable. "Did you hear anything out of the ordinary?"

Mable pointed to her ear. "Sorry, but I don't turn my hearing aids on when I'm in the house alone. Damn batteries wear out too fast. Same with Gerald." She chuckled softly to herself. "Sometimes we just sit around yelling at each other before we realize neither of us has the darn things turned on." A sob escaped from her lips. "Guess that won't happen any more."

The paramedic standing beside her put his arm reassuringly around her shoulder and squeezed. That was the best medicine he could offer at the moment.

Scott waited a couple of beats before continuing. "I'd like to talk to Mable inside. If no one else has anything to offer, Chief, your men can go home. I'd appreciate it if you could stay until the crime scene people arrive, sit with the body. We don't want to disturb anything until they have a look around."

The chief nodded his agreement and asked the driver of the rescue vehicle to stay with him. Everyone else left, eager to get home to spread the news. Murder was a new commodity to this quiet, rural area. As soon as the firefighters got home, stories would spread like cold germs through a kindergarten class. Unlike Scott, they had never been involved in a murder before. This was a big day for them.

As the half-ton trucks were pulling out of the driveway, a dark blue Ford sedan pulled in. Red and blue lights strobed along the lowered sun visors. The trucks pulled aside to allow the car to enter the yard. The drivers strained to see who was inside. A man dressed in a dark suit. He had to be a detective. This was just like on TV. Poor Gerald, he would be embarrassed to be the one causing all this excitement.

Jim Mcdonald stepped from his car and took in a deep breath of the clean country air. By now the sun was fully in the sky. The cerulean sky overhead faded to a robin's egg blue near the horizon with wisps of white clouds haphazardly scattered like a young child's drawing. Despite the day's pleasant appearance, there was a chill in the air.

"Sergeant," Scott Bowen said as he reached out his hand. "This is becoming a little too common."

Jim nodded his agreement and took in the sight of the older man lying on the ground. "They caught me at home. Said I was the most experienced detective for crimes in this neck of the woods. No offence, Scott, but I'm getting tired of meeting you professionally."

The fire chief approached the two policemen. "Chief Brian Cosh, this is Detective-Sergeant Jim Mcdonald from the major crimes division," Scott made the introductions. The two men shook hands.

"You were the first on the scene?" Jim asked without any preliminaries.

The chief nodded. "Answered the call around 6:15 a.m. Gerald was already dead when we got here. We tried CPR…" he shrugged, "… but there was nothing we could do. CPR's not much use against a bullet in the head."

The three men walked towards the body where the paramedics were trying to comfort Mable Booth. She was once again on her knees stroking Gerald's weather-worn face. Jim squatted in front of the woman. "Sorry for your loss, ma'am," he said. "I'm Detective-Sergeant Jim Mcdonald. Do you mind if I have a look?"

Mable looked at the man in the suit. "Of course," she said, deferring to the implied authority that Jim exhibited.

Again the paramedic stepped forward and without comment parted Gerald's hair. Jim studied the small wound that had stolen this man's life. His eyes returned to Mable's. "Are you up to answering a few questions?" he asked. "I know this is a bad time, but the sooner we get started on our investigation, the sooner we will have some results."

Mable stood up and shook off the paramedic's arm. "Let's catch the bastard who did this," she said. "There will be lots of time for mourning after that's done."

Jim smiled despite his efforts to keep a serious look on his face. "Let's do that," he said.

CHAPTER 9

JIM MCDONALD AND Scott Bowen perched on the edges of two hard, uncomfortable antique chairs in Mable's front parlor. Outside, the forensic team was checking angles of flight, ground scuffs, the front of the barn and timing of the motion lights. They were tying to determine how long Gerald might have been down before Mable discovered him, where the shot had come from and if there were any misses. Once these determinations were made, they would move across the road to where the shot had been fired from. With luck they would find the .22 casing and get the exact spot. If the shooter had ejected the shell, it was unlikely he would have found it in the dark. On the other hand, if he only fired the one shot, the spent cartridge may still be in the offending weapon if it was a single-shot, bolt-action rifle.

Jim sipped at the cup of tea that Mable's sister-in-law, Sarah Foley, had insisted on him taking. Sarah, who had arrived 15 minutes earlier, had not spared the tea bags. It was a strong brew.

"Can you tell me more about these young fellows Gerald was having problems with?" Jim asked. When asked if Gerald had anyone who might want to hurt him, Mable had reluctantly suggested some of the local yahoos, as she called them.

"I don't really think any of these boys killed Gerald. They're just a bunch of troublemakers with too much time on their hands and too little to do. They like to show off, but murder..." Mable visibly shivered at the use of the word, "...I can't believe they would do that."

"I noticed a lot of tire marks on the road in front of your house," Scott said. "Is this the sort of thing you mean?"

"That's part of it," Mable said. "Gerald called it the evening entertainment. They would be out there burning their tires, spinning in circles, a few of them even went off the road and into the ditch. Those were the good nights. I wanted to call the police, but Gerald said it was a waste of time. He said you people wouldn't do anything about it anyway." She gave Scott an accusing look. His uniform made him the face of law enforcement more so than Jim's Sears' suit.

"The problem is," Scott started to explain, "that they are long gone by the time we get here." Jim gave him a look that cut him off. This was not a time to defend police action or inaction, depending on which side of the fence you were on.

"So did Gerald do anything at all about it?" Jim asked. "Did he ever confront these," he hesitated, "yahoos?"

"He sure as hell did. He told them everyone in Canada has the right to act like a jackass but he wished they would go act like jackasses in front of their own houses."

"I told him to keep out of it," Sarah said. She had joined the group in the parlor with a tray of sandwiches. "My brother could be a bit of an ass himself sometimes. Just let them be, I told him but he never listened to me."

"How did they react to Gerald's comments?" Jim took a sandwich. His breakfast was still waiting in the toaster at home.

"With language that would make a seaman blush," Mable said. "Then a week or so later our mailbox was smashed to pieces along with several others in the area."

Jim rolled his eyes and looked at Scott with a questioning look.

"No one reported this to us," Scott said.

"A waste of time." A line of crimson crept up Mable's neck and into her cheeks.

Again Jim stopped Scott from responding with a cautionary hand slightly raised from his knee. It was better to let Mable vent and get the whole story out. This may be their best lead.

"How did Gerald react?"

"He was furious, but the first time he did nothing."

Jim sighed. His picture of the quiet country life was coming apart. "The first time?"

"We replaced the mailbox with a new one. $17.95 plus tax from down at the hardware store. That tax goes to pay your salary, doesn't it?"

"I'm sure it does," Jim said. He smiled and got one back in return. "Then what happened?"

"Same thing. A month or two later, Gerald confronted them again. He was always afraid that some innocent person might come around the corner while these yahoos were in the middle of making a doughnut, that's what they called the circles they was making, doughnuts, and there'd be an accident. Could easily have happened. This time they threatened to burn down the barn."

Scott sat forward. Now this was getting serious. "Burn down your barn?"

Mable paused. "Not in those exact words. Just asked if we had fire insurance on our outbuildings. It was obvious what they meant. Of course, they didn't burn anything down. Gerald told them if anything happened to any of his buildings he would come looking for them with a gun."

Sarah blanched at that statement. "Why didn't he just ignore them?"

"Not in his nature," Mable said. "He believed he had the right to peace and quiet in his own yard. Said men of his generation had died to guarantee that right. He wasn't going to let any young punks deny him of it." She gave the two cops an earnest look. "Gerald was only letting off steam when he talked about coming after them with a gun. He wouldn't shoot anyone."

The two policemen exchanged meaningful glances. "Maybe so, but that's a pretty heavy threat," Jim said. He glanced towards the window where a man lay dead, a victim of gun violence.

"Anyway," Mable continued, "it wasn't long before our new mailbox was wrecked. Pounded it to pieces late at night." She sat back in her chair and took a long swallow of her tea. A smile slowly spread across her face. "Gerald got the last laugh on that."

Last laugh. Jim consulted his notes. The escalation of events was frightening. He saw nothing to laugh about in any of this. If these boys had committed the crime, would anyone be willing to testify against them? They seemed to be a law unto themselves in this small community.

"What did he do?" Scott asked. He shared Jim's concerns. This area was part of Scott's jurisdiction although patrol cars seldom made the journey out this far. There was not enough crime to justify moving resources from the more heavily populated areas. He didn't realize how out of control things were becoming.

There was a glint in Mable's eyes. "Something he had heard on the CBC. Seems bashing mailboxes is a universal pastime for yahoos everywhere. He bought two mailboxes, one bigger than the other. Then he filled the space between them with cement and mounted them on a cement-filled steel pipe that was buried about four feet into the ground. The setup weighed a ton. It was all he could do to get it onto the tractor and out to the end of the road. He drilled the hole for the pipe with an auger and filled around it with wet cement as well."

Jim smiled. He didn't have to wait for the end of the story to know what happened. He could visualize it in his mind's eye. There seemed to be no end to man's ingenuity when revenge was the motive.

"He didn't have to wait long. Now these clowns were going out of their way to antagonize us. They couldn't drive by our house without spitting up gravel and burning rubber. Gerald would go out in the yard, shake his fist and yell obscenities at them. He was like a kid waiting for Christmas. He was trying to force their hand."

"Oh my," Sarah said. "Where was my Ralphie while all this was taking place? Surely he could have talked some sense into his uncle."

Mable looked at her husband's sister. "Ralph tried. I tried. We all tried. This was Gerald's own little war. There was no stopping him." Mable realized what she said and fell silent for a moment. "I still don't believe they would shoot him, no matter how upset they were. They thought it was just one big game until they tried to bash our mailbox again."

Jim could see that telling this story was having a therapeutic effect on Mable. He encouraged her to continue even though he knew the results. "What happened then?"

"Gerald was out in the barn. Must have been about 10:30 at night. He was working on one of the tractors, getting ready to harvest some potatoes we grow in one of the back fields. He heard the pra-a-a-n-n-g resonate from the roadway." Mable put some life into the sound of the hit.

"I heard it too from in the house even above the TV, it was that loud. I remember I was watching Coronation Street from the west coast on the satellite. We had been out to a church meeting earlier. That's why Gerald was working so late in the barn. Then, there was a string of oaths that would do a drill sergeant proud. Gerald ran from the barn, causing the outside lights to come on. I guess that scared them. He saw the truck speed away, a blue Dodge, one boy in the back holding both of his shoulders and screaming in pain.

"He ran down to the mailbox. It was unmarked except for a little chipping of the paint along the front edge. On the ground was one of those new metal bats, aluminum I think, with a big dent in it. Gerald's got it out in the barn in case anyone wanted to come and claim it. No one did, of course. At the legion, there were stories about some kid who mysteriously strained the muscles in both of his arms. Some said he couldn't even lift a fork to feed himself. Gerald never claimed any credit. He didn't to it for the glory. Just wanted to have some peace and quiet. That was about two months ago. Nobody has squealed a wheel in front of our house since."

"Your husband seems like a man who defended his rights," Jim said. "Could we see that bat? There may be usable finger prints on it." He signaled Scott and the two men moved towards the door. "Get the forensic guys to have a look at the bat. Humiliation can be a big motivator for revenge. You know his friends would have made a big joke of this. I can only imagine the kind of swing he probably took. It would be the classic unstoppable force meeting the famous immovable object. Male crying may be accepted in some circles but I doubt that this is one of them. A jolt like that would bring tears to anyone's eyes. After the first week or so, that teasing may have been worse than the physical pain. It may have taken a couple of months for his injuries to heal enough to respond."

"Serves him right. Who says there is no justice in this world?" Scott fought back a smile from the image of the bat-swinging thug getting his comeuppance.

Jim waved a "behave yourself" finger in his face but he too could not suppress a smile of his own. Then his face took on a serious demeanor. "It's all fun and games until someone dies."

Jim returned to the room and resumed his uncomfortable perch on the antique chair. "Don't take this the wrong way, but your husband seemed determined to not have anyone put anything over on him. Did this create any other difficulties with anyone else in the community? Was he feuding with any other family?" From experience, Jim knew that petty occurrences could often get blown way out of proportion. The Hatfields and the McCoys were more than just an old country song. Members of these southern families actually killed each other.

Mable looked thoughtful for a moment and peered at Sarah. "Gerald was set in his ways, but generally he got along with most people. Don't you agree, Sarah?"

Sarah set down her teacup and leaned towards Jim. "Don't get the wrong idea about my brother from how he acted with these young punks. They were right on his doorstep and it went on year after year. There was always a new crop of yahoos coming along to take over and some of them never grew out of it." She looked at Mable. "That Karl Tiley from over the road, he's almost 40 and still acts like a teenager. Never grew up. I think he's touched in the head." She looked back at Jim. "Most people like Gerald. His outspokenness put into words what everyone else was thinking. They kind of looked up to him."

Jim noticed Mable's head nodding agreement. She had been too modest to blow her husband's horn. This revelation would cause him to reassess his opinion of Gerald. Everyone had at least one pet peeve. These boys were Gerald's.

"Tell me about Ralph." He looked at Sarah. "He's your son, I assume."

"Yes. He's been helping his uncle for about ten years now, ever since the mill closed down. Mable tells me he was sick today. I didn't know anything about it. He has a place of his own just up the road."

Mable took up the narration. "Ralph came in yesterday morning, around five like always. About fifteen minutes after he got here, Gerald came into the kitchen to get me. Said Ralph was throwing up something awful. Wouldn't go home. Wanted me to come out and talk to him. I tried but Ralph was determined to soldier on. After the third time of talking into the big porcelain phone, Gerald insisted he go home or he was going to fire him. Told him to take today off as well and get better. The clincher was when Gerald said he, personally, was too old to fight off the flu and didn't want Ralph giving it to him.

"First time Ralph's missed work in ten years and look what happened." Again, uninvited, tears welled in her eyes.

Jim passed her a box of tissues from a side table. "I'll need Ralph's exact address. He might know about some problems Gerald was having that he had kept from you. Husbands do that sometimes."

Mable shook her head. "Gerald had no secrets from me. I knew if he wasn't telling me something. I could make him talk."

Jim didn't argue. "We'll still have to talk with Ralph."

CHAPTER 10

THE BUILDING SEASON was drawing to a close. Soon snow would be flying. Josh Daniels wanted to get all his ongoing projects roof-tight before that weather phenomenon took place. In this way he could create employment for much of his staff well after other companies started laying people off. This served two purposes. Most importantly, it allowed him to retain the best tradesmen in the business. Secondly it extended the revenue stream for both his company and Kevin Barnhill's investors.

To be totally honest, Josh saw these investors as merely a necessary evil. Without them, he would not have ten houses still in the works. With each of them taking a cut, the houses Josh built had to be sold at a higher price than he considered necessary. Josh understood the cost of materials and the cost of labour. He even accepted that the real estate agents were entitled to a piece of the pie. His ego liked to tell him that the houses were of such high quality that they sold themselves. In the competitive markets of the real world, he knew this wasn't true. Without people like Victor tracking down the buyers, convincing them this was the house of their dreams and doing the necessary paper work, all his labours would be in vain.

But the investors. They demanded their 30 pieces of silver on a regular schedule, sometimes before the houses were even finished. They didn't care if there had been a delay for some reason. They didn't understand the vagaries of the weather, sometimes materials weren't available when needed or sometimes the fates just connived against you. All they saw was that they were promised a return on their investments and they wanted it, now. At least, that was Kevin Barnhill's problem. Somehow he juggled the finances to keep everyone sort of happy. Josh didn't know how and truth be told, he didn't care what hoops Kevin jumped through.

Josh did understand some return was required in exchange for startup funds. He just questioned the amount of the return. It was not as if this was a risky investment. As fast as people could build good-quality housing, others would be available to fill it. Sometimes Josh wondered where all these home buyers came from. There seemed to be a never-ending supply of them. They were as essential a part of the chain as any other step along the way. Perhaps the most essential. Without the buyers, everything else would be like government work. Everyone would look busy, but the end product would serve no useful purpose.

Today Josh had to leave the building sites to have another meeting with Kevin. This was a task previously filled by Cliff Lawrence. Victor Boyd had stepped up to fill the void of running the real estate company but most of the time Kevin bypassed him and dealt directly with Josh. Victor was a crackerjack salesman. In most cases, he could close the deal on these houses without even breaking a sweat. He made the buyers feel he was on their side. But somehow, he made the investors nervous. They didn't want to hear talk about shaving a little profit here, dropping the price a little there to remain competitive with other builders in the neighbourhood. All these trimmings came directly from their pockets, they felt. Most of the other costs were pretty much fixed.

Today's meeting would deal with the following year's money. Next year was already locked in. Land bought and cleared. Supplies ordered, just waiting for Josh's crew to perform their magic.

Now some of Kevin's backers were threatening to pull out. They had heard about Cliff's death and were worried his absence might affect their bottom lines. Kevin wanted Josh to reassure them that essentially nothing had changed. Cliff would be missed but the people building the houses were still the same as always. The quality, which Cliff had always made a point of guaranteeing, would not change. Josh used to chuckle over this guarantee. Cliff never entered the picture until the houses were finished. It was a promise that he could not affect one way or the other. Still the money people seemed to be more impressed when someone in a tailor-made suit made the promise than someone in a T-shirt and overalls, someone who would actually be producing the quality.

Given time, Victor may develop this gift of gab for sucking up to the investors. For now, he was too honest. He knew who guaranteed quality and who didn't. He lied to no one. Josh, on the other hand, could make that promise with no feelings of duplicity. His reputation rode on every home. He took no chances with it.

Josh entered the upscale restaurant on Barrington Street's south end. This was billed as a breakfast meeting. Josh had finished that meal more than two hours ago and had been spinning his wheels during the interim. The suit Kevin insisted he wear did not fit on construction sites. He had filled the time going over figures for this meeting, figures that required no memorization. He had painstakingly worked them out over and over until they were second nature to him. These were not mere numbers on paper but the essence of what would be required to produce a profit in the following year for all concerned. He could boil down his presentation to these people to one five-word sentence. He knew what they wanted to hear.

"Your return will be $X."

Everything else he said would be wasted breath. Josh knew that. Kevin knew that. Still the charade had to be carried out. It was part of the dance.

The maître d' greeted him with a smile and escorted him to a back room where four men and two women were already waiting. Kevin met him in the doorway. He was not smiling. This meeting had been going on for over half an hour. Kevin's job was to lay the ground work. Josh would come in to furnish the details about projected costs, finishing times and numbers of units that could be built. These people all had questions, all scribbled notes on yellow lined pads, all had no idea what he was talking about. Unconsciously he straightened his unfamiliar tie and took his place at the head of the table and opened his briefcase.

"I hear the bottom is about to drop out of the real estate market," one of the seated men said before Josh even had a chance to say good morning. There were nods of agreement around the table.

Josh looked over at Kevin who simply shrugged. This vitriol had been going on since the meeting began. Obviously, this was phase two of the meeting for the investors. They had met among themselves to plan their strategy before meeting Kevin. They were after an even bigger piece of the pie.

Josh smiled. "I've heard that report as well." He paused and looked from face to face before continuing. "I heard it last year, the year before, the year before that and ..." He appeared to be in deep thought "...yes. The year before that as well."

"But this time I have it from a reliable source," the same voice, obviously the selected spokesman. "The bull market has run its course. Stock prices are falling."

Josh gathered his papers and placed them back in the brown case and snapped shut the closures. "Ladies, gentlemen, I build houses. I don't shuffle papers. I deal in bricks and mortar, not scraps of worthless paper. I have a building season to finish and another one to prepare for. I'm sorry you're going to miss out on the opportunities." He started for the door. Slowly, he counted backwards in his mind: five, four, three, two...

"Wait." A woman's voice.

He continued to the doorway and took the knob in his hand before turning to face the gathered assembly. "You sound like your minds are made up to me. I have the projections here for next year's building season. It will be profitable." He held up the case. "Nothing is carved in stone, but let me assure you, your percentage of the take is not going to increase. If you want to make more money from this, simply make a bigger investment."

A heavy layer of silence settled across the table. Josh had called their bluff. Would they call his? Kevin stepped to the head of the table. He had played this game before but never with this approach. Cliff had always used humour to fight the attempted grab for more of a share of the profits. Sometimes it worked, sometimes there had been concessions. Josh's approach seemed to leave little room for negotiations. He held up his hands.

"Come on folks, let's at least listen to what Josh has to say. You've already blocked off this time in your BlackBerrys. He's the man with the answers to all your production questions. Let's listen to what he has to say."

The spokesman stood up. "My sources are reliable. If I'm taking a bigger risk, I need a bigger return."

A soft clunking sound came from the direction of the doorway. All eyes turned to see its source. The door was closed. Josh was gone.

CHAPTER 11

RALPH FOLEY LIVED a scant five minutes by car up the road from his uncle's farm. His house was small by any standards, 12x20 at the outside. There was a new, red truck parked in the yard and the remains of a small vegetable garden to one side. A neat stack of firewood protected the west side of the house from the ever prevalent westerly winds. No smoke came out of the silver chimney running up the outside of the building, a possible indicator the man was still in bed. Jim knocked heavily on the door, waited a few seconds and knocked again.

The door opened. A big, weather-beaten man of indeterminate age stood there in a set of long johns. His salt-and-pepper hair pointed in all directions. Dark pouches under his eyes testified to a poor night's sleep. On seeing the two policemen on his doorstep he snapped wide awake.

"What's going on?" he asked. He squinted at his watch as the bright early-morning sun shone through the door into the darkened one-room house. It was 9:30 a.m., long after his usual time of rising.

"Ralph Foley?" Jim asked, knowing full well it had to be. He could have passed as Gerald's son instead of his nephew.

"Yeah." Ralph looked confused.

"May we come in? We have some information for you."

Ralph stepped back. The room was neat and tidy. The linoleum floor gleamed from a fresh waxing. The sink stood free of dirty dishes. Clothes hung from hangers on a rack in a corner of the room. A small, gray Sony television sat on a five-foot high shelf in one corner of the room. Two doors were set into the back wall. Jim assumed one would be a bathroom. He was at a loss to know what was behind the other. The main room seemed to be a combined kitchen, living-room, bedroom, everything a man living alone needed.

Jim's eyes did a quick sweep of the room. Being as sick as Ralph was supposed to be, dirtying dishes was not on the agenda for the last day or so. Food was the last thing on his mind, but still the place was exceptionally neat. Somehow, he had expected to see at least a little bit of clutter. God knows his own apartment was never free of it.

The small kitchen table had two chairs. Jim sat in one. He indicated to Ralph that he should sit in the other. Slowly the big man lowered his bulky frame into the chair, his eyes shifting from the uniformed cop to the man in the suit.

Scott walked around the room. Two rifles hung in a rack on one wall, a .303 Savage and a .22. Scott took them down and checked their workings. Both were unloaded. Both had trigger guards. Neither had been fired recently.

Ralph watched Scott's progress. "You're wondering if I went through that stupid registration process?"

Scott looked over at him. Actually, the thought hadn't occurred to him.

"I have my card around here somewhere." Ralph pointed towards the other unopened door. "I took part in that $2 billion boondoggle."

Jim looked towards the door with a questioning look.

"My office," Ralph said. "It's where I keep my computer and files."

Jim looked surprised. Another stereotype shattered. He shrugged and went on. "We just came from your uncle's house. You weren't at work this morning."

Ralph nodded. "I've not been feeling too good," Ralph said. "The flu, I reckon. Uncle Gerald ordered me to stay home."

"So we've been told," Jim said, then came right to the point. "Gerald Booth is dead." Jim watched for a reaction.

"Dead? Uncle Gerald? How? When?"

The news rattled Ralph to his core.

"I should have been there. I've never missed a day in over ten years. I knew the work was too much for him to do alone. I told him that, too. But no, he insisted I take the day off. God, I hope he didn't catch my flu, not at his age."

Jim looked at Scott. Both men tacitly agreed this was not an act. Ralph was genuinely shocked at the news. "Gerald was shot coming out of the barn. You may be lucky you weren't there."

"Shot? Don't be foolish, man. Who would want to shoot Uncle Gerald? He's a pillar of the community."

"That's what we're trying to determine. The shots appear to have come from the direction of Chris Ritchey's farm."

A change came over Ralph at the mention of the name. His previous innocent demeanor seemed to diminish. Sweat broke out across his forehead.

Jim picked up the change immediately. "Is there a problem between Chris and your uncle?"

Ralph composed himself.

"No, of course not. Chris wouldn't shoot Uncle Gerald. He wouldn't. That makes no sense. They've been neighbours for years." Ralph looked away from the two policemen still shaking his head. He appeared deep in thought. "Chris's got religion lately. A lot of his old friends avoid talking to him. He appears to be out to proselytize the entire community."

He gave his head a little shake as if clearing those thoughts. "Not Gerald though, he treated him the same as always. When Chris tried to talk religion, Gerald would just nod his head a few times and then change the subject."

Scott left his position by the door where he had been examining a black cap similar to one worn by Gerald. It, too, bore the chain-saw maker's bright orange logo. This one had no hole in it. He walked over to the table.

"You don't look very good. Did you see a doctor about your sickness?"

"A doctor? No, I've got the flu. I don't need to waste my time seeing a doctor."

"Throwing up is not always the flu. You most likely have food poisoning. Have you eaten anything out of the ordinary in the last couple of days?"

"I cooked some scallops the other night. I thought they tasted off. Do you really think I'm poisoned? Who would want to poison me?" The thought of his uncle being murdered seemed to trigger a paranoid reaction in Ralph.

"No one, intentionally. It happens to people all the time and they think it's the flu. Poor food handling is the usual culprit. It sounds like salmonella, only lasts a day or so."

Ralph gave the policeman a disgusted look. "I don't care what fancy name you want to hang on it. As far as I'm concerned, I've got the flu."

"Whatever," Scott said. "Do you think there is someone out there who would want to harm you? Someone who would kill Gerald and try to kill you?"

Ralph screwed his face into a look of disgust. "We're farmers, for God's sake, not some big city thugs. The whole idea is too stupid to contemplate."

Ralph looked back to Jim. "There's been talk of coyotes running loose on some of the nearby farms. Any farmer who sees one of those killers is liable to take a shot at it, day or night. They can kill a lot of livestock in a short time."

Jim shook his head. "What are you implying? Someone shot at a coyote, missed, and hit Gerald instead?"

"Could happen," Ralph said. "I think it might have been Chris Ritchey who was warning Gerald about them. Two or three farms on that side of the road are within sight of Gerald's farm. A .22 will carry for a mile, according to the warning on the box."

Scott stepped closer to the two sitting men. "Every one of those firemen who were there this morning will be spreading the word about Gerald's shooting. Now that word is out, I can't see anyone stepping forward and admitting they were out shooting in the dark."

"Of course they would," Ralph said. "No one intended to kill Gerald. It was an accident."

"I hope you're right," Scott said. "We'll talk to everyone along that road. See if anyone was out shooting varmints." His voice carried no conviction.

Jim took up the questioning again. "Your uncle was having some problems with the local kids?"

Ralph turned the disgusted look to Jim. "Those young assholes? None of them had enough guts to shoot Uncle Gerald. They only operated under the cover of darkness. Spinning their tires and wrecking other people's property was the limit of their simpleminded ability to act."

"You're referring to the mailbox incident?"

"Yeah. It was easy enough to find out who did that. The lazy bastard couldn't do anything for weeks, not that anyone noticed the difference. I had a talk to him."

Scott let out a heavy sigh. "You had a talk with him?"

"I told them to stay the fuck away from Uncle Gerald's house before someone got seriously hurt. They got the message. None of them shot anybody."

Jim studied the farm hand a little closer. There was not an ounce of fat on the 210-pound frame. His dark eyes had a smoldering quality about them that suggested you didn't want to cross him. If Jim had to guess, he would place Ralph's age as late 30s. No teenage boy would want to be on the receiving end of this man's wrath. His attitude seemed to mirror that of his uncle's.

"Your uncle knew about this conversation?" Jim asked.

Ralph shook his head. "No. You have to understand Uncle Gerald. He was from a different era, a different time. He still believes that kids should respect their elders just because they're older. He doesn't understand that some of these young punks don't respect anybody or anything. They still have a lot of growing up to do before they can get out in the real world." Ralph paused for a second before continuing.

"In a way they have a lot in common with Uncle Gerald. They don't understand how the world today works either. When they get out into the work force with their attitudes, they're in for a big surprise. Employers don't give a damn how tough they had it as kids or how little there was for them to do. They'll just fire their sorry asses if they don't produce."

Ralph looked reflective for a moment. "You know the really sad part of that? These kids don't give a shit. They'll have to be fired four or five times before they realize the world doesn't give a shit either. By then, for some it will be too late. They will turn to crime to survive. There they'll discover a whole new set of rules than the ones they came across as kids. Instead of the gentle slap on the wrist doled out to *young offenders*," Ralph turned those two words into an expletive, "they'll find themselves doing jail time. That's where they'll really grow up in a hurry. Right now they think they're tough. In jail, they'll find out what that word means."

"You sound like you know what you're talking about," Scott said.

Ralph forced a slight smile and slowly shook his head. "No, not me. My younger brother." He fell silent again as if in another place and another time. "Thought he was so damned smart," Ralph said in a low voice, barely above a whisper. Then he looked up at Jim and continued in his normal tone. "Was as big as me, maybe even bigger. But that didn't cut it in prison. I tell you these young assholes around here wouldn't kill Uncle Gerald. My brother was as bad as they came. If he had what it took to kill someone, he might still be alive today."

Jim's head snapped up. "He died in prison?"

"Doesn't matter how good you are with your fists or smart with your mouth if someone slams a sharpened toothbrush into your back. Guy that killed him never felt an ounce of remorse. His world and my brother's world weren't even from the same universe. In that punk's world, if someone farted off key, it was grounds to waste him.

He weighed about one-seventy. Claimed self-defence. Stand him beside my brother and it was an easy call of not guilty. I saw him laughing on his way out of court. To him, it was all one big joke. Now he could have easily killed Uncle Gerald, but not the yahoos around here."

"You didn't try to dissuade your uncle from building the killer mailbox?" Scott asked. "You sound like you think it was a waste of time."

"It was, but that didn't stop Uncle Gerald. He thought it was the stupid mailbox trick that drove them away. All that was going to do was make matters worse. I could see this whole thing escalating out of control. I knew I had to intervene so I talked to them in language they understood. I was young once. I know what it's like living around here with nothing to do. I told them to play their silly games someplace else."

"And that worked?" Scott asked. It seemed too simple.

"Yeah, it worked. Look at the road out in front of my house."

Scott glanced through the kitchen window. Black streaks snaked up and down the roadway in both directions. Black circles created an entrance way to the driveway. Miles of tread wear had been deposited on 50 feet of roadway.

Ralph laughed. "I've done it myself. It doesn't bother me. When you get up at 4:30 in the morning and put in a full day of honest labour, it takes more than the gunning of engines and the squealing of tires to keep you awake at night. I simply moved the problem to someplace where it wasn't a problem. Every so often, I go out and shake my fist at them to keep them interested. Let them have their fun."

Ralph slid back his chair and stood up. "I've got to get down to the farm and see Aunt Mable. Is she all right? Damn, why would anyone hurt Uncle Gerald? It must have been an accident."

Jim stood as well. "Your mother is with her. If you can think of anyone else your uncle may have had a problem with, let us know." He put an arm on Ralph's shoulder and turned him so they were looking into each other's eyes. "Let us know. We will handle it. You take care of your aunt."

Ralph stared back. Their eyes locked. A few seconds silently ticked off the kitchen clock. "Right," Ralph said, "we'll try it your way. If I think of anyone, I'll be in touch."

Jim let go of the shoulder and took a business card from his suit coat pocket. He passed it to Ralph. "Let us handle it." He paused between each word. Ralph reached out for the card but Jim didn't let go. He held the card in his hand, his eyes still held Ralph's. This time Ralph wasn't staring down some scared teenager. Jim showed no signs of being intimidated by Ralph's bulk. He had been in tougher confrontations than this, once or twice with a gun filling in the role of the business card. Finally Ralph nodded again.

"I'll call you."

This time he sounded like he meant it.

CHAPTER 12

ONCE OUTSIDE, THE two policemen watched as Ralph sped towards his aunt's farm. His insight into the whole situation seemed well reasoned and probably true. That did not add to the joy of Jim's day. He had been hoping for a quick resolution to this murder. An out-of-control young punk sounded like the perfect perpetrator to him.

Overhead, Jim noticed the sky was taking on an ominous black colour. Big, dark clouds were rolling in from the west. The air felt as if rain could burst from the sky at any moment. Jim pulled his overcoat tighter and approached Scott's cruiser.

"Ralph gave me the name of the young yahoo..." Jim chuckled at the addition to his vocabulary, "...who beat up the mailbox. I think we've got to talk to him somewhere along the line. That way we can come to our own conclusions as to whether or not murder is part of his psyche. I've heard too many neighbours in too many cases say with all earnestness that 'He was such a nice boy. I can't believe he killed anyone.' Those remarks would be made after I had taken the kid in question into custody. What do you think?"

"Without a doubt, he's still our main suspect. Everyone knew where the old man would be at that time every morning. Every kid in this neighbourhood owns a .22 from the time they are old enough to hold one up to their eye. That gives the young punk opportunity, means and most definitely motive." Scott opened the cruiser door and looked across the roof at Jim. "Chief Cosh also advanced the 'fox in the hen house' theory about the shooting."

Jim gave him a blank look and shook his head.

"He's heard the stories about the coyotes coming out of the woods and into the fields around the farms. Claims the locals shoot varmints on a regular basis. Skunks, foxes, rats, coyotes." He waited while the thought settled in Jim's mind. "Ralph may be right. I saw a dead coyote in the ditch on my way to the crime scene this morning.

This whole thing might have been an another unfortunate accident. Somebody shooting at a coyote in the hen house."

"Two accidental shootings in two months? Could happen I guess. The community must have a real bad karma."

"I looked around the area from the barn. There are gentle hills all around. The only house really in sight is the Ritchey farm, although I could see a few buildings off in the distance."

Jim held up his hands in a defensive pose. "Let's not even go there, yet. Accidental shooting. I hope you're right. But, as you said, no one is likely to flag us down and say 'I killed Gerald Booth. Sorry. Didn't mean it.' We could spend days investigating and come up empty handed. Let's check this kid out instead, just in case you're wrong. It at least gives us a solid place to start."

Scott started up the patrol car and revved the engine. He stopped at the end of Ralph's driveway and looked at the myriad tire marks before heading back in the direction of the Booth farm. "There's the controversial mailbox. Let's see what everyone is talking about before the rain starts. It looks like we're in for one hell of a soaking. Then we'll find that yahoo that Ralph Foley told us about."

Both men exited the car and studied the box in front of them. Jim took hold of it in both hands and gave it a shake. The Statue of Liberty was less solidly anchored in its footing in New York Harbour. The box and the earth beneath it were one with the universe.

Scott smiled at him. "Having seen the bat and the damage to it and now seeing the lack of damage here, I have to say Gerald was a master craftsman when it came to defeating mailbox bashers." He pointed to a small mark on the leading edge of the mailbox. "You can see where the paint is chipped away right here." A closer examination of the side showed a distortion in the paint if you looked into the light exactly the right way.

Jim looked up the road in the direction the truck would have been travelling. "I can picture it in my mind. The young kid standing in the back of the moving truck, feet braced, bat cocked, squealing at the top of his lungs. Then a swing that would have been the envy of Babe Ruth, Hank Aaron and Barry Bonds, a swing for all the ages. A wild, war whoop would be coming from his lips right up to the moment of contact." Jim demonstrated the movement with his arms stopping even with the side of the mailbox. He shook his arms in an accurate demonstration of vibrations travelling up to his shoulders.

"Visions of a home run would be replaced with the sudden realization that the bat was on the ground, the muscles in his arms and shoulders had gone numb and he was lying on his back in the bed of the truck looking up at the stars. His arms would be too stunned to break the fall, so he probably smacked his head as well.

"The kids in the cab would still be living it up, not even realizing the screams from the back were of pain and not joy. It's scary what some people find pleasure in." He shook his head. "Let's go hear how his version of the story agrees with mine."

Scott consulted the address given to them by Ralph Foley and continued down the roadway. Before long they spotted the white numbers on the blue background indicating the house they were looking for. It was a storey-and-half farmhouse set back about fifty feet from the road. Like most of its neighbours, the spruce shingles had been replaced with white vinyl siding. Several junked cars were lined up in a field behind the house. There were two unpainted outbuildings but neither was big enough to be called a barn. To the left of the house were the remains of the summer's vegetable garden. Eisenhauer was written in large letters across the wooden mailbox. Hanging below it were six individual slats of wood, each containing a name. That would indicate a mother, a father and four children. Halfway down was the name: Darrin. This was the subject of their investigation. He appeared to be the oldest son by his placement on the list.

Scott turned into the driveway and brought his cruiser to a halt in front of the open doors of one of the outbuildings. A short, stocky man of about forty appeared in the doorway. He brushed sawdust from his blue smock and removed his hat and gave it a shake. Behind him could be seen a well-furnished woodworking shop.

Jim leaned out the car window in the man's direction. "Looking for a Darrin Eisenhauer," he said.

The man approached the car. No smile crossed his face. "Sorry, you've missed him. He left early this morning. Drove him to the airport myself. Why do the police want to talk to Darrin?"

Jim stepped from the car. The lead suspect being dispatched on an airplane threw a new wrinkle into the case. "Where was he heading?"

"Slow down partner. You're one answer behind. What interest do the police have with my son?" The man held his position, forcing Jim to stand with his backside touching the car door.

Scott exited the vehicle from the driver's side and made his way around the front of the car. He took up a position to the right of the elder Eisenhauer. His hand rested lightly on the butt of the black nine-millimetre pistol at his waist. The man held up his hands in a conciliatory gesture.

"Hold on fellows. Let's not get excited. All I'm asking is why you want to talk to my boy."

Jim took a step forward. If Darrin Eisenhauer was the killer, his father was in danger of being charged with aiding and abetting. His eyes darkened. His voice took on a threatening tone. "Where was your son heading?"

The elder Eisenhauer took a faltering step backwards. He looked up at the cop. "Alberta. Him and two of his buddies got jobs out there. Sure as hell ain't nothing for them to do around here except work at some fastfood joint in town."

"Was this a sudden decision?"

"No. They've been planning it for a couple of weeks or more. They went to a job fair in Halifax a while back and got hired by some big company out there. Darrin was recovering from strained muscles in his arms so they had to wait awhile before they could go."

"What happened to his arms?" Scott asked. He let his hands fall to his sides now that they were getting answers to their questions.

"Kids fooling around. Hit a post with a baseball bat or something stupid like that. I never did get all the details. Learned his lesson though. His arms have been sore for a couple of months. This trip west seemed to speed up his recovery. Now, I'm asking you polite like. Why do you want to talk to my boy?"

"We're investigating a murder and your son's name came up in our discussions. What flight did he leave on?"

"Murder investigation? What would Darrin have to do with a murder investigation? He may have his wild side but my boy is no killer. You guys are barking up the wrong tree on this."

"Nobody is accusing anybody of anything at the moment. What time did your son's flight leave?"

"Seven o'clock this morning. I've got all the details inside but Darrin didn't kill anybody." The man paused and a shroud seemed to pass over his face. "Who's dead anyway?"

Jim looked towards the house, alerted by the sound of the opening door. A woman in a simple cotton dress came running onto the top step. She stopped short when she saw the police car in the yard and two men, one in uniform talking to her husband.

"Merrill, Gerald Booth has been murdered. Why are the police here?"

The two statements gushed from her mouth, fighting for prominence. Her voiced raised on the last "here" as if this was the last place for policemen to be. Jim noticed the woman's eyes were red and puffy as if she had been doing some heavy-duty crying. Scott was the first to react. He headed for the porch.

"Ma'am, are you all right?" he asked.

"No, I'm not all right. One of my neighbours has been shot. My boy has left home to go miles across the country looking for work. I have no idea when I will see him again and the police are questioning my husband. Why would I be all right?" Again the words came out in a torrent.

Merrill looked at Jim as if to explain. "She's been crying off and on ever since Darrin announced he was heading west. These last two days, it's been almost nonstop. She doesn't understand that the boy has grown up and must strike out on his own. Was it Gerald that was shot? I can't imagine anyone wanting to shoot him. Good God, he got along with everybody."

"Including your son?" Jim asked.

"Darrin? I doubt if he even knew him."

"He may not have known him but he knew of him. Your son and a bunch of the local kids have been harassing Mr. Booth for some time now."

"Darrin? I don't believe that. It's bullshit. Who told you this?"

The two men had been walking towards the house as they talked. They were now at the foot of the steps beside Scott and looking up at the distraught face of Mrs. Eisenhauer.

"Darrin wouldn't harass anybody," the woman said, conviction in her voice. "He's a good boy."

Big drops of rain suddenly dropped from the sky like a pulsating shower head, causing puffs of dust to pop up in the dirt driveway. Jim turned back to the senior Eisenhauer. "You were going to show me your son's itinerary. Now seems like a good time." He followed the man up the steps and past the wife. She seemed oblivious of the sudden rain squall. Big wet splotches appeared on her cotton dress, each drop spreading to a two-inch circle.

"My Darrin's a good boy. Why aren't you out looking for Gerald's killer instead of bothering us?"

Jim ignored the comment and slipped into the house. She followed behind him. Outside the rain was now coming down in sheets. The wind had come up and waves of water passed through the air by the front door. Mrs. Eisenhauer took one last look as Mother Nature displayed her artistic talents with water colours and slammed the door shut to the storm.

Inside the kitchen, Merrill handed the piece of paper to Jim. It had been lying on the table where he had tossed it on returning from the airport early that morning. Jim reached for the itinerary as he looked around the old-fashioned country kitchen. It probably measured 14 by 16, with the table taking up the centre space. On the far wall was a pale green and cream coloured woodstove. The word Enterprise was written in raised, metallic script across the oven door. A neat stack of hardwood filled a wooden frame beside the stove. A black chimney pipe protruded from the back, arced upward and disappeared into the ceiling overhead. A pot of soup simmered in an old stainless-steel pot near the back. The spicy smell assaulted his nostrils, reminding him that it must be near lunch time and he suddenly felt hungry.

In contrast to the old stove, a new, all-white Maytag dishwasher was tucked into the corner by the double sinks. A refrigerator, also a Maytag, was along the opposite wall from the stove. Energy conservers would be pleased with this arrangement, maximum separation between hot and cold. Efficiency experts would disagree, thinking the stove and fridge should be within reach of each other. Jim never had to give the matter much thought. The kitchen in his apartment was so small that everything was within reach of everything else.

He looked down at the paper in his hand and read the details aloud. "Flight 803 departing Halifax at seven, one stop in Toronto and arriving in Calgary at 11:10 a.m." He looked at his watch. "Of course that arrival is Calgary time. The plane would still be in the air." He looked at Scott. "We could have someone meet it when it lands."

Merrill snatched the paper from Jim's hands. "What aren't you telling us? You don't go to that much effort for routine questions."

"Does your son own a .22?" Jim asked, again ignoring Merrill's questions.

"Of course he does. He's a boy, isn't he? I gave him one of mine when he turned 12. He knows how to handle it safely. I taught him myself."

Jim said nothing, simply stared at the man.

"I'll get it for you," Merrill said and turned towards the steps. "It's been fired recently. Darrin and his friends were out plinking at cans a couple of days ago, you know, target practice. They do it all the time."

Jim looked over at Scott. He gave a slight flick with his head. "I'll go with you," Scott said. He followed the father up the steps and out of sight down a hallway.

"What time did your son get up this morning?" Jim asked the mother.

She hesitated. "He was pretty excited about this trip. I'm not sure he ever actually went to bed. He was awake when I got up at 4:30, all dressed and ready to go. They told him he had to be at the airport two hours early but we told him that was hogwash. We got him there around quarter to six and that was lots of time." Again her eyes filled with tears. Separation anxiety had been tearing her apart before Jim's arrival. His accusations were not helping her any.

"So you left here at what time to get to the airport?"

"Around five. He almost dragged us out the door before I had a chance to have my morning tea. Made me drink it on the way."

"So he was anxious to get going?"

"This was an adventure for him, Officer. He's been anxious ever since he met those people in Halifax. I tried to be excited for him but I was missing him before he even left. It's a crime that our boys have to go to Alberta to find work. What's wrong with our government that they can't find good jobs right here at home?"

Before he could answer, if indeed he had an answer, Scott and Merrill appeared at the top of the steps. Scott carried a .22 rifle by the barrel. He had a black glove on his hand. Jim looked back at the woman. "Did you know how your son injured himself?"

"Playing baseball," she answered, without hesitation.

"Right," Jim said. "Rough game."

Scott held the gun out towards Jim and turned it in the light. "It's been cleaned. Fresh coat of oil all over it. Looks like some good fingerprints. No one used this gun but the boy so we should be able to compare these prints to the ones on the bat."

"Wait a minute. No one said anything about getting fingerprints." Merrill reached for the gun but Scott put it down at his side.

"Innocent people don't have anything to worry about, Mr. Eisenhauer. You keep telling us what a good boy your son is. This will prove it."

"Or not," Jim added under his breath. Mrs. Eisenhauer looked sharply at him. She had not quite caught the words, only the tone.

CHAPTER 13

JOSH DANIELS BIT into his muffin and looked around at his fellow diners. He felt much more comfortable in these confines, a steaming mug of Tim Horton's coffee in his hand. His fellow patrons covered all walks of life. There were suited businessmen, uniformed cashiers, casually-dressed workers and relaxed retirees. All were enjoying a break. None were trying to hustle someone for more money.

The cell phone on his belt gave a couple of beeps, the ringtone of an English telephone. Josh gave those nearest him an apologetic smile before unsnapping the phone and pushing the talk button. He hesitated before saying anything. A lot was riding on this call. The company needed the guaranteed financial backing that his breakfast meeting investors could provide. Kevin had deduced, correctly as it turned out, that they would be looking for a bigger cut. Josh's dramatic exit had been stage-managed right down to the final look he gave the table before leaving. Now he would discover if the plan had been a success.

"Josh Daniels," he said into the small handheld device.

"Start placing orders for next year's supplies. They folded like a backyard deck chair."

Josh's shoulders noticeably sagged. Tension drained from his body like an open faucet.

"Thank God," he said. "I've watched Cliff carry out these bluffs many times. I never realized how stressful they could be. How much did we get?"

A deep chortle emanated from the phone. "More than enough. They even bought into your idea of investing more than we had asked for. You've got a busy couple of years ahead of you. We'll complete Phase Two and lay out the ground work for Phase Three of Ridgeway Estates. They totally bought into your version of the market place."

"That's no biggie. My version is the correct version. Real estate is still booming. Prices are so high that it may not be a great investment, but from a builder's point of view, this is where the action is. I don't see the demand easing up anytime soon."

"Exactly," Kevin said. "They bought into your sincerity. Next thing I knew they were planning bigger houses, smaller lots, more revenue. I had to slam on the brakes and remind them they only supplied the money. The planning was in the hands of experts."

"Good thing. There is a demand for those oversize monstrosities but the best return is on the smaller houses that baby boomers are downsizing into. They want them practical and well built so they won't have a lot of maintenance to do. Most have just sold a bigger house so money is not a factor."

"Exactly what I told them. They did make one suggestion worth considering. They want to name the main street Cliff Lawrence Drive. Cliff recruited a lot of them into this project. Most of them considered him the principal partner. His untimely death is what prompted today's meeting."

"How touching. I would think one of the side streets would be more appropriate. Cliff Lawrence Crescent. It captures more of Cliff's essence, a big, round, sweeping circle." The investors may not have realized it, but Josh knew that Cliff was merely the mouthpiece of the group. He had the gift of gab, the gift to make the investors feel as though they were an actual part of the whole process. The partnership cashed in on that gift. The real business savvy rested solely on Kevin's shoulders. The vision was his. The drive was his. He saw the investors for what they were: a source of funding. Josh understood his function was simply technical expertise, the ability to build good-quality houses in a reasonable length of time at a reasonable price. If that was to be his role in life, Kevin was the man to be doing it with. Josh didn't care what they called the streets. "Makes no difference to me. You decide."

Again Kevin laughed. "We could make it simpler. The road along the edge of the ravine could be called Cliff Street. In ten years time, when nobody but us remembers who Cliff Lawrence is, the name would still stand up." Kevin believed the naming of the streets was an important part of his developments. He believed in names that fit on a return address label and caused no snickering when read. A real estate salesman's name didn't quite fit the bill as far as he was concerned. At the same time, if the investors wanted a memorial to Cliff, he wanted to oblige. Anything to keep the money flowing in.

Josh took a sip of his coffee. "Sounds good. Whatever you think works. Make sure you get it into the paper work. I don't want any hassle with the authorities over street names. I have enough red tape to deal with now. Did you get actual cheques or just promises this morning?"

"Cheques. I told them the time for talk was over. Commit now or I would go to my other sources. They ponied up an initial investment. It didn't hurt that I also passed out a summary of how much they had made last year with my projected figures for next year. The bottom line is the same as yours. It just lacks the mundane details. They'll still want to know what all the costs are before we get all their money. They have to make presentations to their respective companies and investment houses."

"Yeah, well I'll mail it to them. They missed out on their chance to have it explained in detail. That was a one-time offer."

"I told them that. I think they're intimidated by you. Cliff had told them so much about the quality of work you demanded, your need for perfection, they were in awe meeting you in person. They think you are some kind of a construction god."

Josh blushed at this back-handed praise. "I like things done right," is all that he said.

Kevin allowed that statement to hang in the air for a few seconds. "This new arrangement may work out even better than it did with Cliff being the number two man. Next year we may go for a drop in their percentage return."

Josh nodded his head. "Why wait? I think they're getting more than they deserve right now."

Another booming laugh from Kevin. "Slow down tiger. We don't want to scare them off. At least let me get the cheques cashed first."

Josh drummed the table in front of him with his fingers. There had been something he was wondering about ever since he left the meeting. "Do only six people supply all our backing? Somehow I thought there would be more of them."

Kevin didn't answer right away. When he did there was an ambivalence to his voice. "They've got deep pockets but there is one other. He was already onboard. Nothing you were going to say would affect his judgment one way or the other." Kevin hesitated before continuing. "Let's say he's sort of a silent partner in the whole operation. When the time is right, I'll introduce you to him."

"I'm not sure I understand."

"There is nothing to understand. We have a seventh investor who prefers to remain anonymous. Right now the important thing is to have the cash flow to get rolling on next year's production. We wrapped that up this morning. How are the current houses going?"

The change of direction caught Josh off guard. This was not a question Kevin usually asked. If he wanted to know how things were going, he showed up on the site. There was no bullshitting him. He had been in this business all his adult life. He enjoyed the good life that the money provided him, but at heart he loved to see his dreams and plans come to fruition.

As a kid, he probably supervised the others on his block as they built up little cities with Legos. He had a flare for creating attractive living space. His projects were not simply the ticky-tacky houses from the old song. Each project had a theme of its own and attracted people who wanted to live in a subdivision with that theme – mature seniors, young families or up-and-coming junior executives. Kevin supplied the additions expected by each demographic. Seniors clubs in one, playgrounds in another or upscale restaurants in the third. Victor may have done the actual selling, but Kevin created the demand to start with.

"They're right on schedule. I guess I'd better get out of this monkey suit and back to the site and keep it that way." At this time of the year, the work had a flow of its own. Josh's presence or absence would make little difference. However, like Kevin, Josh took a special pride in seeing the results of his labours. "I'll be in touch."

He slid back his chair and headed for the door. Out the big picture window at the front of the restaurant he could see black clouds rolling in. The rain was only minutes away. He gave a silent prayer that all the current construction was roof tight. The rain would be a nuisance for anyone going back and forth to their vehicles for tools or supplies but it wouldn't interfere with the progress of the construction. He stepped onto the sidewalk and turned towards his truck. Huge drops of rain splatted on the sidewalk. Josh picked up his speed. He didn't wear a suit often and he didn't want to get it wet. It was a special occasion outfit that he hauled out ready to wear when the situation demanded it. A good soaking and it would have to go to the dry cleaners to be at least pressed. He made it to the truck in time and sat there watching the sudden cloud burst intensify. All around him people were scurrying for shelter, their hair already pasted to their foreheads.

My luck is holding, he thought. So far it's been a good day.

CHAPTER 14

"**H**E WANTS TO meet me?" Anthony Dellapinna asked when Kevin broke the connection to Josh. "I didn't think he knew about me."

Kevin shook his head. "Relax. He doesn't know about you. Josh is a smart man. He looked at the investors we had here this morning and knew something was wrong. He knows how much investment money comes in and those six people didn't add up to that supply in his mind. He wanted to know if there were more. My policy is that if you don't lie, you don't get caught up in a web of deceit. You heard what I told him."

"I heard. I also heard that he wants to meet me."

"No, you heard me tell him he would meet you when the time is right. He won't pursue the matter any further. Josh's sole concern is in the building end. As long as there is a hole in the ground for the foundation when he first arrives on the site, wood for the walls when he's ready and shingles for the roof when he needs them, he doesn't give a damn about the administration. Except of course, he expects to keep the cost of the houses reasonable. By that, he means not giving out too much in the way of dividends on the capital we raise."

Kevin put a hand on Dellapinna's shoulder and laughed. "He would approve of the return you get on your money."

Dellapinna failed to share the laughter. He didn't even smile. "I'm not a greedy man. I just like my money to be clean. Clean and anonymous."

The smile stayed on Kevin's face but the laugh lines went rigid. "That's what this morning's meeting was all about. As long as we have a reasonable source of legitimate money coming in, yours will stay lost in the shuffle. You'll just be another businessman struggling to make an honest buck." He squeezed the muscular shoulder. "Take me to lunch. You can write half of it off as a business expense."

Anthony Dellapinna had not attended the investor's meeting that morning. He had been present in the lobby when the others gathered. Like so many people these days, he had the earphones of his MP3 player plugged into the sides of his head. Unlike everyone else, his choice of listening was not music but the audio of the discussions held among the investors. Kevin had placed a small, inconspicuous microphone in the centre of the table as part of the flower arrangement.

Dellapinna trusted Kevin's business instincts. Had trusted them from their very first meeting. That was back when Kevin was first setting up the company and was trying to raise enough money to purchase their first block of land. Cliff Lawrence had introduced them. Dellapinna knew Cliff from the old neighbourhood. Dellapinna had listened with interest to the proposal and bought into it with a modest investment. The return was nothing to get excited about but the company was in its infancy. They built and sold five houses that first year. He remembered Josh as a conscientious builder at the time. Only the best went into these dwellings.

Over the following winter, Dellapinna approached Kevin with a proposal of his own. Practically unlimited funding, as long as Dellapinna controlled where the materials were purchased and there were enough other investors to make the company look legit. The money represented by the six people in that breakfast room was never an issue. What was important was that they think it was. They had to be convinced this was a legitimate enterprise and so did any snooping government agency: police, taxman, whoever.

As far as Josh was concerned the supplies were purchased by the company's purchasing agent. He was happy not to have to bother with that aspect of the building. He submitted his lists on a regular basis and the products showed up at the work sites as requested. Josh chalked the process up as more of Kevin's efficiencies.

Dellapinna never scrimped on quality. He was not trying to turn a quick profit on shady supplies. His concern was taking money from his other enterprises, which might not come under the definition of strictly legal, and having it turned into clean, spendable money accepted by any part of society.

His interest in this morning's meeting was to make sure Kevin was not too glib with the other investors. Kevin had to appear to want their business. Kevin insisted that appearing to take a stand on increasing returns would be expected by the others. Josh's indifference, although all part of the act, had worried Dellapinna at first. He feared the investors might simply walk out of the company taking their financial backing with them. Kevin was right. Kevin was almost always right. That didn't happen and no one backed out. Instead, they raised their investments. More money coming in from them afforded Dellapinna the chance to increase the money he ran through the company. All in all, it had been a good morning.

"Any new word on Cliff's shooting?" Dellapinna asked as they slipped into their seats in the hotel restaurant.

Kevin looked surprised at the question. "No. As I told you before, it was an accident. Cliff was in the wrong place at the wrong time. The police are not even investigating any longer. The issue is closed."

Dellapinna took a sip of the water that the waiter placed at his side before he had even adjusted his chair. The waiter moved on to the next table and refilled their water glasses. Dellapinna lowered his voice. "Excuse me, but I don't see very many accidental shootings. Are you sure Cliff wasn't involved in something nefarious, something that's going to come back and bite us in the ass?"

Kevin studied the other man's eyes. They were dark pools with no signs of emotion. "Cliff sold real estate. He spent his whole life making everyone like him. You were the most dangerous person he knew. You didn't kill him did you?" He softened the remark with a smile. None was returned.

"I did not, but if I find out that somebody did –" He let the remark trail off.

CHAPTER 15

FLASHES OF LIGHTNING lit up the inside of the police car holding Scott Bowen and Jim Mcdonald. Earth-shaking, ear-splitting claps of thunder that trailed off to long, rumbling echoes followed almost immediately. The two men were at the centre of this late fall nor'easter. Rain gushed in little rivers down the windshield, distorting their view of the outside world.

Sergeant Mcdonald pushed the end-call button on his cell phone and returned it to his pocket. "RCMP in Calgary will be waiting for Darrin Eisenhauer when his plane lands. They are going to hold him and his two friends as subjects of an investigation while we try to get some answers here."

Scott Bowen brushed some excess water from his jacket's sleeves. In the few seconds it took him to stow Darrin's .22 in the trunk of the car, he had gotten soaked. "This rain is not going to help our search any. I wonder if the forensic guys found anything before it started."

"They were waiting for the dog to be brought in. That will now be an exercise in futility. Let's go back and see if they had any luck at all." He wiped at the condensation building up on the inside of the passenger window. "Have you ever seen the rain come down like this?"

Another flash of lightning, punctuated with a simultaneous crack of thunder shook the car. Outside the driveway was turning into a muddy quagmire. Scott started the car and slowly edged forward. Even operating at full speed, the wipers were losing the battle to keep the windshield clear. He slumped down in his seat to peer through the clearing arc created by the defrosters as they battled the built-up humidity. "This is the kind of weather we advise people to stay off the roads in."

Jim looked over at the big Mountie crunched into his seat and smiled. "And that's damn good advice too. We'll park the car as soon as we get back to the Booth farm and let this blow over."

Four white-suited men stood in the double doorway of Gerald Booth's red barn staring out at the deluge. Their yellow crime scene tape flapped like party streamers in the wind. A black and brown German shepherd lay on the floor at the end of the lineup. The thunder and lightning didn't bother him. He had been trained to face a gun fired in his face and still keep attacking. His eyes shone like searchlight beams with each flash of lightning. His tongue hung out of his mouth, moving in and out in time to his panting. He was anxious to get back to work.

The others seemed less assured in the face of the raging storm.

Scott parked as near to the door as he could without going over the area where the body of Gerald Booth had been found. He and Jim dashed for the cover of the barn. The other men stepped aside to let them run under shelter. The barn lit up with another flash of lightning. This time the thunder was delayed a couple of seconds but still reverberated through the hollow structure. In the brief moment of bright light, they had spotted the body shape of Gerald Booth lying under a tarp in front of the barn.

"See the coroner has yet to arrive," Jim said.

"Still waiting," Robin West answered. "Sounds like the gods are doing battle over the poor man's immortal soul."

Jim laughed. "Yeah, who's winning?"

"The bad guys. Our crime scene has been wiped clean of any evidence. We did manage to find a freshly fired .22 cartridge in the field across the road just as the heavens opened up." He pointed into the storm in the direction of Chris Ritchey's farm which was totally obscured by the falling rain. One of the trees on the side of the hill split open by the lightning and crashed to the earth in front of us. We called off the search. Sorry, but safety of the team comes first."

Jim took off his overcoat and shook out the excess water. "No arguments from me on that front."

"We followed the trail for about 30 or 40 feet away from the house before the lightning stopped us. But that direction is not conclusive. The shooting location was in a dip between two hills. Banks on the east and west would have absorbed a lot of the sound from the rifle and .22s don't make a whole lot of noise to begin with. The chosen direction of travel was an almost natural trail up the side of the hill. The other choice would have been towards the victim."

Jim studied the forensics man. "I'm not sure what you're trying to tell me."

"I'm simply saying we didn't follow the exit path far enough to draw any conclusions as to the direction of escape. We don't have enough data to form a judgment and I don't want you to misinterpret what I'm telling you. Once out of that dip, the shooter could have gone anywhere."

Jim nodded. Anywhere would most likely be to the Eisenhauer house. "Any chance of picking up the trail after the rain stops?"

The forensic team leader smiled at Jim's optimism. "Not a hope in hell," Robin said. "The path, itself, may not exist when this lets up." He pointed to the muddy swirl of water filling the ditches along the edge of the Booth driveway. The water ran brown as it dissolved any loose soil in its path.

Again, lightning lit up the inside of the barn, dimmed and then lit up every corner. Jim held his hands up to the heavens. "Okay, okay, I get the message."

The thunder cracked and the echo rolled and rolled and rolled across the sky.

"There is one other thing," the forensic chief added. "The grass around the shooting site was well tramped down. It looks like the shooter was waiting for a while. We found the tattered remnants of a cigarette. Someone had field stripped it when they finished smoking. Must have taken the filter tip with them."

"Someone was advancing a fox in the hen house theory. This looks like a deliberate shooting to me. Unlike the last time we met, I wouldn't spend a lot of time working the accidental shooting theory here."

"Scott was telling me he saw a dead coyote in the ditch on his way here this morning."

Scott stepped forward. He placed the folded knuckles of his forefingers into his red, itchy-looking eyes and rotated them vigorously. "I came from the opposite direction of you guys. I was already working."

Robin looked into the irritated eyes. "Not a farm boy, are you? I've got some allergy medication in my kit." He flipped open a pouch and produced a small squeeze bottle of Visine. "We run into a lot of noxious chemicals in our line of work."

He looked up the road in the direction Scott had indicated. The pelting rain obscured his vision. "The dead coyote would have been interesting if we had known about it sooner. A bullet could have easily carried that far and still been fatal. That would have eventually been part of our search field. Not now." He pointed across the road. "We opted to start close and work our way up the road. The lay of the land made that ravine a natural lead-off point. We lucked out. Roscoe led us directly to the spent shell casing. It was buried in the deep grass, but that was no challenge for his nose. There was no sign of weathering on the casing." He pulled a 400 power eye glass from his pocket. "The ejector marks still shone. That's where the shot came from. With the freshly trampled grass, there's no doubt in my mind."

"Hell of a shot with a .22," Jim said.

Scott shook his head. "My father could shoot your choice of left wing or right wing off a fly at 100 yards. You could tell by the direction the fly circled to the ground which wing was missing. There are people out there who could easily make this shot.

"When I learned to shoot, I wanted to use bottles as targets. There's something exciting about the sound of shattering glass. My father insisted that the neck of the bottle face me and the shot was only a success when I shot out the bottom and left the rest of the glass intact. I learned to do it."

Jim, himself, could put five rounds into a one-inch grouping from 25 yards with his service pistol. He, however, had more of an incentive. When he was shooting, it was because his life depended on it. That served to improve your aim.

Jim leaned out the doorway and looked up at the heavens. Dark clouds continued to roil around above them with no letup in sight. Rain washed down his face. "How much longer can this storm keep up with this intensity?" he asked no one in particular.

"I believe the current record is 40 days and 40 nights," Scott answered, a smile spreading across his face.

CHAPTER 16

AS DARRIN EISENHAUER and his two friends descended the escalator into the concourse at Calgary International Airport, he spotted a tall, well-built man dressed in a dark suit holding up a sign bearing his name.

He nudged his buddies with his elbow. "Look, the company sent someone to meet us. How cool is that?" He waved to get the man's attention.

The man smiled and waved back. He threw the sign into a nearby garbage can and proceeded towards the three boys. Another man, equally big, hair worn in a short brush cut, joined him.

"Must be oil field workers," Darrin said to his buddies. "Look at the size of them." From his five-feet-five, most people looked big. These guys easily topped six-three or four. To Darrin, they were giants.

As they reached the group of boys, the sign carrier reached out and encircled Darrin's upper arm in one hand. His other hand produced an identification card. "I'm Detective Robert Hennigar with the RCMP major crimes division. Are you Darrin Eisenhauer?"

Darrin was taken aback. He tried to pull his arm free but the grip only tightened to the point of causing him pain. "What do you want with me? We just arrived this minute from the east coast."

The other cop took the arms of the two other boys. "We'd like to talk to you over here." His head indicated the door of an open office. A uniformed Mountie stood in the doorway.

Again Darrin struggled to free his arm. "No, we've got people to see about our jobs. We don't have time to talk to you. We just got here from back east. We were on that plane that just landed. We haven't done anything wrong." The level of frustration rose in his voice.

The uniformed Mountie started towards the struggling boy. The plainclothes cop gave his head a shake. He lifted his hand slightly and Darrin was on his tiptoes. "Let's keep this civil. We have some questions about a murder that took place in Nova Scotia. You can cooperate and talk to us or I can place you under arrest as a subject of an investigation detention. Your choice."

The man didn't wait for an answer. He turned and started towards the office. Darrin had no choice but to follow, his toes scuffing along the highly polished stone flooring. He was by far outmatched in strength. All around them, people stopped to watch the by-play. They had no idea what was going on but the presence of the uniformed Mountie who seemed to be giving the whole process his blessing prevented them from interfering. Those closest heard the word "murder" and crowded back a few steps, bumping into those behind them who were just exiting the escalator.

"Watch it," someone snarled.

Given the choice of a possible murderer being arrested in front of them and a disgruntled plane passenger behind them, most continued to move backwards into the crowd. Then the office doors closed and everyone went about their own business, some with a story to tell their friends when they got home about their run-in with a killer who had most likely shared their flight from Toronto.

Once inside the office and confronted by two more uniformed Mounties, Darrin Eisenhauer lost all his fight. "I don't know anything about any murder," he said. "We just arrived on our way to new jobs here in Calgary. There must be some mistake."

Detective Hennigar indicated a room off to the left of the office. He took Darrin in there. The other detective took one of the other boys into another room. An additional Mountie joined both detectives. The third boy was offered a chair in the main office and waited for his turn. A trickle of sweat could be seen running down the side of his face. He wiped it away and took a deep breath. "Can I call home?" he asked, a tremble in his voice.

The sergeant behind the desk looked up at him. "Sure," he said, "but why not wait a few minutes? All our phones are tied up right now."

The boy looked at the unused phone on the desk in front of the sergeant but said nothing. He slouched in the chair and studied his sneakers.

In the small interview room, Detective Hennigar offered Darrin a coffee or soft drink. He declined both. The detective shrugged and poured himself a coffee, added two sugars and sat back in his chair. In front of him was a sheet of paper. The type looked like it came from a fax machine getting low on toner. He picked up the top edge and studied it for a minute.

"Raymond's River? Where exactly is that?"

"In Nova Scotia," Darrin answered in a sullen voice.

The detective smiled. "I know that, but exactly where? I'm a Bluenoser myself, but I've never heard of Raymond's River."

Darrin perked up a little. "Oh, where are you from?"

"Truro. Been out here for goin' on ten years now. Good place to live if you behave yourself."

"Raymond's River is in Hants County. It's only a small place, only about 40 people, mostly farmers."

The detective nodded. "I guess it's down to 39 now."

The uniformed Mountie suppressed a smile. The remark had gone over Darrin's head.

"A place that size, I guess you know just about everybody," Hennigar said.

Darrin said nothing. The import of the previous statement was finally registering in his mind. A sheen of sweat broke out on his forehead. He fidgeted in his seat. "Who was murdered?"

Again the cop looked down at the piece of paper in front of him. "Gerald Booth," he said. "Did you know him?"

Darrin looked like he had been kicked in the head. "Ol-old man Booth? Is he dead?"

The Mountie nodded. "That's what it says here." He paused. "Know what else it says?"

Darrin shook his head.

"Says you were harassing the old man."

Darrin shook his head more vigorously. "No. No. I haven't seen him in months."

"Says that, too. A couple of months ago the old man got the best of you. Caused you considerable pain, according to this." He held up the paper. "Then the day he gets murdered, you hightail it for the other side of the country."

Darrin gripped the edge of the table and shook his head. "No, that's not true. I've had this job lined up for weeks. Call the company that hired me. They'll tell you."

"Exactly. You had weeks to plan Mr. Booth's murder and your escape."

"No. It was all harmless fun. I never killed anybody. We were having fun with the old man. Squealing tires and the like, not killing him."

"Fun for whom? Was Mr. Booth having fun?"

Darrin lowered his head. "Yes, I think he was." The voice was so low the two Mounties had to strain to hear him. They gave each other a quizzical look.

"In what way?" Hennigar asked.

Darrin looked up, defiant again. "Don't you have that written on your paper? He rigged his mailbox somehow and almost broke my arms. He thought it was a big joke. I couldn't do anything for weeks. He was having fun, too, I'm sure of that." Darrin noticed the smiles on the Mounties' faces. It was in the report. "There was nothing funny about it and I didn't see any cops knocking on his door. It's only us kids you pick on."

"Right," Hennigar said. "So you took the law into your own hands and you got even. You took your trusty .22 and you murdered the man. You've probably still got the gunshot residue all over your hand and arm. Do you mind if we run some tests?"

Darrin brightened. "If it will prove my innocence, go ahead. I've nothing to hide."

CHAPTER 17

B Y THE TIME Josh got back to Ridgeway Subdivision, blue sky was showing through the clouds. The wipers of his truck were on low speed, leaving blue streaks on the glass and making an irritating squeaking sound. He turned them off and watched the window mist over after a few seconds. He flipped the wipers on and then off. The truck was equipped with an interrupt cycle but Josh could never find a setting he liked. It was easier to do it manually.

As he passed the model home at the entrance to the subdivision, he spotted Victor Boyd's car in the driveway along with two others. Josh smiled. So far every completed house was occupied and seven of the ten still under construction were sold. It looked like Victor was in the process of selling off the remaining three.

Josh slowed down as the door to the model home opened and two older couples stepped out. Retiring baby boomers. This was the target market for this subdivision. Close to shopping, close to hospitals, not a school in sight. The plans called for a community hall where folks could get together for cards, bingo or just plain, old-fashioned socializing. That building was nearing completion, a portion of the sale price of each house contributing to its construction. A committee of locals would be struck to figure out ways to maintain the ongoing costs. That was not a problem. This age group was good at that sort of thing.

Josh lightly tapped his horn twice and waved as Victor emerged from the building. Instinctively Victor's hand went up in a wave, a hundred-watt salesman's smile lit up his face. Then recognition seemed to register in his eyes and the hand dropped like an overloaded express elevator. The smile lost its sparkle.

At first Josh was surprised by this action, then understanding slowly dawned on him. He had heard through an acquaintance that Victor believed he was the one who should have made this morning's presentation. He was, after all, Cliff's successor. Josh couldn't argue with the logic. He, too, thought Victor would fill this role. It was Kevin who didn't see things that way.

Kevin explained that Victor's strengths were in selling the houses. He was liable to scare the investors off with talk of competitive pricing and meaningful negotiations. To the investors this was heresy. Higher was always better.

Josh, on the other hand, fit the bill perfectly. He had a better understanding of the overall picture. He understood all the aspects that went into the final selling price. He could explain every part of the equation, including where the investors dividends fit into the scheme of things. And he could do all these things in a convincing manner,

Kevin would smooth things over with Victor.

But that would have to wait until a later date. Right now, Josh had other things on his mind. He wondered about the company's source of funding. To think that the people at the morning meeting believed real estate was a risky investment made him question their financial smarts. He thought about his performance and the bluff he pulled off and realized he was wrong about them. It wasn't their financial smarts that had to be questioned, it was their lack of nerve in calling his bluff after he had called theirs. He could take no credit for his play. That was totally choreographed by Kevin. Kevin was the poker player. It was he who read the other players, not Josh. Kevin's answer to their bluff was to come over the top with a bigger bluff of his own. It had worked, big time.

Now Josh found out there was another player in the game. One who had been in all along and about whom he knew nothing. His feelings were ambivalent. On the one hand, he was making a good living as the contractor with no let-up in sight. On the other, he had believed that he was a major player in the umbrella company but now had to question that idea. Why was Kevin hesitant about introducing the other money man to him? Were they all equal partners or not?

Prior to the death of Cliff Lawrence, Josh's only role was in seeing that the houses were built on time, on budget. His contributions to upper-level meetings were strictly presenting factual information. These are the costs, these are the returns we need to justifiy the effort. Now Kevin wanted him to take a more active role in the company's administration, to fill the gap left by Cliff. He was willing to step up to the plate and fill that function. However, if introducing him to that role was Kevin's plan, Josh had to be fully informed as to what was taking place. He had to know what Cliff knew. There would be no working in the dark. No sudden surprises. He had to know all the players, silent or otherwise.

He gave Victor a final wave and proceeded to the work site. He did his best thinking with a hammer in his hand. Letting his conscious mind work on the repetitive task of driving nails freed his subconscious mind to roll the underlying problem around so he could view it from all angles. Then, like Paul on the road to Damascus, a solution would suddenly present itself. He applied himself to installing baseboard molding while waiting for the "Praise the Lord, I see the light" moment.

CHAPTER 18

FINALLY THE STORM seemed to be letting up. The time between the lightning and thunder was stretching out to nine or ten second intervals. The rain, although still steady, didn't seem to have the same driving force as earlier. Visibility in the area improved.

Jim and the senior forensics man were still standing in the doorway of the barn. The house across the road was coming back into view. "Did you or any of your team talk to the occupant of that house, Chris Ritchey?"

The man looked in the direction Jim was pointing. "No. Once the lightning started popping trees, we hauled ass and went for shelter."

"So, he doesn't know about the shell casing you found on his property?"

"I would say not. His house was not in view of where the shooter stood." He pointed out a small tree on the side of the hill. "The shooter used the lower branch of that maple as a gun rest. We dusted for gunshot residue. It was positive. It's five feet, one-half inch above the ground. Make the shooter around six feet, give or take an inch or two."

Chief Cosh had been listening to the two men. "Chris stands about five-eleven."

Jim turned towards the chief, surprised at the information he volunteered. "How tall is Darrin Eisenhauer?"

The chief rubbed his chin with his left hand. "Darrin? Darrin's only a half pint, maybe five-four, five-five. Takes after his father. Like a lot of shorter people, he's always causing trouble. Seems he has to compensate for his height with his big mouth."

"You've had trouble with him?" Jim asked.

"We have teen dances at the fire hall. There's always trouble at least once a month. We've banned him a couple of times." He shrugged. "Not much else going on for kids around here, so we always let him back in after one or two misses. He never learns though. Always has to have the last word. I make him as more of a talker than a doer. It would be hard for me to believe he murdered Gerald."

"We hear that a lot," Scott Bowen said. "Still, somebody commits these crimes. What about the people Darrin hung around with? Any of them in the six-foot range?"

"There's a couple of guys he's usually with. One of them is crowding six feet. If Darrin told him to do something, well, he just might do it. They have that kind of relationship. But, I have to be honest. I don't think that would extend to murder. He's probably in Alberta with Darrin."

Scott flipped through his notebook and read off the names of Darrin's travelling companions. The chief nodded his head. "That's him. Still, murder, I don't know what to tell you. I can't believe anybody in Raymonds River is a murderer. You probably hear that a lot."

"Nobody likes to believe there is a killer living next door," Jim said. He glanced at his open notebook. "They left for the airport around five. How does that fit for the time of death? It would have to have been before, let's say, 4:30, 4:45." He looked up at the fire chief. "You say you got the call around 6:15?"

"At 4:45 Gerald would be just crawling out of the fart sack. Most of us don't start our morning chores until at least five."

Robin looked out at the plastic-covered mound in front of the barn. "I think five o'clock is too early. The body was warm to touch when we arrived. It was a cool morning. If your boy was on a plane by then, he's probably not your shooter. The coroner might give you a more definitive answer when he arrives. Got anyone else in mind?"

Disappointment showed on Jim's face. He gave his head a small shake. " Not at the moment. Chief, you got any ideas?"

"How about a random act of violence? We read about those all the time in the Halifax papers. Maybe they are enlarging their territory."

Jim held up his hands in a surrendering pose. "Don't even go there. We want a motive and a person who would follow through. Random murders are almost impossible to solve. If there is no logic behind the act, using logic to figure it out is a waste of time."

He held his hand out through the door and watched the moisture accumulate. "The rain has almost stopped. Scott, let's go over and talk to Mr. Ritchey. He may have seen or heard something. We know he was up when the shooting occurred. Let's get this investigation back on a logical course."

Chris Ritchey knew about the death, of course. He had been there earlier when the paramedic pronounced Gerald dead, but his disappearance before the police arrival did raise some questions. Curiosity alone should have kept him on location. Jim's experience always had the neighbours gathering under these circumstances. Ninety-nine percent of them never saw anything, or at least that was their claim, but they always pooled around the scene of the crime.

"Never heard a thing," Ritchey said when asked if he heard any shots fired, "and I sure had no reason to kill Gerald. No reason at all." His voice dropped off as he volunteered that statement.

He looked down at the floor, avoiding eye contact with the policeman.

"We were told you were at the Booth farm before we arrived," Jim said. "Why did you leave?"

Chris looked surprised that his name had come up in discussions at the farm. "I had to finish milking my cows. People think we own the animals. It's the other way around. They own us and our every waking minute. They don't let you stand around rubbernecking when there is work to do. I had to get back and finish my morning chores."

Scott stopped by a trophy cabinet in the living room and looked over at the seated men. "Is your farm bigger than those of your neighbours?"

Chris shook his head. "They're all comparable in size. Milk quota determines how many head of cattle we own and that's determined by pasture land. Most of the farms in the area are the same size. They were given as land grants by some old British king and pretty much stayed intact through the years. Mine goes back to my great-great-great-grandfather. Gerald's goes back to his great-great-grandfather but he's a lot older than me. Both men fought in the Revolutionary War for the British. Eighty-fourth Regiment."

Scott picked up a trophy from the mantel. Two crossed rifles emblazoned the top. He studied the inscription.

"Most of the other men were finished their milking when the alarm was sounded."

"They don't start the day off with morning devotions. I believe in reaching out to the Lord before reaching out to the secular world. This morning I had to include special prayers for my wife, Linda. She's feeling poorly."

"Oh, what's wrong with your wife?" Scott asked.

"She has the flu. Couldn't keep a thing down all day yesterday. Tossed and turned all night struggling with her internal demons. She's still weak. "

Scott raised his eyebrows at that information.

Internal demons? That was an interesting turn of phrase. Scott decided not to go there. "If she was awake most of the night, we should check to see if she heard any shots," he said

"No, she's not up to any questions," Chris said. "She's sleeping now. She needs her rest."

Scott set down the trophy. "Do you own a .22?"

Ritchey looked back at him. "A .22? No. Yes. A small one." He stumbled over his words, not sure how to answer.

"I'd like to see it."

"I'm not sure I know where it is. Give me a minute. Since I have found my saviour, the Lord Jesus Christ, I avoid blood sports and all their trappings. Guns are toys of the devil."

Ritchey disappeared up the stairs of his house and returned with an older, single-shot .22. He passed it to the policeman. Jim pulled back the bolt, locked it open and looked down the barrel. It gleamed a shiny silver but did not smell like it had been recently cleaned or fired.

"Where is your semiautomatic?" Scott asked.

"My semiautomatic? Ah, ah, I sold it." His voice lacked conviction. "I told you I don't shoot anymore."

Scott gave the man a peculiar look. "Right. Work of the devil. To whom did you sell it?"

Chris looked down at the floor, possibly hoping to find a name written on the floor. "I don't remember his name."

"But you have all the paperwork? The person had a proper Firearms Acquisition Certificate or a Possession and Acquisition Licence?"

Now Chris looked confused. He had his own FAC but these other terms were foreign to him. "Yeah, he showed me one of those."

"So you have the paperwork?" Scott was about to pursue the issue when a voice interrupted them.

"Chris, what are the police doing here?" Ritchey's wife, Linda, appeared at the top of the steps. All three men looked up at her. Despite the lateness of the day, she was still dressed in her nightgown and was fastening a white flannelette housecoat around her waist. Her hair was uncombed and her face matched the colour of her clothing, with one glaring exception: Mrs. Ritchey sported a black eye. The purple bruising stood out in stark contrast against the whiteness of her face.

The edges were just beginning to show signs of yellowing. This shiner was no more than a day old. Someone appeared to have battled with the internal demons in a physical sort of way.

Scott was first to speak: "Sorry to bother you, Ma'am. I understand you're sick. You haven't been eating scallops lately, have you?"

"How'd you know?" she started to say and then quickly recovered and said: "No, I've got the flu. There must be a bug going around." She sought agreement from her husband.

Scott nodded. "Right. Must be." The two policemen exchanged knowing looks. "May I ask what happened to your eye?"

She touched the bruising and winced. Again she looked at her husband before answering. "A cow kicked me while I was milking her."

Chris studied the floor without comment.

"Kicked by a cow?" Jim fought back a smile. "Now that's a new one on me." He flipped open his notebook, found a fresh page and wrote: Kicked by a cow. "I'm sorry. I don't mean to make light of your discomfort. It's just that I've never heard that one before." He gave Chris a meaningful stare. "We'll have a few questions to ask when you're feeling better. Perhaps we can set up a time?"

"Questions about what?" Curiosity trumped a queasy stomach.

Jim looked from the lady at the top of the stairs to Chris and then back to the lady. It was obvious that the morning's events across the road were unknown to her. "There was a shooting this morning at the Booth farm. A man was killed."

Mrs. Ritchey clutched the hand railing of the steps and lowered herself to a sitting position. Her ashen face took on the pallor of a corpse. Her other hand came to her mouth to hold back a scream and instead she let out a painful, eerie moan.

"Gerald Booth is dead," Chris said. He bounded up the steps and took his wife in his arms. "It's Gerald that's dead."

"Gerald? Why would anyone want to shoot Gerald?"

Jim studied the woman's reaction to the news. It seemed genuine. She had asked the question of the day. As of yet, no one could supply a good reason for the shooting. That is, if you discounted the wild actions of a psychotic youth. Jim had not.

"You don't know of any problems Gerald was having with anyone?"

Her face had returned to merely white. She shook her head. "Everyone liked Gerald. He had some trouble with some teenagers a few months back but nothing to die over. So did we for that matter.

They wrecked our mailbox on a couple of occasions. Gerald even fixed it for us the second time. That's the kind of man he was." She paused and ran her fingers through her tangled hair. "But that was kids letting off steam. Ralph Foley put a stop to that foolishness."

Scott looked up with renewed interest. "How do you know Ralph Foley put a stop to it?"

She gave the cop a scathing look and then turned to her husband. "You told me that, didn't you dear? Everyone seemed to know about it."

Chris slowly shook his head. "Not me. Gerald told me he had stopped them himself. Did you see that mailbox he constructed? I hear the kid that beat on it was laid up for weeks." He looked back at his wife. "Where did you hear about Foley?" It was more of an accusation than a question.

She pushed her husband away and stood up. "I've got to go and see Mable. She must be devastated." She turned on her husband. "Why didn't you wake me? Mable needs her friends around her at a time like this."

Chris hung on to her arm. "What Mable needs at this time is to take Jesus into her heart. His love will carry her through this time of trouble. I think you should go back to bed. You're still too sick to be out and about."

A neighbour was dead. There were procedures to be followed. Linda shook her arm free. "Jesus is telling me to look after my neighbour." There was scorn in her voice. "Take one of those casseroles out of the freezer. I'll heat it up and take it over to her. This is so terrible." She shook her head again in disbelief. "Gerald, dead."

Scott smiled. Food, the cure for the misery of death. Soon Mable would have a kitchen full of casseroles and pies. It seemed to be a universal constant in all investigations. When the police left, their presence was replaced with a mountain of food.

"Ma'am, did you hear any shots this morning?" Scott asked.

Mrs. Ritchey stopped and looked at him. "I don't know. I might have. I was sleeping poorly. First I was cold, then I would wake up in a sweat, then I would be cold again. Each time I came awake, I was having these awful dreams. At one point, I thought I heard sirens. I guess they were real." She shook her head. "I don't know what was real and what was not."

"So you may have heard shooting?"

She looked at her husband and hesitated. "No, I don't think I did. I remember Chris getting up and going to the barn. I don't think I had more than five minutes sleep up until that point. Then I thought I heard the sirens. The next thing I remember after that is hearing voices down here. What time of day is it anyway?"

All three men looked at their watches. "It's almost two o'clock," her husband said. "You still need more rest. You look terrible."

Scott put his hand on the bottom stair newel and stared up the 12 steps into the sickly, pale face of the woman. His eyes searched hers for the truth. "Perhaps when you're feeling better, you might remember more." He took a business card from his pocket and inserted it into a crack between the bannister and the post. "Call me." His gaze shifted to Chris's face. "Find the paperwork for when you sold your rifle. We'll be back."

Detective-Sergeant Jim Mcdonald and Corporal Scott Bowen sat in the white RCMP patrol car in Chris Ritchey's yard. "What do you think?" Jim asked. From the distance, the low rumble of thunder could still be heard.

Scott slowly shook his head. "She and Foley being sick at the same time. Black eye. Seeks permission from her husband before she speaks. He seems to be a Jesus-freak. I think this guy needs a closer look."

Jim nodded. "I agree. Couple that with Foley's response when we mentioned Ritchey's name. There is some kind of history between those two men. It looks like someone may have been carrying that country friendliness a little too far."

"We've got to get her separated from her husband the next time we talk. It may have nothing to do with the death of Gerald Booth, but I think we may be looking at a battered wife."

Jim paused. "That, I must admit, is more your area. Most battered wives I see are dead. Those that aren't are widows and are chief suspects in the death of their husbands."

"Let's intervene before either of those things happens here. With Booth's death, we have the perfect excuse to be nosing around asking questions. I don't want to sidetrack our investigation but I've seen too many of these problem relationships go bad. We've got a chance here to step in on this one before someone becomes seriously hurt. This is probably not the first time she was 'kicked by a cow.'"

Jim stared into his partner's intense eyes. "I thought there was something wrong with the man from the time we walked through the door. Altogether too edgy. He's definitely guilty of something. It may just be that he was beating his wife, but I think it goes farther. Do you think Ritchey shot Booth by mistake? Was Ralph Foley the intended target?"

Scott held the other's gaze. "That trophy I was looking at: Canadian small bore shooting champion. I don't care if he found Jesus or not, he has the ability to make the shot."

"Do you think his wife knows?"

"I don't think she believes her husband would shoot somebody even if he did find out about an affair, but," Scott rubbed his chin as he thought about the rest of his answer, "some of her answers were guarded as if she didn't want to accuse her husband of doing the wrong thing."

"If Ritchey's beating on her and she's having an affair with Ralph Foley, why protect her killer husband?"

"That's the thing, there might be a lingering doubt but she still lives with the man. Deep down, I would say she doesn't want to suspect him. She doesn't look like a stupid woman. She'd get the hell out of Dodge if there was a real belief in her mind that he was our shooter."

"That's where we disagree. As I said most of the battered women I meet are dead. The one question we always ask and never answer is why didn't she leave him."

Scott nodded. "I know what you mean. I'm the guy that was at the house five or ten times before. I see the nonfatal results. We do our best to encourage them to leave. Some do. Most hang around, truly believing it won't happen again." Scott shook his head. "It does. It keeps repeating until he moves on, looking for a new victim or until you get the call."

"What does Dr. Phil call that? Insanity? Stupidity? I don't remember. Doing the same thing over and over and expecting different results. It boggles the mind." Jim smiled. "Look at this." He had been multitasking, discussing the issue with Scott with his left brain and working the in-car computer with his right brain. "The Canadian Gun Registry has three more rifles in the house. Besides the .22 he showed us, he has a Remington 30-06, a 12-gauge shotgun and another .22, a semiautomatic."

Scott looked at the screen. "Right. I knew he had a semiautomatic. A fine looking rifle too, I might add. He's holding it in the pictures with his trophy. Despite guns being the toys of the devil, he still has the trophies on display. I'm not surprised he still owns the rifle. He didn't have a clue what I was talking about when I asked to see his paperwork from when he sold it. Jesus or not, I doubt he parted with that gun. In the picture it looks expensive and finely crafted, as much a tribute to his shooting skills as the trophy it earned him. If he's the shooter, that's the murder weapon."

"That sounds so logical. If only we could convince some ivory-towered judge of that, we could get a search warrant to search his house and barn. God, I hate all the paperwork involved in trying to do that. I guess it's got to be done."

Scott reached across and touched his shoulder. "Maybe we can get lucky. The gun could be stashed outside somewhere. Let's get the dog back over here and see what he can find."

"The storm has washed away any traces he could follow. Robin told us as much."

Scott smirked. "He found the spent cartridge. Any additional searching would be considered hot pursuit. Haven't you ever seen the Littlest Hobo? London would be able to find the gun in any kind of weather. Who's to say our dog is not as smart? He's trained to sniff out weapons."

Now Jim was smiling. "Randomly search the area until he finds something. Why not? We can be sure his prized gun is not out in this rain and I'm willing to bet he didn't take it back into the house. It's probably tucked safely under something in the yard. It's worth a try. In the meantime, I'll start the wheels turning for a search of all the buildings on the property."

"And let's talk to Foley again. This is all hinged on him having an affair with Ritchey's wife. Our evidence of that is pretty thin. Neat and clean bachelor pad. Both sick at the same time from apparently eating the same food. Her knowledge of Foley talking to the kids." He held up a finger with each point he made. He looked at his little finger still held down by his thumb. He released the finger. "A wild hunch on our part. Like I said, it's pretty thin."

"It feels right," said Jim. "I can't take that to court but it has carried me a long way in solving other cases." Jim looked at his watch. "That plane should have landed in Calgary by now. Let's give them a call and see how our other suspects panned out.

"I know Gerald Booth was supposed to still be in bed when they left. With Ralph off sick, maybe Gerald got an early start on the chores. The kids might have seen the barn lights on." Jim shrugged as if the next step in this scenario was obvious.

"If they've confessed, Ritchey may simply be a wife-beater as you suggested. If he is, we'll nail him for that at least."

Within a minute, his call was patched through to William Hennigar at the Calgary Airport. The news was not promising. None of the boys had tested positive for gunshot residue and the initial questioning did not seem to indicate any of them were involved in the shooting. They had had the fear of God put into them, though. Hennigar figured they would be better citizens in Alberta than they might have been back home. He promised to keep tabs on them in case Jim came up with any new evidence to implicate them. Jim thanked him for his troubles and signed off.

"I agree with his gut instinct," Scott said. "In reality, our forensic evidence is pointing away from them now. The time line doesn't seem to work. Locked up tightly inside a giant can flying across the country when the crime was committed is a pretty air-tight alibi."

Jim nodded. "At least they know we know about the mailbox bashing. Hennigar may have told us he believes they are innocent of murder but he hasn't passed that information on to the boys. They'll be looking over their shoulders. They don't know who killed Booth either. If their imaginations start to run wild, they may think it was one of their buddies back here. In their minds they all think they are tough guys. The fear of being implicated may keep them in line out there for awhile."

Scott gave a short, gruff laugh. "Let's hope so. They deserve some kind of punishment for harassing the old man. I guess Mr. Ritchey moves to the top of our suspect list. Let's see what kind of a case we can build against him."

CHAPTER 19

CHRIS RITCHEY STOOD back a few feet from the closed curtains of his living room. He could see outside through the white, lacy sheers. The police cruiser still sat in his yard, the two cops inside, still talking and looking at his house.

"Chris, get that casserole from the freezer." His wife was descending the stairs, She had quickly dressed and had run a brush through her hair. Her face was still pasty white. A touch of red had been added to her cheeks. A dusting of flesh-coloured powder tried to hide the purple from the black eye. It had been unsuccessful. She had dismissed all thoughts of being sick. She was a woman on a mission. A neighbour was in distress and it was her duty to be there for her.

Chris turned from the window. "I tell you, you're too sick to be going over there. Mable has all the help she needs. Her sister is there and there are a bunch of other cars in the driveway." His voice was firm. "Why don't you wait until tomorrow when the excitement has died down a little?"

Linda walked by him and went into the kitchen. He could hear the freezer door open and then Linda poked her head through the living room door. "This is no time to be thinking about one's own suffering. It's time to help in any way we can. Doesn't your new religion teach that?"

She disappeared again and Chris heard the microwave door open and close. Linda appeared back in the doorway. "Besides, in all the years I've lived in Raymond's River, there has never been a murder committed. Aren't you a little curious about what is going on over there?"

This question caught Chris by surprise.

"I can't imagine anyone shooting Gerald on purpose. It must have been an accident." Linda joined him at the window and looked out at the police car in her driveway. "You know all about guns. How far could a bullet travel and still kill someone?"

Chris didn't answer. His attention was devoted to the police presence in his yard.

"Why are the police still in our yard, Chris?" Linda grabbed his arm and gave it a pull to get his attention.

Chris snapped out of his reverie and looked at his wife, then back out the window. "I don't know. They must be deciding what to do next. You're probably right about it being an accident. Maybe a jacker was out hunting in the dark. No one is going to come forward and admit to that. It wouldn't bring Gerald back and they might end up in jail."

"Why did they want to see your old rifle?" Linda asked. "They don't suspect you, do they? You haven't used that old thing for years. Where's your shiny, new one?"

Chris forced a harsh laugh. "Of course they don't suspect me. They are probably going to check on everybody who lives close enough to have shot Gerald. They call it eliminating suspects so they can concentrate on the actual shooter." He looked sharply at his wife. "Why would I want to shoot Gerald? We've been good neighbours all my life."

"I know that," Linda said. "I'm just wondering what they are doing at our house."

Chris looked back out the window. "Ralph Foley's truck is up by the house. I don't remember seeing him there earlier."

"Earlier? Were you already over there? Why didn't you wake me?"

"Because you are sick and need your sleep. There was nothing you could do."

"You still should've woke me up. What will Mable think?"

Chris gave an exasperated sigh. "I doubt Mable is thinking about you at all. Now Foley, he may have expected to find you there."

"What is that supposed to mean?"

"You know darn well what that means. I'm not stupid, Linda. I know what is going on."

"No you don't. Ralph and I are just friends. We've known each other since we were kids."

"Well, you're not kids anymore. Stay away from him."

Linda subconsciously reached up and touched the swelling around her eye. "Stay away or what? You'll show me what a man you are?" She turned and stomped back into the kitchen.

Chris watched her disappear and then looked back at the police car. "Damn," he said under his breath. He debated following her into the kitchen and apologizing, but he didn't. He wasn't the one violating their marriage vows. He wasn't the one violating the laws of God.

Chris did not go to the local church. Instead, he belonged to a parish in the city, a parish where the teachings of God had not been forgotten. Sure, he thought, everyone cites the verse in Leviticus about homosexuality being an abomination in the eyes of God, but none of them seem to remember that three verses before that it says that when a man commits adultery with his neighbour's wife, both the adulterer and the adulteress should be put to death.

Linda did not share these beliefs. Linda did not join him when he went to the city. Oh no, Chris had discovered, she had other things on her mind. Was he trying to put her to death when he hit her the day before? No, he knew he wasn't. He was upset, however, upset and angry. So angry that he had struck out and given her that black eye, something he had never done before; something he would never do again. He still loved her and was willing to forgive. That came from the New Testament.

But what about the adulterer? The Bible said he should be put to death. What a fuck-up. Could he blame one and not the other? Despite her actions, he loved his wife too much to even contemplate doing that. The fault had to rest with that smooth-talking Ralph Foley.

Chris dropped into his Lazy Boy chair, closed his eyes and silently wept.

CHAPTER 20

KEVIN BARNHILL SLOWLY sipped his third cup of coffee. Anthony Dellapinna had picked up the bill for their meal and left. He had an empire to run, he had told Kevin. He couldn't waste all morning sitting around in a restaurant.

Kevin also had an empire to run, not as big as Dellapinna's, but it was his own empire. An empire that Kevin controlled and not the other way around. As a boy, he knew he would one day be a successful entrepreneur. At the time he didn't know what his line of business would be, but that was unimportant. The important part was that it would be his business. And now, here he was, the president and chief shareholder of a successful development company.

Kevin had a flair for matching other people's money to his dreams. That was the big breakthrough he had made in the business world. He had discovered the way to success was with OPM – other people's money. All the dreams in the world wouldn't generate a plug nickel if you couldn't put them into action. Putting them into action required capital. The best source of capital for a boy of limited resources was tapping into other people's.

Along with that secret, he had discovered his mission in life. During his junior year at university, his parents decided it was time to downsize their living arrangements. They sold their big, old house that had served them well in the raising of three children, but was now showing signs of wear and demanding too much attention. They moved into their dream home. His mother and father had spent months laying out exactly how everything in the new house would mesh together. She would have her living space, he would have his workshops and the common area would be designed for entertaining their baby boomer friends.

The house was perfect.

The location was not.

Kids from the local elementary school took shortcuts through their yard wearing paths in the lawn. Older kids hung around the nearby playground until all hours of the night banging on tennis balls or bouncing basketballs, loudly cheering each other on. When these sounds emanated from your own offspring, these things would be tolerated. That time had passed. The Barnhills wanted peace and quiet along with people their own age to share it with.

Kevin immediately saw the opportunity this dilemma presented. He would design a subdivision for baby boomers looking to downsize their houses and leave the joys of supporting children behind them. The beginning was modest, only five houses the first year, but five solidly built houses. The demand became overwhelming. The second year, all the houses were presold before the first nail was driven. He doubled his output. He reserved the corner lot on the first intersection for a small pub, the local was the British term. A place where you could go for a drink with like-minded people and if that drink turned into three or four or five, you could walk home without any problem.

From the start, Josh Daniels and Cliff Lawrence were on board. They weren't rolling out production line houses. The buyers were invited to offer their input. After 25 or so years in their old houses, they knew what they wanted in the new ones. Most were prepared to pay for their individual tastes. Josh proved to be remarkably flexible at adapting to the small changes most requested – bigger closets, different kitchen layouts and the like. If the changes got too crazy, Josh recommended the architecture firm which had originally designed the houses. Josh never gave an outright no to anything. In the end, it would boil down to a question of money. If the buyers wanted the changes badly enough and they could cough up the extra dough, they got them. If not, they were still getting a top quality house that was more than livable. Their reputation spread like wildfire thoughout the community.

Kevin, Cliff and Josh shared the same dream and made it work. Kevin was the creative genius behind selection of locations and target markets. From that beginning, his touch was on subdivisions in all parts of the suburbs surrounding Halifax. He went after all demographics, not just the baby boomers. He planted subdivisions near elementary schools aimed at young families. He built seniors' complexes with medical centres and easily reached shopping. He even blended a few of these ideas together for those families that like to have all the generations within easy touch of each other. But even these blendings were aimed at the older generation of buyers. The ones who had the money. Schools and playgrounds were put on the periphery of these subdivisions.

The one thing all these developments had in common: As fast as they were built, they were filled.

Kevin took another sip of his coffee and watched Tony's SUV pull out of the parking lot. This success raised an interesting question in Kevin's mind. Why was he still involved with a hood like Dellapinna? Did he really still need that tainted money? The answer was yes and no. With the company's success, their yearly output was limited only by the amount of seed money they could pour into the developments. The houses may have been presold but no one paid the full amount upfront. That transfer of funds took place on closing day.

From the beginning, Kevin vowed not to operate in the red. Investors knew the risks up front. They were investors. If things went down the tubes, they weren't owed anything by Kevin et al. If things worked out as planned, they were handsomely rewarded. To date, everyone fell into that latter category. That made raising funds fairly easy. That also gave him the option of dropping his association with Tony Dellapinna. The one problem with that scenario: Who told Tony? By far, the safest route was to allow Tony to keep doing his laundry in your laundromat and tell yourself that you really weren't the one doing anything illegal.

CHAPTER 21

ROBIN WEST CLAMBERED up the slippery, muddy trail going up the hill beside the Ritchey farm. The dog master had given Roscoe the order to find the gun and now Roscoe was a dog on a mission. The starting point of this adventure was the point where the spent cartridge, the cartridge believed responsible for the death of Gerald Booth, had been found.

Both Robin and the dog master were in agreement that any trail left by the shooter would be totally destroyed by the torrential rains that had fallen for the last hour or so. But Roscoe wasn't a one-trick searcher. Give him a new target to find and he was off like an angry Jesus after a sinner. This time his destination was a recently fired rifle. When given the command, Robin could see the dog running through the database stored in its mind for the smell in question. Then, once released, he was off like a shot. The challenge for the men was to keep up.

Roscoe paused at the top of the rise, lifted his nose in the air and sampled the available smells. Without further hesitation, he took off in the direction of the Ritchey farm.

Robin was now soaked from the knees down by the wet grass. His white coveralls had acquired brown legs from the mud. Running in the wet grass had all the challenges of running on slick ice and he concentrated on maintaining his footing with only brief glances at the bounding Roscoe. His fellow officers shared his concerns as they struggled to keep up with the dog. Roscoe appeared to have a destination in mind. This was not a blind search.

The dog master led the searchers and encouraged Roscoe on. "Find the gun, find the gun," he kept calling. He had followed Roscoe on many searches in the past and he was four or five steps out in front of the others. He disregarded the rough, slippery terrain under his feet as he tried to maintain close contact with his dog. Then, without warning, he caught a toe on a clump of grass and tumbled headlong down the slight grade of the path, doing one complete somersault before landing on his back. Robin tried to fetch up and was forced to jump over the sprawling figure. He, too, went down in a heap. The two trailing Mounties slammed on their brakes, skidded in the wet grass and plunked down solidly on their butts.

Everyone did a quick personal inventory of their bodies and decided they were unhurt – no broken bones, no cuts, no abrasions. Despite the seriousness of their cause, laughter rang out across the hill. Roscoe, for his part, ran several more steps up the path before realizing he was the sole searcher. He trotted back and gave his handler a few encouraging licks on the face. Roscoe saw no humour in the situation. He had a job to do. He barked once, sharply, and then started up the path again, looked back, gave another sharp bark and headed towards the Ritchey farm. The others scrambled to their feet and followed along, this time with a larger degree of caution.

When they reached the barnyard, Roscoe stood outside a small outbuilding, barking and pawing at the door. A padlock held it shut. Robin gave the door a shake. A decision was called for. Sergeant Mcdonald had made the case for this search to be considered hot pursuit because of the bullet casing found earlier. At the time, that sounded like a plausible argument for what they were about to do. Finding the gun outside somewhere or even inside an open barn or shed could be argued to be the simple product of the search. Now he was looking at a locked door. There were extra legal ramifications involved. Some judges would agree they were still in hot pursuit. Others would rule that any evidence found if they broke that lock would be inadmissible.

His decision was quick. He triggered the mike on his portable radio and put in a call to the sergeant.

Mcdonald and Scott Bowen were still back at the barn. Ralph Foley was with them. This time the interview concentrated more on Ralph's relationship with Linda Ritchey than about who might be considered enemies of his Uncle Gerald. With friends like Ralph, Gerald didn't need enemies.

Ralph did not hide the fact that Linda had been to his house two nights previous. She had shared the scallops that may have given them both flu-like symptoms. And no, this wasn't the first time they had been together, alone.

However, Ralph drew the line at admitting that anything untoward was taking place. He and Linda were friends, had been since they attended grade school together. There was nothing romantic about the friendship. This was not an affair. This was not adultery. Linda needed a friendly face to talk to; Ralph provided it.

Chris had gotten himself involved in some freaky, religious cult. Linda was having no part of that and their relationship was suffering as a result. When her pleas to her husband had fallen on deaf ears, she had turned to Ralph to intervene on her behalf. Ralph was considered by people in the community to be a smart, level-headed person who could be relied on.

Ralph had been hesitant. He and Chris had been acquaintances for several years. They worked on side by side farms but they were not what could really be called friends. Sure, they had shared the odd drink of rum outside one barn or the other. That drink usually followed sharing a job like splitting a load of hardwood or gathering a wagon load of hay. It was not the "let's get together for a drink" kind of thing.

If Linda had asked Ralph to suggest Chris shouldn't purchase a certain bull or breed of cattle, he would have had no problem. This was the familiar territory on which their acquaintanceship was built. But to intervene in the man's religious beliefs, especially when Ralph could only describe his own views on the subject as ambivalent, was not a step he was prepared to take.

Instead, he and Linda would get together when Chris was in the city and as The Boss, Bruce Springstein, so aptly put it, talk about the glory days. These sessions were having a therapeutic effect on Linda and she harped less and less at Chris about his strange new friends. Chris should have been glad to see his wife's improved mood but that wasn't the case. He became suspicious and morose. Finding God only had an uplifting effect when he was in the presence of his fellow church members. At other times, he questioned everyone who did not share his new beliefs, especially Linda, especially now that she was happier. Who was putting this new smile on her face?

With some prodding from the policemen, Ralph accepted that Chris might get the wrong idea about what might be going on. He was surprised to hear that they suspected Chris of being a batterer. Linda had never said anything about being abused. They were close enough that she would have told him. Ralph had never seen any evidence. The black eye surprised him.

Ralph would also not accept the idea that Chris would try to shoot him. Murder was a big-city concept. It was not how things were dealt with in Raymond's River. There might be a confrontation in the local pub on a Saturday night, but there wouldn't be a sneaky, sleazy bullet under the cover of darkness. No, Ralph insisted, that was not the country way.

The discussion was interrupted by the radio call from Robin West.

"More good news, bad news, Sergeant."

"I'm only interested in good news at this point," Jim said.

"We think we've found the murder weapon."

Jim hesitated before reluctantly asking: "What's the bad news?"

"It's in a locked shed."

"Can you see the gun?"

"No, but Roscoe gives every indication that it is there."

The dog master nodded his head in an emphatic manner. "It's there. Roscoe is never wrong."

Robin keyed the mike again. "The dog master says Roscoe is never wrong."

More dead air while Jim pondered his choices.

"I'll be right over," he said. He looked back at Ralph. "We've got to talk some more. Try to wrap your head around the idea that Chris Ritchey may have beat his wife and tried to shoot you. Think back to anything he or Linda may have said to you. This is important. We have to know if we're looking for someone with a grudge against Gerald or a grudge against you."

"I'm telling you, Officer. I wasn't doing anything wrong. We were just talking."

Jim shook his head. "Good, but that doesn't matter one way or the other. The facts are not important. The only thing that counts is what Chris Ritchey believed. Could he have mistaken your friendship with his wife for an affair? Would he have tried to kill you if he did?"

Again Ralph shook his head in disbelief. "I don't think so."

"You know he was a crack shot with a .22," Scott said. "He has trophies all over his living room."

"Canadian champion," Ralph said. "Everyone knows that. He's the pride of the community. Could shoot the stinger off a mosquito at 100 yards." He smiled. "Used to be in the army. Some kind of special force."

No smile came on Scott's face. "Or put a bullet in your brain at 200 yards. Do you mean JTF2?"

The smile dropped off Ralph's face like someone had closed a shutter. "The army. That's all I know. Signed up right out of high school. Everyone thought he would make a career out of it. But when his Dad died, he came back home and took over the farm."

"Did he tell you he was a member of JTF2?"

"Not me. But if JTF2 is Canada's version of the special forces, then that was the word in the community. Could just be a rumour for all I know." Ralph shrugged. "Then he got religion and gave up shooting."

Scott gave Jim a meaningful look. "Definitely something worth looking into."

Jim nodded in agreement. "We'll be in touch."

The two cops left the barn to see what Roscoe had found.

CHAPTER 22

A S THE POLICE cruiser reentered the Ritchey driveway, Chris Ritchey was exiting the side door of his house, pulling on an older, black and red checked woolen jacket. He was yelling something to the knot of men standing in front of one of the outbuildings but neither Scott nor Jim could make out the words. It didn't take much imagination to figure out what he was saying, however, especially if a certain .22 calibre rifle stood behind the locked door of that shed.

Scott gave the cruiser a shot of gas and the big car lunged forward with a roar of the engine. All eyes turned in the direction of the vehicle. As the car skidded to a stop, Jim was jumping out, his jacket open and his hand on the butt of his 9 mm pistol.

"Hold it right there, Ritchey," he said.

Involuntarily the two other Mounties reached for their own pistols. By now Scott was out of the car and around in front of Chris.

"Face that wall," he said, and at the same time turned the man in the direction of the shed. "Get your hands out in front of you and spread them."

"You guys are trespassing on private property," Chris said. His voice lacked the conviction of his words. "You have no right to be here."

"Search him," Jim said. He looked over at Robin. "Is this the shed in question?"

Robin nodded. He was a scientist. He was surprised by the sudden escalation of events.

Scott had the hunting jacket pulled up and was patting down Chris. He pulled a jack knife from his pocket and threw it on the ground beside him.

Jim turned his attention to the dog. "Okay Roscoe, is there a murder weapon in this shed?"

Roscoe raised his head and barked. He ran to the door and then back to his master.

"That's good enough for me," Jim said. He looked back at Chris who was now sporting a pair of handcuffs. Scott turned him from the wall to face the group of policemen. "Do you have any objection to us looking in this shed?" If he could get Chris to give permission for a search, it would save a lot of time.

Chris was shook up but was getting control of himself.

"There's nothing of interest to you in there," he said.

"Good, then you won't mind if we have a look."

The quandary was evident on Chris's face. If he refused, he looked guilty. If he allowed the men inside the shed, he knew what they would find.

"What happens if I say no?" he asked.

"We stand here and wait for a search warrant to arrive and hope that the rain doesn't start again," Jim said.

"Even if I'm innocent?"

Scott tapped him heavily in the centre of the chest with two extended fingers. "If you're innocent, hand over your keys. You have nothing to worry about."

"I'd like to call my Pastor," Chris said.

"You're not under arrest," Jim said. "You can call anybody you like." A pastor sounded like a better idea to Jim than a lawyer.

Chris twisted to bring the cuffs into view. "If I'm not under arrest, what are these all about?"

"They are there for your protection and ours," Scott said. "We don't want anybody getting hurt here. Promise to be good and I'll remove them."

"And I can order you to leave my property." Chris was getting a little confidence back in his voice.

"Not going to happen," Jim said. "We have reason to believe there is material evidence to our murder investigation in that shed. Roscoe, here, led us directly to this shed from the suspected scene of the shooting. We found a spent cartridge at that site. This site is now directly connected to the other. It's all part of the same crime scene."

Scott was standing behind Chris. He smiled at Jim. He knew Jim was making it up as he went along and had to agree it sounded convincing.

"I want to make my phone call, alone."

Jim pointed towards the house. "Be my guest. But don't go anywhere. We want to talk to you some more."

Chris disappeared into the house. One of the other Mounties went inside with Chris, another went around to watch the front door.

"Now what?" Robin asked. "When I called you to come over, that isn't exactly what I expected."

"We were hoping if we shook him up enough he would simply let us open the shed and find the rifle. Didn't work. Now we wait for a warrant."

"He's our man," Scott said. "Not once did he proclaim his innocence. He should be wildly indignant about how we're treating him. We can only hope his pastor tells him to turn himself in."

"In the meantime, Robin, give headquarters a call. We've already applied for a search warrant but your new information may speed things up. Make it technical and make it convincing. Make it sound like of all the sheds in Nova Scotia, this is the only one that can contain the murder weapon."

"I don't fudge on my work," Robin said, "but in this case, what you are asking is the absolute truth. I can almost smell that rifle sitting in there myself."

Twenty minutes later, Chris Ritchey reemerged from his back door. "Pastor Dave is coming out to pray with us for a quick resolution to this terrible event," he said to the waiting men. "In the meantime, he advised me to cooperate in any way I can."

Bless Pastor Dave, Jim thought. Aloud, he said: "You can start by unlocking this shed door."

Chris fished through his pockets for some keys. He was no longer wearing his black and red jacket. Instead he wore a lined, black, nylon wind breaker. The padlock released with a snap into his hand. He withdrew the lock and stood back. Robin stood to the side and pushed the door open. Caution came naturally to him. The only sound was the creak of the old hinges as the door swung outward. He snapped on his flashlight and stepped inside the door. A few seconds later he looked outside again. He pointed to the search dog.

"Roscoe," the handler said. "Find the gun."

Roscoe bounded inside, sniffed around the door and sat down. "Woof," he said.

Jim looked in through the door and then to the handler. "Can you translate that, please?"

"Whatever he smells is right there in front of him," said the handler. He, too, had a look inside the door.

Roscoe scratched at the floor. "Woof. Woof."

Robin shone his light over the floorboards just inside the door. "I think that last woof means 'Right here, stupid.'"

Scott got down on his hands and knees and looked under the shed. He fished a small but powerful flashlight from a pouch on his belt and shone it around. Then he crawled in a little further.

"I don't see the weapon, but there is a wooden box nailed to the floor above."

He squirmed in further still. "I don't seen any way in. It must open from the top."

Robin knelt down and ran his hand across the floor. "There's a loose board here." He pointed.

Jim withdrew a maroon-coloured Swiss Army knife from his pocket, picked out the proper blade from the selection offered and opened it. He gently pried up the board in front of Roscoe. The dog backed off and started barking again. There, in a little, wooden pocket under the floor lay a gleaming .22 semiautomatic rifle.

Jim looked back at Chris. By now, Scott was back on his feet. He took hold of Chris's upper arm. Chris had a dismal look on his face. He had dedicated his life to looking after animals. Now one had tripped him up.

"I have nothing to say until Pastor Dave gets here."

CHAPTER 23

THE FOUR MEN sat around the narrow metal table in the interrogation room at Halifax Police Headquarters. On one side was a solemn looking Chris Ritchey and a smiling man known simply as Pastor Dave. The pastor had been called on his cell phone and redirected from the Ritchey farm to police headquarters.

On the other side of the table were Detective-Sergeant Jim Mcdonald and Corporal Scott Bowen. Two cups of freshly brewed coffee and two bottles of spring water sat on the table. Pastor Dave said his flock restrained themselves from the use of stimulants like coffee and alcohol. Neither policeman shared the pastor's smile.

"I trust you're familiar with the Good Book?" Pastor Dave opened the conversation.

Jim nodded his head. "You mean the one that says: '*You shall not commit murder*?'"

Pastor Dave's smile increased. "That is the one. Are you also familiar with the next verse? *Neither shalt thou commit adultery.*"

Now it was Jim's turn to smile. "I am, but here's the thing. I'm a detective from Major Crimes. That's homicide and burglary. Adultery comes under the civil codes. Your boy here is charged with committing murder. That's the Criminal Code."

Ritchey's head snapped up. "I didn't murder Gerald. We were lifelong friends. His death was an accident."

Jim and Scott exchanged a cynical glance.

"That's your defence?" Scott said. "You meant to shoot someone else so this was an accident?" He could not hide the sarcasm from his question.

Pastor Dave held up his hands in a placating manner. "You are aware that Chris's wife was carrying on an adulterous affair with the farm hand next door, the nephew of the victim? Adultery is not a venial sin in the eyes of the Lord. In fact, the Bible calls for adulterers and adulteresses to be put to death."

"Well, Father? Pastor? Reverend?" Jim shook his head. "I'm not sure what I should call you."

"My congregation refers to me as Pastor Dave. We like to run a friendly church."

"Okay, Pastor it is. I'm sure I'm not telling you anything new, but your Good Book also reads '*Justice is mine, sayeth the Lord, I will repay.*' It goes on to say to let the proper authorities handle these issues."

Pastor Dave nodded. "That's the New Testament teaching. The Old was not so forgiving. It doled out severe punishments for a whole list of crimes."

"Solomon also warns that *A man may think he is always right but the Lord fixes a standard for the heart.* You'd best advise Mr. Ritchey to be checking if that standard gives him free rein to commit murder."

Pastor Dave raised his eyebrows with a look of surprise. "I must admit that I'm surprised at your knowledge of the Bible, but, and I don't mean to doubt your sincerity, I'm sure you'll agree that I can find a quote to cover any situation one might want to cover."

Now it was the Sergeant's turn to grin. "That's exactly my point. In or out or context, everything seems to have a biblical justification. I hope that is not the defence Mr. Ritchey plans on using in court. It won't fly for two reasons. One, in this country we have a separation of church and state and two, and most importantly, Ralph Foley claims there was no adulterous affair taking place. I believe he quoted Bruce Springsteen when he described the relationship; they got together and discussed their *Glory Days* from high school. Rock and roll music also has a wellspring of quotes to cover every situation."

Both men laughed. Pastor Dave was not the tight ass that Jim had expected.

"On the serious side," Jim continued, "Linda Ritchey claimed to have a problem with your church and the effect it was having on her husband. She was only seeking advice from Ralph on how to best handle the situation. She wanted Ralph to intervene and free Chris from your control; he refused."

Now it was the pastor's turn to look skeptical. Before he could speak, however, Chris jumped to his feet. "Don't give me that line of bullshit. Every time I left the farm, they were getting into each other's pants. I tried to encourage Linda to follow the path of the Lord, but she was caught up in the snare of the devil. Ralph Foley deserves to die for his sinning ways and for leading an innocent woman down that same path." His voice shook with emotion as he made the last proclamation.

The other three men in the room were taken aback by this outburst. Up to this point since his arrest, Chris had been quiet and controlled. This was the first time he had raised his voice.

Jim turned to the pastor. "Mr. Ritchey has been advised of his right to retain a lawyer. He chose to call you instead. I should point out that anything he says can be used against him in a court of law. Your presence here doesn't make this privileged communication or protected by seals of confession or anything of that nature."

The pastor gave his head a little shake. "We understand that. There is a lawyer on the way. Leon Goldstein, perhaps you've heard of him."

"Goldstein?" Jim said. "Farming must be more lucrative than I thought. He's one of the most expensive lawyers in the province."

"He makes a good living," Pastor Dave said. "He's also a member of our congregation. His firm has been known to help fellow members out from time to time with legal problems," the pastor raised his eyebrows, "for free. When I called him about Chris, he said he would personally be over to intercede on Chris's behalf. Something about it being an interesting case."

"He's crazy if he thinks this Bible defence will free his client," Scott said. "He murdered an old man in cold blood. One, I might add, who is neither a devil nor sinner. From everyone we talked to, Gerald Booth was a pillar of the community."

Pastor Dave shrugged his shoulders. "Maybe Leon is not the crazy one in this case."

Jim sat back in his chair and sighed. It was all beginning to make sense to him. Pastor Dave had been sent in to control the flow of the interview but not to prevent Chris from making any wild statements or claims. He and Scott were going to be part of the defence's case for an insanity plea. Scott had already used the phrase " he's crazy." Granted he was talking about the lawyer, but it wouldn't take much talking on the part of a lawyer as skilled as Leon Goldstein to twist that around to mean it was Chris whose thinking was crazy.

With Chris's current fundamentalist approach to understanding the Bible, it would be a difficult call to decide if he really understood right from wrong in the secular sense of the words. Chris's total lack of remorse and limited efforts to hide what he had done suggested he didn't fully understand the magnitude of the crimes with which he was being charged. He truly didn't believe he had done anything wrong.

It was true that Chris had hidden his rifle, but Leon Goldstein could twist that around to make it appear that Chris felt guilty about still owning this egotistical token from his earlier life. Merely owning this glorified weapon made him appear to be a braggart.

The addition of Leon Goldstein to the case meant that no "i" could remain undotted, no "t" uncrossed. Jim looked over at Scott and motioned with his head towards the door.

To Pastor Dave, he said: "Excuse us, we're going to give you a chance to talk to Chris. We want to be sure he understands the seriousness of what's happening here."

Both Mounties pulled back their chairs and exited the room. Once outside, Scott gave his fellow policeman an inquiring look. "What's up? He was just starting to open up."

Jim nodded in agreement. "I think we're being set up for an insanity plea. We've got to reconnoiter. Forensics is going to confirm his guilt. Ballistics will match the killer bullet to his gun; powder residue on his face and hands will put that weapon in his hands. We know what his motive is."

Scott nodded in agreement with each of these statements. "A confession would tie it all up with a neat little bow."

"You're not familiar with Leon Goldstein. There's never been a confession he couldn't either have thrown out or turned to his favour."

Scott looked back through the one-way mirror into the room. Pastor Dave and Chris were deep in conversation. Pastor Dave did most of the talking, Chris most of the nodding. From somewhere Chris had obtained a cigarette. He simultaneously sucked it into his mouth while pulling it free with his pinched thumb and fingers. Smoke came out in short puffs while Chris appeared to explain something to his spiritual leader. Agitation was written all over his face. When he finished talking, he sat back in his chair and stared at the ceiling.

"Why are we allowing this Pastor Dave guy to sit in on the interrogation? Now that we know he has Goldstein as a lawyer, we could put the boot to the good pastor."

Jim thought about this for a few seconds. "I think Ritchey will be more inclined to talk in the pastor's presence. He is trying to prove how well he understands the teaching of the Old Testament to the pastor. He no doubt thinks we are soulless infidels. Part of this understanding ties in with his actions. We won't have to prove that Chris did it. Instead we have to show that he knew what he was doing was wrong in the eyes of the secular world."

"I'm not sure he thinks that."

Jim studied his partner. "Well, if he doesn't, he's not guilty in the eyes of the law. Insane, but not guilty."

Scott rubbed his chin while contemplating this statement. "He's guilty as hell. He did try to hide the rifle and during the first interview, he did lie to us about owning it. This shows knowledge that he had done wrong. Damn it, I don't want to see him kill an innocent old man and just walk away from it scot-free."

"Me either. I've thought of one way they could cover that up. I doubt that Chris has but I'm willing to bet that Goldstein will come up with something. When we go back in, we'll start with his hiding the gun. If he can't come up with a plausible explanation, we'll push it to the limit. If he has some crazy defence, we'll move on to his denial at once."

Scott gave his head a frustrated shake. "Oh, for the good old days when Jimmy Cagney played a cop. He would simply beat a confession out of him."

"Then send him up before Judge Isaac Parker and he would be dangling from a rope by week's end."

Scott blushed. "Damn right," he said, but the enthusiasm had left his voice.

Again Jim laughed. "Even lawmen can fantasize."

Scott's smile faded. "Getting justice for the victim shouldn't be a fantasy."

Back in the interrogation room, Scott resumed his seat across from Chris. He brought both forearms up and rested them on the table. "Word in Raymond's River is that you're one of the best shots in the country with a .22 rifle. Sort of a local hero."

Chris wasn't buying into this line of questioning. He made no comment.

Scott tapped the crossed rifles on the cuffs of his uniform jacket. "I know something about competitive shooting myself. We should get together some time and see who really is the king of the shooters in this area."

"Any time, any place." There was no friendliness in the response from Chris.

"Chris no longer shoots competitively," Pastor Dave said. "That sort of sport is an abomination in the eyes of Jesus."

Scott ignored the pastor. "Of course, at that level, the gun is almost as important as the shooter."

"My gun was a prize for winning my first national competition," Chris said. "I was a champion first."

"That gun means nothing to Chris anymore," Pastor Dave said. "He has put useless possessions behind him."

Again Scott ignored the interruption. "You may not have used it the first time, but I bet you've used it every time since."

"Be a fool not to. It's a finely crafted weapon. In the right hands, it's almost impossible to miss with it. Don't try to tell me you just grab any old gun off the rack when you're competing."

"I have my favourites," Scott said. "They don't look as fancy as yours," he paused," but if you take care of them, they get the job done."

Chris nodded. "That's the trick. You treat your weapon with respect, it will do what you ask of it. The fancy chrome is just for show."

"Too true," Scott said, "that's why I was surprised to see yours under the floor in that outbuilding. That seems like a funny place to store a weapon of that quality. What were you thinking?"

Chris's cheeks reddened. "It was a stupid thing to do. I guess I wasn't thinking straight at the time."

"It looked like you were trying to hide it." Scott stared directly into Chris's eyes. "Is that what you were doing, hiding the gun?"

"That's enough," Pastor Dave cut in. "We already told you that gun means nothing to Chris anymore."

Scott turned his attention to the pastor, said nothing, then looked back at Chris. "That's coming from a man who has never felt the thrill of a successful shoot. What would he know about the pride you feel when the person in the butts indicates a bulls-eye for all on the firing line to see?"

Chris's head was nodding up and down, his eyes sparkled. His mind was at some shooting competition somewhere.

Scott's face took on a momentarily confused look and he shook his head. "You must have been really disturbed to treat that fine rifle with such disregard."

Chris's eyes clouded over. He looked around the table, his view settling on the disapproving look coming from Pastor Dave.

Jim heavily placed his coffee cup on the table. "It's obvious he was just trying to hide it." Now the attention of the other three men focused on Jim as he made this comment. "If it hadn't been for Roscoe, we'd have never found it under those floor boards. You were hiding the rifle, Chris. You knew the police would be looking for it, so you hid it in the shed and then told us you had sold it when we asked. Why Chris? Why deny your prized possession?"

"There's no proof of that," Pastor Dave said.

Jim turned on the pastor. "We know that rifle is the murder weapon. Ballistics has confirmed that. We know whoever shot it murdered Gerald Booth and we know Chris, here, hid it. This is not rocket science, Pastor. Chris Ritchey murdered Gerald Booth and tried to hide the evidence. Isn't that true, Chris?" Now he addressed his full attention to Chris. "Confession is good for the soul. Ask your pastor here, I'm sure he'll agree with that. You killed Gerald Booth, didn't you? And then you tried to cover it up. It was a good hiding place but you can't outsmart a dog as intelligent as Roscoe."

"I didn't kill him on purpose. It wasn't supposed to be Gerald coming out of that barn. He always stayed behind and made sure all the equipment was shut down. Years ago he had some lazy kid helping him. The kid left a compressor running and it caught fire. Nearly took the entire barn. Gerald has done his own shutdowns ever since. Ralph was always the first to leave. It was supposed to be Ralph coming through that door."

"Not another word, Chris." Pastor Dave put a hand on Chris's arm. "Leon Goldstein will be here any minute. Don't say another word until he gets here."

"I didn't mean to kill Gerald. Doesn't anyone understand that? It was an accident."

Jim slid a pad across the table. "Accidents do happen. Why don't you write down exactly what you remember about the sequence of events. That way we can see what we can work out for you."

Chris's eyes brightened. "I know things. Important things you should know about. Things about another one of your cases."

The two cops exchanged confused glances. Chris was trying to plea bargain a murder conviction. Scott wasn't working on any other major cases in this area. What could Chris know that would be of help to Jim, a cop from the city? Jim shrugged and decided to play along. "What things?"

Pastor Dave stood up. "Things he will discuss with his lawyer first." He pushed the yellow pad back across the table to Jim. "If there's going to be any deal made, Chris is going to be well represented in his part of the negotiation. I have authority from Mr. Goldstein to end this interview any time I think is necessary. Now I say it is ended."

"You have the authority?" Sarcasm dripped from Scott's voice. "Authority granted by whom? Chris is the only one who has the authority to end this interview."

Jim put one hand on Scott's arm and reached for the power button on a tape recorder that had been running during this session. "We can wait for Mr. Goldstein before continuing. He looked at his watch. "This interview ended at 6:47 p.m." He flipped off the switch.

"We've run through supper time. Can we get you something to eat? Pizza? A sandwich?"

Both men shook their head.

Jim slid back his chair. "You sure? It could be a long night."

CHAPTER 24

JOSH DANIELS BROUGHT down the handle of the mitre saw and cut through the piece of hardwood molding. His nostrils twitched as the distinctive scent of the freshly cut oak surrounded him. His eye unconsciously approved of the swirled pattern made by the grain in the wood. The stain, a honey maple in colour, complemented the warm green of the living room walls. He checked the fit of the two angles. Perfect. He picked up his air hammer and secured the beveled wood against the bottom of the wall. His practiced hand made the joints appear to be seamless.

Josh had done this procedure so many times that while maintaining this high-quality workmanship, he could devote a good part of his brain to thinking about other things. Right now, prominently perched at the top of this list of other things stood the identity of the mysterious money man. More importantly, why should there be a mysterious money man? Hell, business was booming. They were building houses. Creating communities. This was not something to be ashamed of. Nothing shady or illegal was taking place. Why be secretive?

His finger hesitated before firing the next brad into the wall. Were they doing something illegal? He sat back on his haunches and looked around the room. Everything was built from quality material. No corners were being cut, no codes violated. Nothing of that nature could be done without his knowledge. He oversaw every aspect of the building. If anything, the houses were overbuilt. So why the mystery?

He rocked forward again and applied the last few brads to hold everything secure. Maybe there was no mystery. Maybe Kevin was simply too busy at the time to fill Josh in on the details of this other investor. Kevin didn't work as physically hard as Josh did on the houses, but he logged almost as many hours. He was always working three, four or five years in the future. Planning, studying demographics, buying up appropriate parcels of land. Josh had heard Kevin make his sales pitches. This wasn't a money thing with Kevin, well not just a money thing. These

116

communities were a vision, a labour of love. There was no way Kevin would do anything that would jeopardize his grand scheme of things.

Cliff had been a little slow to come on board to the targeted market aspect of these communities at first. He believed in diversity, a broader range of prospective buyers.

Josh lay his hammer on the floor. Poor Cliff. Whenever Josh started thinking about the esoteric aspects of their plan, his thoughts turned to Cliff. Kevin wanted the buying public to know that they were building specialized communities, places where people could live among like-thinking neighbours. At the same time, he didn't want other developers jumping on this bandwagon. For Cliff, this was a dichotomy. Make the idea seem like the best thing since sliced bread to the buyers and at the same time downplay the significance to his fellow realtors.

This task would be a difficult challenge for a believer, but Cliff was not deterred. He was a salesman. If he found himself stranded in the Nevada desert, he could convince people roaring towards Las Vegas that he was the sole source of a special, lucky sand. Buy it quick and make your gambling adventure a success. He could scoop it from the ground right at their feet and they would still pass over a mittful of money. Kevin would be proved wrong but not because Cliff hadn't given it his all.

Reality proved the opposite was true. Before the first five houses were sold that first year, Cliff was a believer. The house buyers immediately bought into the idea as though they had started their search with a homogeneous development in mind. Families with children wanted families with children for neighbours. Older people wanted people of their own age and experiences as neighbours. It appeared to be a self-evident fact. But it wasn't, except to Kevin. Cliff quickly grasped the knowledge that they were sitting on a gold mine of an idea. He developed a sales team to make this approach work.

And now, just when they were really starting to reap the rewards of their efforts, Cliff was dead. Shot out of a tree by a quirk of fate. Josh knew life wasn't fair. Life just was. But he couldn't help being discouraged when he thought of the hand destiny had dealt to his partner and more importantly, friend.

Josh gave his head a little shake to dismiss these depressing thoughts. He would give Kevin a call and arrange to meet for a couple of beers later in the week. This would give Kevin a chance to bring him up to speed about this silent partner with the big purse. He picked up the next piece of molding, checked the corner and firmly nailed it into place.

CHAPTER 25

LEON GOLDSTEIN LOOKED up as the two policemen came through the doorway of the small, closed-in interview room. He gestured towards the recording machine still parked in the middle of the cigarette-scarred table. "Fortunately for you, that tape is reusable, unlike the contents, which are worthless. The dulcet tones of your well-thought-out questions will never be heard inside a courtroom."

Jim reached out his hand. "Detective Sergeant Jim Mcdonald," he said. He turned towards Scott: "Corporal Scott Bowen. Scott, this is the famed lawyer, Leon Goldstein."

"Pleased to meet you," Scott said although his eyes spoke the opposite.

Goldstein stuck out a limp hand and briefly touched those of the lawmen, without any enthusiasm. He looked at Scott. "The sergeant and I are already acquainted. I hope you're a more reasonable man than he is."

"You've listened to the tape already, then," Jim said. "Good, that will save us some time."

"I don't have to listen to the tape. It's inadmissible."

Jim canted his head to one side and made a tsking sound. "You should have listened to it. Very early on we have it on the tape where I told Mr. Ritchey that we could use anything he says in court. His pastor was with him at the time providing him with advice, supposedly with your knowledge and under your guidance. The pastor understood and gave us permission to continue. Should I find Pastor Dave and bring him back in?"

"The pastor is a good man, but he's not a lawyer. The tape goes."

"Well, Mr. Goldstein, here's the good news as far as I'm concerned. We can make this case without your client's confession. Whether the tape stands or not is not a decision I have to make, as you well know. We both know you're merely practising your own fine delivery for when you get in front of a judge. So let's save a lot of time and move on to the real issue here."

"My client's guilt or innocence is the real issue here, Sergeant. What could be more real than spending the rest of your life in prison?"

"My point exactly. Mr. Ritchey seems to think he has some valuable information that could reduce that prison time. You've discussed this?"

Leon Goldstein's face remained stoic. He gave no indication one way or the other of his knowledge of additional factors.

Jim turned his attention to Chris Ritchey. "You have told your lawyer what you told us? You have important additional information that can help us in another case?" Jim raised his eyebrows and his voice to punctuate the sentence with a question mark.

Chris was nodding before the inquiry was finished. He said nothing. Obviously, the lawyer had impressed his client with the seriousness of his situation. Chris was letting Leon Goldstein do all of his talking, but actual words are only a small part of the communication process. Jim had his answer. He looked back at the lawyer, extended his hands in front of him, palms up.

The lawyer shot his client an evil look before facing Jim again. "I don't think we're at that point in the proceedings yet. I have to see what kind of a case you have against Mr. Ritchey before I start giving you freebies. There may be nothing to negotiate."

Jim forced a disappointed look onto his face. "I could understand that tactic if you were being paid for this defence. Drag it out as long as possible. Run up the billable hours. Is that a habit you simply can't break?" He looked at Chris. "Counsellor, your client is guilty as hell and my understanding is that you're doing this pro bono. Let's wrap this up so we can both get on with our other work."

Goldstein's face blazed into a dark red hue. He leapt to his feet, sending his chair sprawling against the wall. "Every one of my clients gets the best defence I can give, Sergeant Mcdonald. Money does not enter into the equation." He was leaning across the table inches from Jim's face.

Jim did not flinch.

Before he could answer, Scott spoke up. "Dragging this out is not in your client's best interest. Gerald Booth was a well-liked, well-respected member of his community. His killer will be held in utter contempt. If Chris can do anything to redeem himself in the eyes of his neighbours, it had better be sooner rather than later. Two months down the road, any plea bargain will only disgust the good people of Raymond's River. They will see it as a sleazy, lawyer trick to reduce a murderer's just punishment. And they won't forget why he got out early, if he gets out early. Murder doesn't leave much room for negotiation."

"Damn it, it was an accident." Now Chris was on his feet. "I did not mean to kill Gerald Booth. Why doesn't anyone understand that? Gerald shouldn't have been walking through that door. I didn't know it was him."

Jim smiled. "It's confession time again. This time he's represented by and in the presence of one of the best lawyers in this jurisdiction. What now, Counsellor?"

Goldstein said nothing. He retrieved his chair and plunked down into it. Then he rubbed his forehead with the fingers of both hands before looking up. "Listen to the man. It's obvious to anyone that he doesn't understand what he's saying. An insanity defence will be a walk in the park. Next thing you know he'll be saying God told him to do it."

Scott glanced sideways to see Jim's reaction. The sergeant had called the shot.

"Did God tell you to do it, Chris?" Jim asked. "You're a God-fearing man. What does the Good Book tell you about taking another man's life? Does it say murder is wrong?"

"Don't answer that," Goldstein said before Chris had a chance to express his opinion.

Chris shrugged. "Why not? The Bible is quite clear. Thou shalt do no murder, but it also says an adulterer should be put to death."

Goldstein sighed a heavy sigh. "Please, Chris. Say nothing more."

"You should have listened to the tape, Counsellor. We're not covering virgin territory here." Jim gave the lawyer a piercing look. "But you know that. Pastor Dave was sent in to establish the grounds for your insanity plea. We are to believe that Chris is so caught up in his fervent religious beliefs, that he can't determine right from wrong in the secular world. I find it hard to believe the good pastor went along with your plan. Surely, he believes these holy words to be truths to live by as well. Is this a publicity bid to build his congregation and Chris here, is the sacrificial lamb?" He pointed an accusing finger at Chris. "This man is going to prison for murder."

Again Goldstein said nothing. He was a master of knowing when not to talk.

"Doing God's will is not murder," Chris said in a low voice.

Scott shook his head in disgust. "God's will. Remember, Gerald Booth is not guilty of committing adultery. You were not carrying out God's will. You were committing murder."

"Gerald's death was an accident." Chris slammed his open hand down on the table causing the others to jump slightly.

"Your Bible covers that, as well," Jim said. "In Joshua it tells us to set aside cities of refuge for those who kill inadvertently. In your case, the killing wasn't accidental; the choice of victim was. We have places set aside for people in your circumstance. Kingston, Dorchester, Millhaven, a number of maximum security facilities where you will be safe from the relatives of Gerald Booth. How long you stay there will depend on this new information of yours."

Goldstein reached up and placed a hand on Chris's shoulder. With a slight pull, he guided his client back into his chair. "Gentlemen, emotions are running a little high here at the moment. Let me talk to my client and I'm sure we will be able to come to a mutually satisfying agreement. We all want to do what is in the best interest of the community as a whole. Let's meet in the morning before Chris is arraigned and see if we can save the justice system a lot of time and a lot of money."

Scott and Jim's eyes briefly consulted before Jim answered. "Why not? We have a nice comfortable bed for Chris just down the hall. Court convenes at 10 a.m. See you at nine?"

CHAPTER 26

AN UNUSUAL SILENCE filled the downtown law office. Unusual because the two men present were both noted orators; both used to filling the surrounding air with forceful, well-thought-out arguments; both used to being listened to. Now they were at an impasse.

"For God's sake, Pastor Dave, insanity is the only defence I have." Leon Goldstein broke the silence. "That blubbering fool has already confessed to everyone who has crossed his path. They have it on tape, twice. Once in your presence and once in mine. When you first called me you agreed our best defence would be that he was following the words of the Bible. You said it was time to test religious belief in court. I advised against it, but you said we could win."

Pastor Dave looked towards the 14-floor window behind Goldstein. His own image stared back at him in the night time window. Lines of strain filled his usually gregarious face. Goldstein was right. He had made that claim, but now he was having second thoughts.

"Things have changed since then, Leon. I thought Chris had killed the man having an adulterous affair with his wife. He was incoherent when he called me this morning. He was crying about his wife being unfaithful. He vilified the neighbouring farm hand. He quoted Leviticus." Pastor Dave lowered his head and gave it a gentle side-to-side shake. "I thought the dead man was the adulterer. Adultery is abhorred in both the Old and New Testaments. Chris is a true believer. We could have justified his actions."

He looked up at the lawyer. "Instead the victim was an innocent, old man. We can't claim that God told Chris to kill Gerald Booth. It doesn't make sense."

Goldstein's voice took on a harder edge. "Ritchey thought it was the lecherous cheater exiting the barn. That's what counts. What was in his mind at the time. He thought he was doing God's will.

"I don't get to make up the facts in this case, Pastor. I have to play with the cards that are dealt to me. It's still a stretch but we could make this insanity plea stick."

Pastor Dave's head was shaking in disagreement all through this statement. "Leviticus tells us that if any person sins unwittingly, he must accept responsibility. There is no biblical defence for murdering the wrong man."

"We're not going to be arguing before God." Leon Goldstein knew he and the pastor had been on different pages from the beginning. Pastor Dave was attempting to justify Chris Ritchey's actions with his religious beliefs; lawyer Goldstein intended to prove Chris didn't know what he was doing because of his religious beliefs. "We're going to be arguing before a jury of his peers. We have to convince twelve men and women that Chris believed he was following the will of God. That's all it boils down to. Did he know the difference between right and wrong at the time of the shooting? Did he honestly believe he was carrying out God's will? Your job is to paint a picture of Chris as an ardent follower of the written Bible. A man who believes there is no room for interpretation in the Good Book. You take it as you read it."

The pastor leapt to his feet. "*My lips shall not speak wickedness, nor my tongue utter deceit.* Chris is not the only believer in the written word here. I thought we all were. The book of Job forbids me to be a part of this charade. I won't have my beliefs manipulated to serve your ends. I will not be involved in legal chicanery."

Goldstein sat back abruptly, a shocked look on his face. "I'm not asking you to sell your soul, Pastor. I'm asking you to help a fellow parishioner. Was Chris a believer?"

The scowl left Pastor Dave's face. "You know that he was."

"Did he take the Bible as a literal instruction book from God?"

"You might say that his beliefs were of a fundamental nature."

"Come on. You know he believed the Bible was the literal word of God. I've heard you two arguing about it many times. There was no might about it."

Pastor Dave just shrugged.

Goldstein continued his questions, building his case for Pastor Dave's help. "Was his wife involved in an adulterous affair?"

"So Chris says."

Goldstein stopped abruptly and studied Pastor Dave.

"You don't know if there was actually an affair?"

"Linda was not a member of our church. She came once and never returned. I can only go by what Chris said. He believed there was an affair. He came to me in tears seeking advice."

"And what did you advise?"

"That the two of them come to me for counselling. She never showed up. Her solution was for Chris to leave the church and seek outside counselling."

"Oh, shit," Goldstein said. "He's already killed the wrong man. If there's no affair, we're up that proverbial creek without a paddle. Who do you know that can confirm this for us?"

Pastor Dave sat down again, a look of deep concentration on his face. For several seconds, he said nothing. "Most people go out of their way to keep these things a secret. We'll have to ask Chris how he knew."

Goldstein gave a heavy sigh. "Not a very reliable source. The man really is crazy."

"Believing in the word of God does not make you crazy."

"It does if it tells you to go around shooting people and you actually do it." There was no smile on the lawyer's face. He was deadly serious. "I'm also a member of your church, remember. I've never heard you advocate killing anyone in the name of the Lord. Chris really is crazy. Now we have to prove that he meets the legal definition of insane – knowing right from wrong." Goldstein shook his head. "It's not even that simple. It's not just what Chris believes, it's what Chris thinks society believes. Is there a faction in your church that believes killing adulterers is right? Some bunch of crazies I don't know about? That's what he will be judged on."

Pastor Dave scowled at the lawyer. He got to his feet and started to pace around the spacious office. This whole situation was bleeding his mind and body of strength. "There may be some elements that carry fundamentalism a little too far, but there is no bunch of crazies. Besides, Chris knows what he did was wrong. The police know he knows. He lied to them. He hid the gun. He refused them access to the shed where the gun was hidden. He did everything he could to cover up his actions. If only he had admitted to the shooting right from the start, then we might have had a chance with the insanity defence. You could have stepped in and exercised your sophistry." He turned to face Goldstein, a look of total defeat on his face. "That opportunity is gone. We need another defence. What is this information he claims to have?"

Goldstein looked insulted. "Sophistry. Do you know what you are implying? Many say the same thing about your job." He gave a wave of his hand as if to dismiss the subject. "As for the other, he hasn't told me what he knows, but he thinks it is of major importance."

Now it was Pastor Dave's turn to sigh. "It had better be or the congregation is going to be down one very active member for the next twenty-five years."

CHAPTER 27

JOSH DANIELS WIPED the back of his hand across his mouth, obliterating the foam mustache left there from the long swig of beer he had just finished. He raised the half-empty mug to Kevin Barnhill. "To another successful season now drawing to a close," he said.

"That's something I'll always drink to," Kevin said. "Sweet success."

"We're finishing up the last of 39 houses in Phase Two this year. Eleven more will be finished in the early spring and then we open up Phase Three if the streets, water and sewer are in." Josh set his mug down on the table. "We should be able to finish 50 houses next year if the weather holds."

Kevin laughed. "Don't worry. Everything will be ready. I've had more than that many inquiries about Phase Three. They're going to be a little higher-end than One and Two. It will sell out fast. There's a whole new batch of baby boomers moving up the pike." Kevin discreetly glanced at his watch but said nothing. Josh had invited him to meet for this beer. Kevin knew that beer was not the main reason for this meeting. That wasn't Josh's style. He didn't stop in the middle of the day to drink beer. For that matter, Kevin knew, Josh seldom drank beer at all.

Josh, ever alert, caught the wrist motion. "Tell me about our silent partner," he said. The foreplay had taken less than a minute. Now they were down to the short strokes.

"Sure. What do you want to know?"

"How about who is he for starters?"

Kevin sipped his beer. He wondered how much information he should give up. "Originally he was a friend of Cliff's. They grew up in the same neighbourhood. He's a businessman who helped us with start-up money that first year. I guess he knew a good thing when he saw it and has been part of the team ever since."

Josh slowly nodded his head, his eyes never leaving Kevin's. "Part of the team? I've never heard the investors referred to in that way before. They always seemed to be an outside component that had to be wooed each year to bring them back. They never seemed to share the vision. They were only interested in the rewards. I've always felt it was the vision that made us a team." Josh touched the mug to his lips, the level of the beer inside almost remained constant. "Has this investor got a name?"

"You make it sound so mysterious." Kevin laughed. "Anthony Dellapinna and he's more than just an investor. He's our supplier."

Josh leaned forward, his look becoming more intense. "Our supplier?"

"Our supplier. At the beginning of each building season, you submit a list of materials you will need and when. Every week or so, you issue a supplementary list based on progress. These supplies show up at the site and you use them up. Mr. Dellapinna is the person who fulfills your wishes and quite well I might add."

"Never heard of him. The person I deal with is Ronald Sutherland. He handles all our supplies."

Kevin was nodding as Josh talked. "Ron works for Tony. Ron does the actual ordering. Tony pays the bills. We buy from Tony."

"That seems like an unnecessary step. Wouldn't it be cheaper to skip that step?"

"We are a minor part of Tony's business interests. With his contacts, he can make deals that we can't even dream of. Believe me, you couldn't get the products any cheaper if you went right to the factory yourself and picked them up. Bringing Tony into the deal was one of the best moves that Cliff made for us."

"Why haven't I ever met the man? It seems logical that I would be the one to be dealing with the supplier of our raw materials."

"Because you deal with Ron. Tony likes to keep a low profile and as I said, we are one of his many interests and not that far up the ladder. It's only because of Cliff that we were able to get this sweetheart deal."

Josh swirled the beer in his mug and watched the bubbles dissipate. Slowly his gaze returned to Kevin's eyes. "Is this all legal?"

Kevin laughed, a little harder than was necessary. He engaged Josh's stare. "What can be illegal about buying lumber and nails? His prices may seem like a steal, but that is the power of buying in bulk." Kevin raised his beer stein in a salute before drinking down the rest of the contents. "And that is why we can make the profits that we do."

"I've seen our invoices. Our prices don't look to be that deeply discounted to me."

Kevin's countenance took on a serious air. "Those are the retail prices; the prices we show our other investors." He noticed the shocked look come across Josh's face. He leaned forward in his seat. "They also don't look excessive. If we were doing our own purchasing, these are the kinds of prices we would be paying, maybe even a little more. They stand up to the scrutiny of our more ambitious investors who check these things out."

Now Josh looked even more horrified.

"You mean you're keeping two sets of books?" he said, his voice a low whisper but with a harsh edge. Both of his fists bunched up as if he wanted to hit somebody.

Kevin reached across the table and grabbed one of the wrists.

"Don't be stupid. I told you we're not doing anything illegal."

Josh shook off Kevin's hand.

"Well, you'd better try explaining this to me one more time because it sure as hell looks that way to me."

Kevin smiled and leaned down towards the floor and brought up his briefcase. "I thought you might want to see it in writing. I came prepared."

The sombre look stayed on Josh's face. "Don't try to dazzle me with figures. I just want the truth."

Kevin rifled through the pages of a report taken from his briefcase. Then he flipped back a few pages and laid the statement open on the table between them. Josh leaned in for a closer look. A list of investors stretched down the page with amounts and dates following each name. Each transaction was listed separately.

He looked up at Kevin. "So? This should mean something to me?"

"These are the people and companies that put money into our projects." Kevin tapped the page to emphasize the point. Then he picked up the report and flipped though to near the end. He studied a few passages and then laid it down for Josh to see again.

"Here are the payouts to these investors."

As before, listed on the page were the names, dates of transaction, amount of money and percentage of return. Also listed were the houses sold that returned this investment. The figures were not in neat columns but more of a paragraph style. Josh had to study the page a little closer to dig out the information being presented.

Again he looked up at Kevin and spread out his hands. "I repeat. So? I've seen this information before. We give back too much money to these people who do absolutely nothing to build a house and are not even taking a risk, given the state of the housing market today. It's as close to a sure thing in the investment world that you're going to find anywhere."

Kevin smiled. "I'm not here to argue that today." He tapped the sheets of paper in front of him. "If you closely study these figures, you'll see that Mr. Dellapinna gets a very low return on his investment."

"Oh," Josh said, "I hadn't noticed."

"You're not supposed to."

"I'm only a simple carpenter. You'd better explain."

Kevin laughed. "Right, a simple carpenter. It's all legal and above board and lawyer approved, but that's how our discount on the building materials is returned to the partners and not the investors."

Again Josh shook his head. "I don't understand."

Kevin looked around the room at the others. No one was paying any attention to them. Their interest was strictly in drinking their beer and discussing last night's sport scores. He turned back to Josh and lowered his voice. "Let's say he takes funds from his other enterprises, runs them through our company and then can legitimately spend them anywhere."

"Money-laundering." The words shot from Josh's mouth before he had a chance to control them. Now it was his turn to check out the other patrons. Those at the closest table had looked his way but without any real interest. They resumed their original conversations, more distracted by Josh's sudden outburst than his actual words.

Kevin was shaking his head. "Not really. This is all on the up and up."

"Then why is it such a secret?" Josh was leaning into Kevin's face again. Traces of anger flashed in his eyes.

"Because some people might misconstrue what is happening," Kevin said in a placating voice. "I told you I've run it by our lawyers."

Josh settled back in his chair. His dark eyes bore into Kevin's. "Has any of this anything to do with Cliff getting shot?"

"What?" All traces of a smile left Kevin's face. "Tony and Cliff have been friends all their lives. If Tony thought that Cliff's death was anything but an accident, he would be beating the bushes to find out who had done it."

He gathered the papers into a neat stack, returned them to the folder in which he had brought them and tossed it across the table to

Josh. "Take these. Study them. Show them to your attorney. Whatever. We're not doing anything wrong. Thanks for the beer." With that, he got up from the table, leaving the virtually untouched glass. "Call me if you have any more questions. I'm not hiding anything from you. It's all right there in black and white."

Josh put his hand on the folder to keep it from falling on the floor. "Don't go away mad, Kevin. If I'm going to take a bigger role in this partnership, I want to be fully up to speed on what's going on. That's all." A smile came across his face. "I have no complaints about our successes to date. You haven't seen me returning any dividend cheques."

"You're right," Kevin said. "There are no other secrets. Read that report. It's all right there if you dig through the legal bullshit." Now it was his turn to smile. "You're just a simple carpenter; I'm just a dreamer who likes to design places for people to live. Let's both continue to do what we do best and leave the legal crap to the lawyers and bookkeepers."

He started for the door of the bar, walking past Josh in the process. He closed his fist and gave him a light tap on the shoulder as he walked by. This had gone as well as he could have hoped. Josh appeared to be completely onside.

CHAPTER 28

AT 8:55 A.M., Corporal Scott Bowen and Sergeant Jim Mcdonald stood on the courthouse steps sipping from Tim Hortons coffee cups. The temperature was hovering around the freezing mark. The sun was breaking over the tops of the buildings along the street, promising a rise in temperature as the day went on.

A green Mercedes pulled up to the curb and discharged Leon Goldstein and Pastor Dave. Both men looked up at the two policemen and waved before ascending the steps in their direction.

"Your client is waiting inside in the cells," Jim said. "I arranged for him to be brought over early so you could meet with him before our joint meeting. Did you get my message?"

"Chris didn't want to meet early," Pastor Dave said. "He said such a meeting would be a waste of time."

Jim looked at Pastor Dave. "Sorry Pastor, but you won't be able to sit in on any negotiations."

Pastor Dave shrugged. "If you say so. I'm sure Chris and Leon will keep me up to date about what is discussed. Chris might be more amenable to talking if I'm there. It could save time."

"We'll have a nice, comfortable chair right outside the door for you. If we need you, we'll send for you." He turned back to Goldstein. "A Crown prosecutor has agreed to stand by in case your client really has anything to offer that could earn him a plea in a murder case. What's your opinion? Are we wasting our time?"

Goldstein shook his head. "I don't know. He hasn't told me anything."

A surprised look flashed onto Jim's face. "He hasn't told you anything? I'm amazed you're agreeing to meet under those circumstances. That doesn't sound like your style."

"I'll be honest. I'm against holding this meeting, but he really feels he has something important to bargain with. He's not your typical client. Insanity is still an option as far as I am concerned."

Scott gave a half-grunt, half-laugh. "So you come out a winner either way? Either he's crazy or he's a real negotiator. Both work for you."

Goldstein looked over at Scott. There was no smile on the lawyer's face. "As your partner said, that's not my style. The only reason I've agreed to meet under these circumstances is that Chris said he was meeting with you whether I was there or not. No offence intended, but letting him meet you two alone would be throwing an innocent to the lions. I only hope he at least has something legitimate to offer."

Jim turned his attention back to Pastor Dave. "Did he tell you anything, Pastor? I hate to be holding up a Crown prosecutor if there is not going to be any real offer to consider."

"Chris may lean a little too far towards fundamentalism for my tastes, but he's not crazy and he's not stupid. If he says he has some important information to offer, I think you'd better listen to what he has to say." He stopped and thought about what he had just said. "Hopefully, it will be relevant to the secular world. I still think it would be wise to let me sit in on the discussions."

"Can't do that for two reasons, Pastor," Jim said. "You have no legal standing to be in on a sentencing negotiation and more importantly, Mr. Ritchey specifically said he didn't want you in the room. So that's one point for him already. You've been excluded."

The pastor's mouth fell open but no words came out for a few seconds. "He doesn't want me in the room?" he finally said. "Why the hell not?"

"That's a question I can't answer," Jim said. "I can only comply with the prisoner's wishes." He looked at his watch. "Mr. Goldstein, shall we go in and find out what Ritchey really knows? He now has aroused my curiosity."

The four men sat staring at each other across the table. Jim had already asked Chris what he had to offer, but as of yet there had been no answer. Chris slowly looked around the room, studying the corners and the line along the ceiling. Jim looked up to see what he was looking at.

"There are no cameras in here, no microphones, no two-way mirrors," he said. "This is a room designed for defence lawyers and their clients to meet before and during the trials. It is as secure as any room you'll find in this building."

Chris looked at him. "So you say."

"So we all say, Chris," Leon Goldstein said. "What do you say we ask these two men to step outside and you can tell me what you have to offer? Then we can decide how best to present it to them." He gave his client an encouraging smile.

Chris didn't return it. "The time for playing games is past. I just want to unload my burden and get on with whatever life now has to offer me. How is Mable Booth making out? I feel so guilty for what she had to go through."

"Mable is doing as well as can be expected for someone who has just had her husband ripped from her life for no apparent reason," Scott Bowen said. "She can't believe you'd do such a thing. A full, honest confession might at least bring her a little peace of mind. She'll know there's not some deranged killer running around out there."

"Whoa, hold up there," Leon Goldstein said. He held up his right hand, palm out, in a stop sign gesture. "Let's not get the cart before the horse here. We've got to work out some kind of deal before we have any talk of confessions."

"Any deal will be based on what information Chris can bring to the table," Jim said. "The clock is ticking, Chris. You will be before the judge in less than an hour. Let's hear what you have to offer."

Three sets of eyes turned to the accused man. Various degrees of skepticism were apparent in each of them. Scott believed the offer of new information was a scam. Jim looked a little more hopeful, if for no other reason than he had several open cases on his plate and help in any of them would be a welcome bonus. Lawyer Goldstein tried to dispense a neutral look. He didn't want to be surprised if there was a real offer, but at the same time, he didn't want to look duped if the offer was only another of Chris's biblical fantasies. He didn't quite pull off the look. Traces of doubt were visible.

"Pastor Dave can't hear me, can he?" Chris asked.

"Pastor Dave? No he's waiting outside," Jim said.

Chris licked his lips. He took a sip of water to relieve the dryness in his throat. "I'm not sure where to begin," he said. His gaze shifted between the two policemen. They both waited to see what, if anything, the man had to offer.

He started, slowly at first, in a tentative voice. "There was a shooting in the woods a couple of months back? Some hunter was shot out of a tree? I heard some of the search and rescue boys talking about it."

It was true. The local search and rescue team had been brought in to scour the area to see if they could find anything out of the ordinary. It was more of a training exercise for them than an actual search. By then the conclusion of accidental shooting was pretty well accepted by everybody involved. Nothing they turned up changed that belief.

"That was determined to be a hunting accident," Jim said. "You are going to have to do better than that."

Scott slid back in his chair and stood up. "I knew this was a waste of time."

"What if I tell you it wasn't an accident?" Chris said. His voice carried a little more authority. Instead of defeating his claim of important knowledge, the attitude of the two police officers seemed to boost his confidence. "Someone went to a lot of effort to make it look like an accident and from what you're telling me, they succeeded. I know differently."

"Do you now?" Jim said. His voice carried no evidence of belief in Chris's claim. He didn't need an already closed case reopened. "Tell us what you know and how you know it. We'll decide if it's worth acting on."

Scott remained standing behind his chair, both hands clutching the padded back. He showed no indication he intended to resume his seat. Chris looked up at him. "Are you going to join us?" he asked

Scott shook his head. "Not until I hear something to convince me it's worthwhile. Start with the good stuff, the stuff that proves our forensics people don't know what they are doing."

"I may not be able to prove that," Chris said. "I may only be able to prove they were the victims of a really smart criminal, someone who knew what they would be looking for and made sure they found it."

Scott's eyes narrowed and moved to Jim's. This didn't appear to be the same God-fearing, Bible-thumping man they had arrested the day before. His eyes had became clearer, his face had a new intensity. What did this farmer know that they didn't? Manufactured evidence was something they always had to be on guard against. He slipped into his chair but didn't settle himself in for the long haul. He still had to be convinced.

Chris cleared his throat and took a longer drink of water. He had the full attention of his three table mates. "It happened about a three months ago," he began, "maybe a little longer."

CHAPTER 29

SERGEANT MCDONALD PULLED a small tape recorder from his pocket and held it towards Chris Ritchey. "Do you mind?" he asked. "Saves taking detailed notes."

Lawyer Goldstein started to object but Chris overrode him. "Go for it. I don't want to have to be repeating this story over and over."

Jim set the machine in the centre of the table and switched it on. He gave the location, the time and date and the names of those present. Then he looked up at Chris. With a gesture of his hand he encouraged him to continue.

"It was about 3 months ago," he said again. "I took my .22 back to the Burn's Field to do a little target practising." He noticed the inquisitive look on Jim's face. "The Burn's Field is a little over a mile back in the woods from Raymond's River towards Mary Jane Falls. It sits behind a hardwood ridge so you can shoot back there and the sound doesn't usually travel out to the civilized part of the community. It's often used by hunters to sight in their rifles." A smile crept across his face. "And I spent many hours there before attending the nationals to hone my shooting eye.

"As I got closer, I could hear some shooting, rifle fire. Not a lot, it seemed to come in little bunches of three or four shots at a time. Even these shots were spaced farther apart than normal target shooting. At first, I was disappointed that someone else was there and I was going to head back home." Chris paused as if reliving the few moments when he changed his mind. "Then curiosity got the better of me and I decided to see who was there. I stayed on the old woods road and kept walking. Most people shoot down the valley away from the road. It's a common courtesy and safety thing. Still, I was cautious in my approach."

"Is this area organized as a target range in any way?" Jim asked. "You know, distances marked, targets set up?"

Chris shook his head. "No, it's just a big open valley with hills all around it. The hills act as a backstop when you're shooting. A few people use real targets stuck to the trees but most just use bottles or beer cans. There are a few distance markers scattered around. They don't really have any meaning except to whoever put them there."

"There's a good combination," Scott said. "Beer and bullets."

Chris looked over at Scott. "We can't all shoot on government-paid ranges with all the fancy gadgets. Some of us just have to make do with what God provides us."

Scott grunted. "Which did God contribute? The beer or the bullets?"

Jim fought back a smile. "So you snuck up? Who was there shooting and why do we care? This was a week or so before hunting season opened. I'm sure a lot of people were out tuning up their rifles, getting their eyes in shape. What makes this shooter a person of interest as we like to say in our business?"

Chris gave his head a small shake. "I don't know who it was. I had never seen the man before. That in itself was unusual. I've shot a good many targets in that field in my day and I know most of the people who go back there shooting. We're sort of like an unofficial club. That is before I found the Lord and turned my interests to other more important things."

Jim looked at the man, willing him with his eyes to go on. He needed something more than a stranger using the local target range to ramp up his interest in this story. Chris had stopped talking and his eyes were starting to resume that religious fervour they had shown at the time of his arrest. Jim did not want to go back there. Before he had a chance to speak, Scott slid back his chair again.

"You've got nothing to tell us. This is merely a stall to keep you from being indicted at this morning's session." Scott's gaze swung to Leon Goldstein. "Are you behind this stalling tactic? What do you hope to accomplish?"

Goldstein was caught off guard by the attack. He was momentarily speechless, then his oratory skills kicked in. "My client is not stalling. He's trying to tell his story in his own words, but you keep sniping at him. Stop your theatrical jumping up and down. Sit in your chair and listen to what he has to say." He turned back to Chris and gestured with a sweep of his hand. "Go ahead, Chris. Tell them the significance of this stranger in your backyard." Jim could sense that deep down Goldstein hoped there was some significance. He momentarily felt sorry for the frustrated lawyer, but it quickly passed.

Chris looked from Goldstein to Sergeant Mcdonald to Corporal Bowen. The religious zealot had been replaced by the no-nonsense farmer again. Scott looked over at Jim and winked.

"It's your story, Chris," Jim said. "Tell it your own way. But, I've got to point out, the clock is ticking. You will be indicted for murder this morning unless you come up with something more convincing than what you've told us so far."

Chris nodded. "I understand. Your hunter was shot out of a tree, right?"

Jim nodded.

"And the tree was on the side of a hill?"

Again Jim nodded.

"And he was shot with a .30 calibre bullet." This last was a statement, not a question.

The two cops exchanged glances. This last bit of information had never been made public. They were holding it back in case the forensic team had come back with a verdict of murder instead of accidental death. It wasn't exactly a secret, but only the police on the scene knew what the killing weapon had been.

"My man," Chris said in a firm voice, "used an M1 carbine, shooting at a target on the side of a hill and measured the exact distance from firing point to target point with a jury-rigged measuring tape. He had one of those big encased rolls like surveyors use, 100 feet or so, attached to a couple of hundred yards of baler twine. The twine was attached to the target tree and stretched tight down to his shooting point. He was getting the as-the-crow-flies distance and not the amount of ground covered with its hills and dales. The distance a bullet actually travels.

"He shot from a tripod with a large scope and the range was well over 250 yards. Nothing was left to chance. He had a five-inch target fastened to a blaze orange background positioned up a tree about ten feet. The rifle was being sighted for exactly that distance and that angle of attack. He shot from various points, always to the same target, and recorded the settings for the scope, angle and distance in a little book. There is no doubt in my mind that he had a particular target in mind."

He looked from cop to cop with more of a smirk than a smile. "Do I have your attention yet? The story gets better."

CHAPTER 30

JOSH DANIELS THREW the narrow strip of paper from his adding machine onto his desk. He glanced once more at the digital readout of the machine. All zeros. His mini audit of the company's books showed everything balanced completely.

These weren't the records he had been given by Kevin but copies of all the reports issued by the company since its inception. Josh had seen too many of his fellow contractors get caught up in hassles with Revenue Canada over the years because of shoddy bookkeeping. He kept meticulous records.

Even the kickbacks from Anthony Dellapinna were all listed. Kickback wasn't the technical term Kevin had used. Kevin had two substitute terms: rebates for volume purchases and refunds for returned merchandise. Nonetheless, they were all noted and accounted for. Josh picked up one of the pages before him and read it over again. Half-way down the page, he found a rebate for a volume purchase. This was not a large sum but a frequent one. There were a number of smaller sums scattered throughout the reports throughout the year, no single amount big enough to really attract attention. Considering they had purchased all the materials from Tony's company for over 40 houses this year, these rebates did not seem to be out of line.

It was the refunds that disturbed Josh more. After a really, really close look, although the numbers of his company were completely accurate, Tony's numbers had some discrepancies. Not discrepancies that would be obvious to most people, but Josh had an intimate relationship with all the materials that went into these houses.

An extra sink here, a marble vanity there, a whirlpool tub, these things added up in a hurry. Without consulting the actual blueprints of the houses, who was to say how many bathrooms each had? Josh. He knew right down to the last fixture. Some items were listed as returned but the numbers still didn't add up.

A few returns would cover the bases if anyone happened to stumble on the extra items. They would not be able to do a simple inventory of the house involved but would have to do it for all the houses the company built. Everything was priced in bulk. To Josh, this was definitely a money-laundering operation on Tony's part. Tony was carrying inventory that only existed on paper.

Josh ran his fingers through his hair with one hand and added the page back to the report. He was no expert on the money-laundering business. He wasn't even sure any laws were being broken from Kevin's point of view. If things went to hell, with a good lawyer, Kevin could claim he was an innocent victim. Josh knew better. Kevin was never a victim.

Josh's thoughts turned to Cliff. Was Cliff a victim? Did the money-laundering have anything to do with his death? Josh had never met Anthony Dellapinna. He didn't want to rush to judgment by the sound of the man's name. Then he physically shook his head. Kevin would never be a party to Cliff's murder. Kevin was a dreamer and a schemer, but he was definitely not a murderer. He could take that thought to the bank.

He flipped to the back page and looked at the bottom line. His cut of the profit margin was nothing to be scoffed at. That was something else he could take to the bank. Who was being hurt? Why rock the boat?

CHAPTER 31

NOW SCOTT BOWEN was not only sitting in his chair, but was leaning into the table to pick up every word Chris Ritchey had to say. Chris had Scott's attention. Initially, Scott thought that even if Chris had anything to offer, which he doubted, it would not involve him. Jim was the man from major crimes, Scott was a highway patrol officer. Scott figured that by some long shot, Chris might know some tangential information about one of Jim's cases. But the hunting accident, he had been involved in that from the start. He was the first officer on the scene. From the start, he had believed it was an accidental shooting. Now this murdering, religious, wife-beating farmer was causing him to question his own judgment. That was a condition Scott did not enjoy.

"An M1 carbine? That's not exactly a sniper rifle. Are you sure?"

Chris shot Scott a contemptuous look. "You're not the only one who can recognize one gun from another, Corporal. I've practised quite a bit with a .30 calibre myself. It's a good varmint gun when a .22 is not quite up to the task, coyotes in the hen house and things like that."

"Have you now?" Scott shot back. "I didn't see one listed when we checked to see what guns you owned. Are you confessing to owning an unregistered weapon?"

Chris pointed a finger in a gun-like motion at Scott. "Gotcha," he said. "Mine only had an 18-inch barrel. When the silly registration laws came into effect, it became an illegal gun. I turned it over to you guys to be destroyed. There must be records." This last statement was not a question, but its tone raised the matter of the efficiency of the multi-million-dollar gun registry. "Basically, I'm a law-abiding citizen."

"Yes you are," Scott said, his voice dripping with sarcasm. "That's why we're here negotiating whether to charge you with first-or second-degree murder."

Chris fell silent. His face lost all its elasticity. It was as if he had momentarily forgotten why he was here crossing swords with a member of the Mounted Police. Scott's words jerked him back to reality.

Jim slipped into the good-cop role. "You said your story gets better. Would you care to elabourate?" He did not have to fake a genuine interest. Chris's story had also captured his attention.

Leon Goldstein interrupted before Chris could speak. "Hold on a minute, Chris. It is obvious my client has something important to offer. What kind of deal are we talking here? I'm thinking manslaughter, suspended sentence. He's not some demented killer who is a threat to the community. He will never re-offend."

Scott gave a harsh grunt. "Suspended sentence. Like that's ever going to happen. Your boy killed his neighbour in cold blood. His intended victim still lives in the neighbourhood. How do we know he's not going to take another kick at the can at his first opportunity? You said yourself that the man is crazy."

Goldstein looked at Chris. "Not in those exact words, I didn't and besides I was talking in the legal sense of the word." He turned his attention to Jim. "If we are going to have a meaningful negotiation here, Sergeant, you had better get control of your boy. It sounds like we have a real killer who is likely to re-offend running around without a care in the world. There's nothing like pulling off the perfect crime to encourage you to believe you can kill at will. To date, that is what he has done unless we can work something out here."

Jim settled back in his chair. Scott had expressed his exact thoughts. They were out in the open so it was not necessary to repeat them. Lawyer Goldstein also made a very good point: There was a killer running loose who had pulled off the perfect crime. No one was investigating Cliff Lawrence's death. No one ever would. It was an accident. All the evidence confirmed that as a fact. At least that was the general consensus among the investigators. Which was the lesser of the two evils? Both men were murderers.

Also as Scott had pointed out, Chris's intended victim was still living in the same neighbourhood. Both of the policemen knew that Ralph was innocent of the adultery charges levied by Chris. They would have to convince Chris of the truth of that statement. If that could be done, it was unlikely there would be any more trouble. Even if they couldn't sell that idea to Chris, now that everything was out in the open, he would be crazy to have another try at killing Ralph. And that was the big question: How crazy was Chris?

"Okay," Jim said. "Let's bring in the Crown attorney and work out a deal. But," and he looked meaningfully at Goldstein, "this all hinges on the information we obtain standing up to an investigation." His gaze shifted to Chris. "So, my friend, you'd better get it right the first time, because there are no do-overs. There will be a lot of people out there who will think that reopening this investigation is a silly waste of time. We sure as hell won't be able to do it twice."

"There's no reason for profanity, Sergeant. As God is my witness, every word I tell you will be the truth."

Scott rolled his eyes as he got up from his seat and went to the door. "We all know that statement is gospel." He stopped at the door and looked back at Chris. "Especially during yesterday's initial interview. Was anything you said then the truth?"

Chris held Scott's eyes for several seconds. He slowly shook his head. "None of it. I was weak and ashamed of what I had done. While you were waiting for me to open the shed, I called Pastor Dave and confessed my sins. Then, I prayed fervently to God for advice on how to proceed. Everything from that point on has been the honest truth because the truth will set me free."

Scott scoffed. "Don't count on that, pal. The laws of man are not so forgiving. I'll get the Crown attorney and we'll see what he has to say."

Negotiations were brief and to the point. The Crown attorney was already up to speed on Chris's murder case. Scott quickly briefed him on the accidental shooting of the hunter along with the reasons for the conclusion of accidental.

Despite his apparent antagonistic attitude toward Chris, he painted a vivid picture for the government lawyer of the other killer—a man who had planned in detail not only the killing of Cliff Lawrence, but also how to cover it up. This had all the markings of a professional hit. Chris Ritchey was small potatoes compared to this murderer if that were the truth. There was no doubt in Scott's mind which killer should be brought to justice if they had to choose between the two. He just hoped Chris had enough evidence to offer to allow them to catch the other shooter.

Chris agreed to plead guilty to manslaughter with a sentence of five to ten years. Goldstein pointed out to Chris that if he behaved himself, he would probably be out in less than two. Not quite the suspended sentence he initially sought, but an outcome he was happy with, nonetheless. Chris had killed a man. Punishment of some sort had to be administered.

There was one minor detail to complete the deal. Chris had to have a story that would live up to his advance claims. He had to be able to refute all the compelling evidence that brought a panel of experts to rule that Cliff Lawrence had died accidentally. He started slowly.

CHAPTER 32

"**R**IGHT AWAY I realized there was something strange taking place," Chris Ritchey began again. He paused as if searching for the right words. "There was a device fastened to the front of his rifle and sticking out about a foot in front of it. At first I had no idea what it was. I sensed that I should exercise caution with this man. Instead of just walking up to him, I examined what he was doing through my binoculars. I always take them to target practice so that I can see how tight a group I'm shooting without having to walk up to the target each time."

He looked at Scott Bowen. "I find the bull's-eyes on most targets too big to bother shooting at so I draw one centimetre dots between the rings and aim at them. That way I can get about ten groups on each target."

Scott smiled. "I know what you mean. I try to shoot the eyes out of the man-sized targets we use. Then I go for the buttons on his shirt."

Chris grunted. He didn't know if the policeman was being serious or just egging him on. He waved his hand in the air as if dismissing Scott Bowen's assertion. He returned his attention to the sergeant. "The man was shooting through a piece of deer hide. It was on a roll and after each shot he moved a fresh piece in front of his muzzle."

Silence filled the room while Chris's last statement hung in the air like snowflakes on a calm winter day.

"I'm sorry," Jim said, "he was shooting through what?"

"A deer hide. It was a narrow strip of deer hide on two hand-rollers. I had to study it for a few minutes to realize what he was doing. Each shot passed through a deer skin before heading towards the target. It's the strangest target shooting I've ever seen.

"I checked his target through my glasses. The groups weren't as tight as I would have liked to see them, but all the hits were within a couple of inches. If you're shooting at a man, that's accurate enough."

"Son of a bitch," Scott said. "That would certainly distort our forensic findings. No wonder they found traces of deer hair in the wound. He must have been shooting from where we thought the deer deflected the shot. The indentations in the leaves are where the shooter was lying, not the deer."

Jim leaned back in his chair, a thoughtful look on his face. "And that would move him about 50 yards closer to the target," he said. "That makes the shot a little less amazing for a .30 calibre. From that spot, he would have laid out his own blood trail for the dog to follow. He really went to a lot of trouble to set this up."

Scott nodded in agreement. "A hell of a lot of trouble to kill a man who had no enemies." He looked back to Chris Ritchey, his dark eyes penetrating those of the accused man. "You've had this information for several months. Why didn't you come forward before? Reopening a closed case is not going to be easy. We're going to be starting at square one months after the crime was committed. Hell, you might have even saved Cliff Lawrence's life if you had come to us right away."

Chris slowly shook is head and lowered his eyes to the table. "I had given up the life of guns and shooting. They weren't a part of Jesus' teachings. There was no way to justify why I was at the target range other than to confess to contemplating murdering that adulterous Ralph Foley." His eyes returned to stare into Scott's. "I wasn't in a place that allowed me to do that. I had too much hatred in my heart." He looked at the door. "That's why I didn't want Pastor Dave to sit in on this discussion. I didn't want him to know what a sinner I had been."

He turned his gaze fully to Scott. "Besides, I'm a simple farmer. Unlike you, my first thoughts didn't go to murder. I thought it strange, but I've done some innovative things to make target practice more of a challenge. It's like that when you're really good.

"By the time I heard the details of the hunter who had been shot, it had been declared an accident. Sitting in jail overnight gave me a chance to think about what I had seen. I wasn't sure there was any connection. Your obvious reaction verifies that there is."

"You said earlier you didn't know who the shooter was," Jim said. "Please tell me you got his licence number or something."

Chris gave his head a little shake. "Sorry. There was a vehicle out beside the road. One of those big, black SUVs. I never noticed what kind it was. They all look alike to me. Unaffordable. They nearly cost the price of a tractor and do the work of a car. They don't make sense to me. This one did have some mud on it covering the shine a little. It may have been off the pavement once or twice in its lifetime."

"Something like that may have attracted attention in Raymond's River," Scott said. "We'll start interviewing the neighbours. But, it was months ago." He wrote something in his notebook. "How about a description? Can you tell us what the man looked like?"

Chris's eyes brightened. "That I can do. He wore light brown camouflage pants and jacket. Blended nicely into the leaves. That's why I knew he was no hunter. They all wear blaze orange that can be seen for miles. This man had no intention of being seen. He was about 5'10, 5'11 and weighed between 160 and 170 pounds, dark brown hair and," Chris paused while both policemen were scratching away in their notebooks, "he walked with a limp in his left leg."

Jim stopped writing. "How distinctive a limp?"

"It was noticeable. He probably swayed about two inches off centre with each step."

"Hmm," Jim said, "that's something to go on."

Leon Goldstein tapped the face of his watch. "It's almost court time. Are we going to amend the charges? If it's going to be manslaughter, let's make that the initial charge and not start with homicide and downgrade it later. People never accept the revised charges as truth. They think they are just the work of some fancy lawyer."

"The wisdom of the masses," Scott said. "You can't fool all of the people all of the time."

The Crown attorney looked at Jim. "What do you think, Sergeant?"

"This is all interesting," Jim said, "but let's not jump to conclusions." He turned to Goldstein. "If you don't want a homicide charge, you won't mind holding your client over for another day without him receiving his due process. Tomorrow we will be in a better position to decide."

"I don't understand." Chris said. "Why wait?"

Jim studied the man for a minute before answering. "You've got a good story there and it may all be true."

"It is true," Chris said.

Jim held up his hands in a placating manner. "It may be true, but there is no real indication that this man killed Cliff Lawrence. He may have just been some eccentric out target practising. Nothing you've said actually ties him in to the death of Clifford Lawrence. I'd like to do a little investigating first." He turned back to lawyer Goldstein. "This is not a cold case; this is a closed case. It was thoroughly examined the first time around."

"Come on, Sergeant," Goldstein said. "You don't believe that. All the evidence points to Chris being right. Why else would the man be doing all these things which are exactly like your crime scene? You're not going to try to cover up some shoddy police work, are you?"

"There was no shoddy police work," Scott said. "The facts indicated an accidental shooting."

Jim put a hand on the corporal's arm to quiet him. "Mr. Goldstein, if Chris's story is tied in to our hunter, what difference does another day make? He is going to go to jail for shooting Gerald Booth. We're just arguing about how long he'll spend there. Let's meet again tomorrow morning.

"In the meantime, Chris, how would you like to go for a walk in the woods?" He extended his hand towards Leon Goldstein. "Counsellor, you're more than welcome to come along."

"I have court this afternoon on another case." Goldstein chewed on his lower lip while contemplating what to do. "If Chris goes with you, there can be absolutely no discussion of his own case. This is strictly to point out what he knows about the other shooting. Anything he says," he turned to look at Chris, "and I'm telling you to say nothing, cannot be used in evidence against him if this case ends up in court. Do we all agree on that?"

"Sure, Counsellor," Jim said as he slid back his chair, "we already have an airtight case against your boy. We don't need anything else."

CHAPTER 33

KEVIN BARNHILL DISCREETLY stole a glance at his watch and then returned his gaze to the doorway of the darkened tavern. He and Josh Daniels had been sitting here for nearly a half-hour, each nursing a glass of beer.

"I don't think he's going to show," Josh said.

"What?" Kevin said, surprised by the statement.

"Dellapinna. He's not coming."

Now Kevin looked overtly at his watch. "He's not that late. Let's give him a few more minutes."

Josh looked around at the patrons at nearby tables and lowered his voice. "You know he's involving us in money-laundering. We could get in a lot of trouble."

Kevin showed no surprise at the statement. He sat quietly for a few long seconds. He understood Josh's concerns. He himself had shared those same doubts years ago when Cliff Lawrence had first introduced him to Tony Dellapinna and Tony's plan to do business with the development company.

Cliff, the silver-tongued salesman, had convinced Kevin that the company was free of any liability in the scheme. Now Kevin had to sell Josh on the same story. Had he even believed the tale Cliff spun or was he blinded by the opportunities the extra income would offer the company? It had never been about profits, only increased opportunities.

Sometimes when he was preparing for an investors meeting, he would tell himself that he really didn't need these demanding, mollycoddled people anymore. The company could be self-sustaining without them as long as Tony Dellapinna kept pouring money into the pot. The truth, he realized, was exactly the opposite. It was Dellapinna he didn't need anymore. They could flourish quite well without Tony's input. As always, when he contemplated this scenario, he had to face that one big problem: Who would tell Tony he had outlived his usefulness?

Maybe that task could be assigned to Josh. He smiled inwardly. Kevin would never do that.

"That's not true." Kevin looked around the room and leaned forward a little more. "Tony is money-laundering. There's no doubt about that. But we are not active participants. We are no more involved than the chartered banks who handle his money for him."

Josh scoffed. "You don't believe that."

"I do and it's true."

Josh leaned back and took a long, slow drink of his beer. His eyes never left Kevin's. "We are accessories before the fact, after the fact and during the fact," he said after he set down his drink.

"No more so than the banks," Kevin said. "Are we guilty of not turning in someone we are suspicious of? Maybe. Are we legally required to turn him in? No. Do we have absolute proof of his guilt? None at all." He made a dismissive gesture with his hands. "We haven't broken any laws."

"Kevin, I've studied our books. You can see where the money goes in and out. We may not be laundering the money ourselves, but we are enabling him to do so. It's the same thing."

A dark wave seemed to pass over Kevin. His voice took on an icy tone. His eyes hardened, penetrated Josh's gaze, making him turn away. "What is illegal is having conversations like this. It confirms our knowledge. You say you've studied the books. Only someone with your intimate knowledge of the day-to-day operations of the company could ever detect anything wrong. I know you. You've studied those reports every year since we started doing business together. Was there ever a problem before? Did you feel guilty a month ago? Did you think you were doing anything illegal? Did you think the company was being run dishonestly?"

"No, but I didn't know..."

"Exactly," Kevin cut him off. "You didn't know. Nothing has changed in how we are doing our business. We have negotiated a good deal with Tony to supply us with our building supplies. That's what we're supposed to do. Negotiate the best deal possible. We have."

The smile returned to Kevin's face. His eyes softened. "Now relax and enjoy your beer. I'm going to try to call Tony." He withdrew his cellphone from his pocket and poked some numbers on the keypad.

Josh reached across the table and placed a hand on Kevin's arm. "I have to ask this once more," he said. "What about Cliff's death? Is there any connection?"

Kevin stopped dialling. Any signs of friendliness fled from his face. "I can't believe you asked that again. What kind of an asshole do you think I am?"

Josh interrupted him. "It's not you I'm accusing, Kevin. It's Tony. He's the criminal in the crowd. Are you sure he's an innocent babe in this death?"

"I'm sure. Do you know why I'm sure? Because I asked him the same thing." He waved a finger in Josh's face. "If I thought there was any chance of a connection, I'd not only sever any ties with him and his company, but I'd be down at police headquarters reporting it to that detective who questioned us about Cliff's death. The cops are positive that it was an accident. They've completely dropped the investigation. I'd advise you to purge your mind of any thoughts that involve Tony. Tony and Cliff were friends from childhood. He's not involved."

"I'm sorry, Kevin, but I had to ask. Cliff was also a good friend of mine. It's still hard to accept that he's gone."

Kevin's features softened again. "I know. I still feel partially responsible for insisting that he take the tree stand. It could have been me up in that tree. Cliff wanted so badly to get himself a deer. He talked incessantly about this being his year. Putting him on the side of that hill seemed like the best way for him to do it. Now I wish I hadn't tried to help him out."

Josh shook his head. "You can't blame yourself. Sometimes bad things happen to good people. This was one of those times."

CHAPTER 34

"IT'S JUST AROUND this bend," Chris Ritchey said. He pointed to the upcoming corner in the rut-filled, overgrown woods road ahead of them. Branches swept along both sides of the RCMP Ford Explorer. Sergeant Jim Mcdonald tightened his grip on the bar set into the side of the door as the vehicle lurched to the right again.

"I think we should have walked this last kilometre. It would have been easier on the body."

Scott Bowen, who served as the driver, stomped down on the gas pedal to bring the truck back up from the dip and at the same time yanked the steering wheel hard right to steer clear of the eroded ditch running into the left side of the roadway. The driver's side wheel dropped into the gully and the truck canted violently to the left, all its occupants following along with it.

The torrential rains of the day before had filled all the ruts, making it impossible to tell how deep they were. Several times the truck had bottomed out. Only the experienced foot of the policeman on the gas pedal, alternating between light and heavy, kept them moving forward.

"Walk and miss all this fun?" Scott said. "People pay big bucks to get a thrill ride like this at Disneyland."

He looked back at the other man sitting in the back seat with Chris. "Besides, Robin has that big forensics case with him. That's too heavy to be lugging through the woods."

Robin West forced a smile. "I appreciate your concern. I just hope nothing is broken back there with all the sliding around the case is doing." He indicated the trunk area of the Explorer.

Robin had been the forensic team leader on the initial investigation of Cliff Lawrence's death. These were his conclusions that were being called into question. When Jim told him where they were going and why, he had dropped everything to come along. If his office had been set up to come to the wrong determinations, he wanted to find out how it had been done. For now, he would wait and see. He had yet to have been proven wrong.

"Guess I should have warned you," Chris said. "Most people who come back here these days use ATVs and they don't always follow the road. They just shoot off and make their own trails. Personally, I walk."

"Did the suspect you saw here walk or have an ATV?" Jim asked.

"He walked. His SUV was parked out by the main road. I told you that before."

"Sorry," Jim said. "You did tell us that."

Scott suppressed a grin. He knew the detective was simply trying to find discrepancies in Chris's story. Score one for the bad guys.

An opening appeared on the right-hand side of the road. "Park here," Chris said. "The range is just over these hills. I don't hear any shooting so there's probably no one there. Once hunting season finishes, no one wastes time practising anymore."

"You mean big-game hunting season," Scott said. "There are still hunters out here searching for partridges and rabbits. Let's not get careless. There are traffic vests in the back. Each of us should wear one."

The four men got out of the truck and walked around to the back gate. Scott threw each one a plastic yellow and orange vest.

"I hardly think I'll be mistaken for a rabbit," Chris said. "Give the locals some credit." He dropped the garment back into the truck.

Scott picked it up and gave it back to him. "Stick a gun in some people's hands and they shoot at anything that moves or rattles a bush. Wear this. We don't want to be responsible for you having any accidents."

Chris shrugged into the vest. "This is foolishness," he said in a low voice.

"Show us where you saw the shooter," Jim said before Scott had a chance to respond. "Let's see if that carnival ride was justified."

Chris turned and slowly started trudging up the hill at the end of the clearing. By now, most of the hardwoods had deposited their leaves onto the forest floor. The fall winds had dried the leaves to the consistency of brittle newspapers. A rhythmic crunching sound came from the boots of the three lawmen as they followed along behind him. No one spoke. Each man reflected on what this new turn of events meant to them personally.

Corporal Scott Bowen served as a highway patrolman. Sergeant Jim Mcdonald had a way of getting him involved in Jim's murder investigations, especially when they were in the rural parts of the province. Jim kept encouraging Scott to apply to join the detective branch of the force. He assured him he would be a shoo-in to be accepted. Scott continually declined. He preferred life behind the wheel of his cruiser to life behind a desk. He told Jim that detective work was mostly boring.

Jim dreaded the thought of reopening a murder investigation that had been closed for over a month. The death had occurred at an isolated location miles back in the woods. His initial work on the case showed it had accidental shooting written all over it. Now this suspect in another murder was attempting to bargain his life sentence into something considerably shorter by suggesting that the accidental shooting had been a homicide. Jim wasn't buying into this scenario without some compelling new evidence showing up.

He watched as Robin West lugged a backpack of forensic tools up the hill. Robin had not declared the previous case an accident lightly. Making a decision like that immediately closed the case. Like Jim, Robin wouldn't be looking forward to resuming it a month later. Several fall rainstorms had swept over the area, giving little chance of finding new evidence. Only the day before, both men had watched evidence be flushed away before their eyes from a fresh murder scene as the heavens opened up with torrents of water. Both scenes were in the same area. Jim would bet that Robin held out little hope that this area would offer anything of use. Still, it was Robin's job to look and Jim knew that Robin took his job seriously.

Chris Ritchey stomped along up front, leading the pack. Jim reflected on how Chris's life had gone to hell since his last trip up this hill. In that short time, his lifelong neighbor was dead. He was charged, not only charged, but guilty of the murder. His marriage was in tatters. Jim knew that Chris had never accepted that Linda and Ralph's liaisons had been anything but sexual. Chris probably believed that the adulterous son of a bitch who wrecked his marriage was most likely consoling his wife at this very moment. Jim noticed the downcast eyes. He wondered how bearing witness against a complete stranger in order to bargain a better deal for himself fit into Chris's distorted religious views.

As they crested the hill, Jim sped up his pace. He caught up to Chris. Before them lay a 300-yard dish with scrubby underbrush sticking up everywhere. Several paths were evident. Most seemed to be going nowhere. Here and there, broken beer bottles and overturned pop cans could be seen on various stumps. Long-faded signs carried numbers like 100, 150, 200. They ran in a variety of directions. Obviously yard markers, but no indication of the starting point was evident. A ring of apple trees skirted one edge. Still-ripe fruit hung from the branches. A stone foundation was visible at the near end of the field. At one time this had been a prosperous farm. Nature was now in the process of reclaiming the land.

"Which way?" Jim asked.

Chris pointed. "Down by the foundation. He shot from various points down there in about a 50-foot range. He was shooting up into that hill over there." Chris turned to the right. The base of the hill was about 200 yards from the foundation. The incline was similar to that at the scene of the Cliff Lawrence shooting.

Scott stepped up beside them. His eye followed the sweep of the land. "The target tree should be about two-thirds of the way up. I'll see if I can locate it." He looked back at Chris. "Any thoughts on which tree it is?"

"See that big pine by the little brook?"

Scott nodded. The rogue pine stood taller than all its neighbours. Its sturdy branches covered all the directions of the compass. Few trees grew beneath its canopy.

"The ash tree to its left. About ten feet up. He used a stick to put the targets in place. I think they must have had two-way tape on them. Small targets, blaze orange background. He didn't change them until they were filled with holes."

Scott studied the two trees. Neither one had any lower branches. He would need a ladder to examine the tree closely.

"I have climbing spikes in my kit back in the car," Robin said. "Ever use 'em?"

"No, but it can't be that hard."

Robin smiled. "You wouldn't think so." He focused a pair of binoculars on the tree in question.

"That's a white ash. Wood's as hard as a prostitute's heart. You won't get much usable evidence from it. All the bullets will be compressed into solid pancake of lead."

Scott nodded in agreement. "It will be proof that someone used the tree for target practice. That's a start." He searched the side of the hill until he found the tree. "I can see where the wood is all chewed up. Must have hit it 15 or 20 times. I should be able to dig out one massive wad of metal. It'll make an impressive exhibit for the prosecution to clunk down in fromt of the accussed."

"Okay," Robin said, "you get the climbing gear; I'm going to check the firing sites. Not sure what good it will do. There is nothing illegal about sighting your rifle in before hunting season. Our best hope is to find an empty casing that matches the one we found at the scene of the shooting."

"Won't find anything," Chris said. "He picked up his brass."

Robin looked at him with a disparaging look. "I'll look anyway. Criminals aren't as smart as they like to think they are. Yesterday, for example, I investigated a scene; found an empty casing; it led to the murder weapon and that led to the killer. The case was wrapped in less than a day."

Chris said nothing.

"He's talking about you," Scott said.

Chris lowered his head. "Yeah, I know," he said. He made no other response.

Scott shook his head. "I'll get the spikes."

Jim Mcdonald put a hand on Scott's arm. In a low voice, he said: "Bring back the rifle, too. I want to check it for accuracy."

Scott smiled but said nothing.

CHAPTER 35

THE THREE MEN made their way to the valley floor in single file. Chris in the lead. Jim close enough to grab him if he decided to run. Robin trailing, his eyes taking in the surroundings, looking for potential forensic evidence.

At the bottom of the path, Chris pointed to a bare patch of forest floor. "This is where he was shooting from when I first arrived."

All three men looked down at the spot and then let their eyes drift up to the victim tree. Each was doing the mental calculations necessary to figure out the distance of the shot.

"Just shy of 300 yards?" Jim said.

Robin nodded in agreement and then put the high-tech binoculars to his eyes. He made a couple of adjustments then hit the small button on the front. He looked at a small display screen. "Two hundred seventy-two point four yards," he said, "or, as we will say in Canadian courts, 249.08 metres."

"Hell of a shot with a .30 calibre," Chris said. He hesitated. "Of course, he was using a scope and a tripod. That leaves little to chance."

Robin looked around the area at his feet and then let his gaze take in an ever-increasing circle. "Don't see much that will be of help to us. You say there were other sites?"

Chris walked a few yards to his left. "Somewhere around here." He indicated another clearing. "And over there." He pointed to another spot further down the trail. "Fired about five shots from each spot. All at the same target."

Jim looked at his watch. This was turning out to be a waste of time. Even if Cliff Lawrence's killer had been practising at this spot, there was nothing that would tie the two events together. The area had been swept clean of any potential evidence. He went over to the foundation and sat down.

Robin checked out the various sites, made measurements and recorded it all in his field book. He then scoured the underbrush for some tell-tale clue that could prove his previous conclusions were wrong. Jim watched the systematic searching. One thing about Robin, he harboured no emotional tie to the case. He dealt only in facts and was willing to let the facts lead him wherever they went. His previous decision would not influence his interpretation of anything he found at this site.

The sun popped out from behind a cloud, forcing Jim to squint and look away. Something in the basement floor of the foundation caught his eye. A one and a quarter inch brass cylinder lay partially submerged in a puddle of water. His pulse quickened a little.

"Robin. Have a look at this," he said.

Robin glanced up with an inquiring look.

Jim pointed. "I think we have what we're looking for. There's a .30 calibre shell casing down there."

A smile came across the forensic scientist's face. "All right," he said. "There is a God after all." He hurried over to where Jim was sitting. He looked down at the shell casing and then back to where Chris had said the shooter had lain.

"That's the thing with an M1 carbine. They kick the spent shell out to the right with a fair amount of force. This one must have hit a rock and deflected back this way."

He took out his camera and photographed the shell, the designated shooting spot and a rock protruding from the ground about five feet from where the shooter would have been. He then stood back and took an overall shot encompassing all three locations in one frame.

"Now the icing on the cake would be to find a fingerprint on that little baby," he said. "That's highly unlikely, though. The heat from the burning powder makes the metal of the casing so hot that any fingerprints are usually obliterated." He shrugged. "But, sometimes we get lucky."

He took off his heavy coat and laid it on the wall. He then swung his leg over the foundation and started climbing down the ancient rocks.

"Watch yourself," Jim said. "That wall doesn't look too sturdy."

The words had hardly been formed when the rock under Robin's extended left foot gave way. In vain, he tried to tighten his hand grip on the moss-covered rocks. All he accomplished was a series of fingernail scratches through the green covering. He landed feet first before toppling backwards to land on his ass. Water and debris from the puddle arced into the air around him. Muddy water covered his seat and legs. His hands sunk into about two inches of dark brown mud.

"Jesus Christ," he said, as the air exploded from his lungs.

Jim leaned over the side, a look of concern on his face. "Are you all right?"

Without waiting for an answer, he turned to face Chris Ritchey. "You. Sit right where you are. Now." He pointed to the ground at Chris's feet.

Chris started forward.

"Now!" Jim made a move towards his holstered gun.

Quickly, Chris dropped to the ground. "I just wanted to see if I could help," he said. "Is he all right?"

Jim glanced back over his shoulder and into the depression. Robin was rolling over onto his hands and knees, a string of oaths coming from his mouth. Jim smiled. Robin didn't sound too hurt, unless you counted pride.

"I can't find the goddamn shell casing," Robin said. "I must have knocked it into the mud when I landed in this slop."

The previously clear water had taken on a murky, dark brown hue. Mud and water dripped from the closest walls of the cellar and ran back into the area where Robin knelt.

"More to your left," Jim said, pointing at the same time to where he remembered the shell casing to be. Robin's hand disappeared up to his wrist. Jim noticed the tendons in Robin's arm flexing as he slowly finger-walked across the bottom of the puddle.

"Watch out for broken glass," Jim said. From his vantage point, he see could numerous broken beer bottles on the floor area.

Robin looked up and scowled. "Keep an eye on your prisoner, Coach. I've done this before."

Jim held his hands in front of himself in a placating manner. "Just looking out for your welfare. A little fall on your ass seems to make you testy and by the way, you're not getting in my vehicle with those muddy clothes." Jim laughed.

"Got it," Robin said. His hand appeared from the puddle with the cartridge gently held by the bottom part. A smile lit up his face. He looked up at Jim. "Now, what were you rambling on about? I wasn't listening." He withdrew an evidence bag from his shirt pocket, shook the water from the casing and dropped it into the bag.

"I just said: Good work. I knew you'd find it," Jim said. "Let me give you a hand to get out of there."

Robin shook his head. "Don't worry, this time I'll be more careful." He looked around to find the best site to exit. He moved down the wall a ways and this time tested each rock before putting his full weight on it. As he swung over the wall, he said: "What have we here?"

Jim looked to where Robin was pointing. Robin pulled a pair of tweezers from a leather pouch on his belt. He reached down and picked up a cigarette butt. He held it up to the light.

"It's in good shape. These rocks protected it from the weather."

Jim came over for a closer look. "Do you think it's from our shooter?"

Robin shrugged. "Might be. Smoking is one of those things surrounded by habits. No matter how careful the man may have been about everything else he did, he may have just reflexively flipped this cigarette over here without a second thought. He probably was aiming for the cellar and fell short." He pulled out another evidence bag. "With luck, this might prove important. It's in good enough shape to light up again. Should produce some DNA if we can come up with a shooter to match it to."

He looked over at Chris. "Like I said, they're never as careful as they think they are."

Chris's look expressed disbelief at the find. He said nothing.

CHAPTER 36

"**W**HAT IN HELL happened to you?" Scott Bowen asked as he came down the path from the top of the hill.

Robin West's pants were still caked with wet mud. He had wiped his hands clean on a towel taken from his backpack but daubs of drying mud still spattered his face. Despite the cool weather, he was not wearing his coat. He was waiting for the mud to dry a bit before putting it back on.

"Just gathering evidence," Robin said. "Forensic science is a dirty job, but somebody's got to do it." He instinctively wiped at his butt in a vain effort to clean himself up. Then he looked at his hands and brushed them vigorously together in an attempt to clean them again. "Give me those spikes. It's my job to collect the evidence."

"I don't mind," Scott said. He held on to the climbing apparatus.

"Let him have it," the sergeant said. "I want you to test that rifle to see how accurate it is." He indicated a rifle case slung over Scott's shoulder.

Scott passed over the climbing spikes to Robin and unslung the rifle. "We've already got a confession. Why bother?"

Chris looked up, interested. "Is that my gun?"

"It's the rifle we found in your shed," Scott said. "The one you claimed to have sold."

"Why do you have it out here?"

"To test its accuracy," Jim said. "We want to see if it is properly sighted in to make a shot of the required distance. A target range seemed like a good place to do it."

Chris reached out his hand. "Pass it over. I'll show you."

"No," Jim said. "The corporal will conduct the test. We don't want another 'if the glove don't fit, you must acquit' type of case."

He turned to Robin. "What was the distance from where the shot was fired to where Gerald Booth was standing? One hundred fifty yards?"

"About that," Robin said. "One hundred fifty-seven to be exact."

Jim walked over to Robin's coat and picked up the binoculars sitting on top of them. "Let's find a stump that distance away." He brought the glasses up to his face and made a quick sweep of the area. The laser distance finder flashed the numbers as it passed over the distant trees.

"Over there," Scott said. He pointed to an uprooted fir tree. "That looks pretty close."

Jim swung in that direction and pushed the distance button on the high-tech binoculars. One fifty-five," he said. "Close enough." He pointed to a spot behind where he stood. "That's your spot there, Scott. Now we need a target."

"Got just the thing," Scott said. He reached into his jacket pocket and extracted two cans of diet Coke. The silver can with the red lettering flashed in the bright sunlight.

"Not very big," Chris said. "One hundred fifty yards is quite a long distance even to see something that size, let alone hit it."

Scott gave an arrogant tap on the crossed rifles on his uniform jacket. "A .22 is not my rifle of choice but I think I can hit these."

"Oh, big words," Robin said. "This is evidence. Let me film it." With that, he pulled a small camcorder from his sack. "You take them down and set them up, Sergeant. I'll record you from here. That will give us some perspective as to the distance."

It took Jim a couple of minutes to pick his way through the brush and blown-down trees to get to the target site. He placed the two cans side by side, then he waved for the camera before moving out of shooting range.

Scott snapped the clip into the rifle and jacked a shell into the bore. He brought the gun up to his eye.

"Which one are you shooting at?" Chris asked. "The right or the left?"

Scott lowered the rifle. He gave Chris a contemptuous look. "The right," he said and brought the weapon back up to the shooting position.

"That's our right?" Chris asked again. "Not the right as they look at us?"

Scott kept the rifle sighted on the target. "Our right. Now be quiet and let me shoot."

"Just making sure," Chris said.

Scott lowered the rifle. He looked back at Robin who was still recording. "This is an official government test," Scott said. "I'm ordering you to be quiet."

Chris put the thumb and forefinger of his right hand together as if he were holding a key. He brought them up to his mouth and made a locking gesture.

Scott looked down the range again towards the cans. He shouldered the rifle and took careful aim. The sound of the shot rang out and one of the cans toppled over backwards.

Chris tried to stifle a laugh. Scott turned and glared at him. "Sorry," Chris said, "but most people would call that the left can."

Scott looked down the range again. "I only see one can standing," he said.

"I know but it's the left can that is missing." Chris looked at Robin for support. "Rewind your camera. Let's have an instant replay."

"That's not necessary," Scott said. "The sights must be off."

"Something is off," Chris said in a low voice. Both policemen heard him clearly.

Scott walked over to a nearby stump and knelt down behind it. "Set up the can again, Sergeant. I'm going to take another shot." He waited for Jim to comply and then leaned forward onto the stump and lined up the target again. The rifle cracked. The left-hand can flew through the air one more time.

"You didn't tell us which can you were shooting at that time," Chris said.

"It's the rifle," Scott said. "The rifle is not accurate."

Now Chris laughed out loud. "It's not the rifle; it's the shooter. Let me show you."

"Don't be foolish. You're our prisoner. I can't give you a loaded weapon."

"Afraid I'll show you up. There is nothing wrong with the gun. Maybe you didn't allow for the wind." Chris stuck his finger in his mouth and held it up in the air. "Wait, there's no wind blowing. If you've got any guts, you'll give me a shot."

Scott looked back at Robin. The camcorder was still recording. Scott winked.

"Sergeant," Scott called out. "Chris here insists there is nothing wrong with the rifle. He wants us to let him have a shot."

"Not with me down here," Jim said. He picked up the can with the two holes already in it and started back to the firing line. "If we let him shoot, there are going to be restrictions."

"I'm opposed to this," Scott said as soon as Jim arrived back at their location. "We shouldn't be letting him handle a firearm. He's charged with murder. Besides, Leon Goldstein told us not to involve Chris in anything regarding his own case. You know what a pain in the ass these lawyers can be when you ignore their instructions."

"You're just afraid I'm going to show you up," Chris said. He gave the Mountie a challenging look. "Come on Sergeant. Let me prove there is nothing wrong with my rifle. Mr. Goldstein told me not to talk about my case. I'm going to let the gun do the talking."

Jim looked at Scott and shrugged. "Why not? Chris's a grown man. He can make up his own mind. Here's the rules. The barrel of the rifle is pointed down range at all times. We take all the shells out of the clip leaving only one shot in the chamber. We both have our pistols drawn and pointed in your direction. That barrel moves 20 degrees left or right, you're dead. Do you still want to shoot under those conditions?"

"Under any conditions. I just want to show him how easy it is to pop a target," his gaze shifted to Scott "if you have a steady hand and a good eye."

Scott's features froze. He gave Chris a granite-like stare. "Bring it on," he said. "Give him the damn rifle, Jim."

Jim ejected the clip from the .22. With his thumb, he flicked the bullets into his other hand and returned the empty clip to the gun. "One round," he said to Chris, "and don't even think about pointing it anywhere but at that can." He lay the rifle across the stump that Scott had shot from.

"I don't need any stump to support me," Chris said. He wrapped the rifle strap around his arm and brought the gun up to his shoulder. His breathing almost stopped as he aimed at the can then looked back at Scott. "No heckling? I'm disappointed."

"Show us what you've got, hotshot," Scott said. "I don't want you to have any excuses."

The shot rang out across the small valley. Four sets of eyes were concentrated on one small silver and red diet Coke can sitting on a dead tree. The can didn't move. A smile swept across Scott's face.

Robin was the first to speak. His eye was glued to the view finder of his camcorder. His fingers were controlling the zoom button.

"I see black liquid running from the can," he said. "Looks like he got it dead centre."

"Oh yeah," Scott said. "It was a perfect shot. I can see the foam running down the side of the tree." He turned towards Jim. "I guess there is no doubt he was capable of making the killing shot. We've got it on tape."

Chris was still looking down range. His face was glowing with satisfaction. Then, slowly the smile started to fade. "What are you talking about?"

"To shoot a man in the head from 150 yards is a pretty spectacular shot. We didn't want you coming up with the idea that you were shooting at a fox or skunk or whatever and accidentally shot Gerald Booth. We now have proof that that shot is easily within your abilities." He tapped Chris in the centre of his chest with an extended forefinger. "And it was your pride that gave us this extra piece of evidence. You had to prove you were a better shot than I am."

He snatched the now empty rifle from Chris's hands.

Chris's eyes darted from one cop to the other. "You can't do this. Mr. Goldstein said you were not to discuss my case in any way."

Jim gave a dismissive shrug. "Who was discussing your case? We were just test-firing your rifle. Nobody even invited you into the conversation. You imposed yourself there voluntarily and we thank you for your contribution."

Various emotions reflected on Chris's face: disbelief, resignation, fear and finally anger. "At least I showed you who is the best shot."

Scott laughed. "Nah, you didn't. You shot at the whole can. Anybody could do that." He turned to Jim. "You brought my can back? The first shot should have been through the 'o' in Coke; the second should have filled in the hole in the 'e'."

Jim produced the can from his pocket. It was exactly as Scott described.

"No," Chris said. "You were shooting at the right-hand can. You hit the left."

Scott shook his head. "If you thought I had hit my target, what would you have to prove? That you are as good as me? Why bother? There's no upside to that equation for you. You had to think I missed. You had to be able to prove you were better than me."

He threw the can to Chris. Instinctively his hands shot out to catch it.

"Keep it as a souvenir," Scott said. "I can do this anytime."

CHAPTER 37

"JOSH DANIELS? TONY Dellapinna. Sorry I missed you the other day. As I'm sure Kevin told you, I was unavoidably detained. My flight into Halifax was rerouted back to Moncton. Too foggy to land."

Josh was caught off guard by the unexpected phone call. The other day he had been full of fire and brimstone, ready to interrogate this Tony Dellapinna. He intended to get to the bottom of this money-laundering scheme and to find out what, if anything, Tony had to do with Cliff's death. Kevin had deterred him from pursuing the former and gave him assurances that Tony was not involved in the latter. He once more reminded Josh that the police had declared the unfortunate event an accident.

"Mr. Dellapinna," he said, instead, "I was disappointed, too. Perhaps some other time."

"I'm sure there will be numerous other occasions now that we are working closer together with the construction business. Was there anything in particular I could help you with?"

The voice was well-modulated. There was no trace of an accent, Italian or otherwise. Josh wasn't sure if he had expected Tony to sound like Marlon Brando with a mouth full of marbles or be swearing like a trooper as they did on the Sopranos. He knew he expected something different, something out of the ordinary. He was disappointed. Tony sounded like any other guy Josh dealt with every day.

"No, nothing of importance. Just thought we should meet." He paused for a few seconds before continuing. "I have to admit I was surprised to hear you even existed. I though Ronald Sutherland was our supplier."

"Ron, a good man. Been working for me for years. Deals with all the contractors. He handles things so well I don't actually have to get involved too much. No problems with Ron, are there?"

Josh laughed. "Hell, no. Best supplier I've ever worked with. I give him a list for each house and a time line and then forget about it. Never had to wait for anything."

"Glad to hear that. No problems with the quality of the materials? Everything's up to code?"

"Everything's great, Mr. Dellapinna. It's actually a pleasure dealing with your company."

"Cut the Mister, shit. Call me Tony. We're compatriots, all one big happy family."

One big, happy family, Josh thought. Let's not go that far. He had seen The Godfather, I, II and III. He knew what happened to family members who asked too many questions. Josh still had a lot of questions that needed answers. He would have to exercise some discretion in choosing the targets of these inquiries.

"Tony it is," he said instead. "We'll have to set up a date to meet sometime real soon."

"Where are you working today?" Tony asked. "I'll drop by the site. See how things are going."

Alarms sounded in Josh's head. This hadn't been just a "sorry I missed you" call. Tony had something else on his mind. Meeting him today seemed unavoidable. Short of saying he would be out of the province, and Tony had already burnt that excuse. Josh had no other options open to him since Tony was willing to do all the work and come to him. He told Tony the name of the subdivision where the current work was taking place. Tony knew where it was.

"We are just putting the final touches on these units before we turn them over to their new owners," Josh said.

"Final touches?"

"Yeah," Josh said, "vacuuming the carpets; polishing the chrome; making sure all the light bulbs work. Nothing turns a client off more than flipping a light switch on his first night in his new house and seeing nothing but darkness. All that other hard work just goes down the drain because of a five-dollar light bulb."

"Five-dollar light bulb? I'd better check up on Ron after all. He sounds like he's ripping you off."

"All our new houses are environmentally friendly. Nothing but the latest technology including those low-wattage light bulbs that cost so much."

Tony laughed. "And give off half the light," he said. "I'll see you later on this morning." He hung up without waiting for Josh to say goodbye.

Josh stared at the dead phone in his hand. He had been summonsed. Well, not quite. Tony was going to come to him. All he could do was wait and see what the visit was all about. At least he would get to meet the man behind the money.

Less than 15 minutes later a silver Ford Escape pulled into the driveway out front. There were two men in the front and one in the back of the big machine. Two men emerged from the right side of the vehicle, one from the front, one from the back. The driver remained seated. The front-seat passenger had on work boots and carried a silver hard hat. He wore blue cargo pants, a dark brown leather jacket over a dark shirt and a red tie. His companion wore a black suit under a light parka. The parka added to his already enormous bulk. On his feet were black, well-polished, leather boots. Not work boots, but every bit as substantial.

Josh turned to his foreman who had joined him at the window. "Who the hell is that? Haven't we had all our inspections?"

"Sure have," the foreman said. "Everything passed with flying colours." He stepped closer to the window and studied the two approaching men. "Don't see any clipboard. Don't think they are inspectors. Maybe they are the new owners and are anxious to see their finished house."

"We'll soon know," Josh said. He went to the doorway. Could this be Tony Dellapinna? If it was, he had gotten here very quickly. He couldn't have been calling from his downtown offices. But, Josh realized, he didn't know if Dellapinna had downtown offices, or any office for that matter. He knew nothing about the man. Josh did know that this wasn't the image he had formed of the money-launderer.

The man in the work boots stood about 5'10, weighed about 170. He wasn't fat but he wasn't muscular either, simply fit-looking. His dark hair broke over the tops of his ears much like that of a young John Lennon, once thought long but now considered mid-length.

Josh studied the two men through the door sidelight. The second man, 6'2, 240 pounds, looked like he could start a fight in an empty room, had to be a bodyguard. He fit the stereotypical image. Josh had one hand on the knob prepared to let them in. The big man approached the door and reached for the doorbell. Josh opened the door before it had a chance to ring. This startled the man and he instinctively reached inside his coat.

"Sorry to have given you a start," Josh said at once. "Can I help you?"

"You Josh Daniels?" the big man asked.

Josh hesitated. He momentarily considered asking "who wants to know?" but thought better of it. If his assessment was correct, a sense of humour wasn't necessarily part of this man's job description. "That's me," he said instead, "and you're –?" He left the question hanging in the air.

The smaller man stepped forward, his hand extended. "Tony Dellapinna," he said. "Glad to finally meet you, Josh."

Josh accepted the outstretched hand. The grip was solid but not challenging. "I didn't expect you this early. Were you in the neighbourhood?"

Dellapinna held up the silver hard hat. "Just making the rounds of the construction sites I'm supplying. Never hurts to keep on top of things and see which way the wind is blowing, especially this time of year when business drops off." His eyes swept around the inside of the house. "Looks good from out here."

A slight blush slid up Josh's face. He stepped back and held the door wide open. "Please, come in. I'll show you around. As I told you earlier, this one is pretty much wrapped up. The owners will be taking over at the end of the week."

"You sell them before you build them," Tony said. "That's a good deal. Reduces the stress in your life, I'm sure."

"Quality workmanship with quality products," Josh said, pride evident in his voice. "Victor takes care of the selling. He doesn't have too much trouble with these starter units."

"So this is a starter unit?" Tony examined the quality of the kitchen cupboards. He couldn't help but smile as he ran his hands over the finished product.

"Starter unit for those who already have the ability to make big monthly payments but don't have a down payment put together. They are moving out of high-end apartments into something they will proudly own themselves. Kevin arranges the financing to cover the lack of down payment. He hasn't been wrong yet and we all reap the benefits. It's a team thing."

Tony nodded involuntarily. He liked innovative thinking. "I hear you walked out of the investors' meeting the other day."

Josh was taken aback. This was not common knowledge. Kevin had to have shared the information with Tony, but why?

"They had their minds all made up before I got there. Why waste my time making a presentation when no one was going to be listening? I have better things to do."

Tony reached out and patted him on the arm. "A man after my own heart. These financial whiz kids don't understand that real work has to take place before money is made. They think the work consists of shuffling papers around. I'd like to have seen their faces when they realized you were gone."

Josh couldn't help but smile. "I would have liked to have seen that myself. You realize I can't take the credit. This was all orchestrated by Kevin. He surmised they would be looking for more money. It was prearranged that I would walk out if they pushed their own agenda."

"Maybe Kevin concocted the idea. You carried it off." Tony reached out for Josh's hand. "It's been a pleasure meeting you. Cliff always spoke highly of you. I see he wasn't bullshitting me." The meeting was over.

"Strange," Josh said. "Cliff never mentioned you at all." He gave Tony a sardonic look.

Tony didn't miss a beat. "No," he said. "People like to know me but don't like to admit they know me. Even those from the old neighbourhood. I'm not sure I understand why." He continued to hold out his hand.

Josh smiled and took the hand. "Well Tony, if we're going to be friends, I won't hide it from anyone. You can count on that. The rest of the house? You haven't seen it."

"Don't have to. I recognize quality when I see it. When I bite into a scrumptious slice of pizza, I don't have to eat the whole pie to know that it will all be good. I'm satisfied with what I've seen. I've got other places to get to this morning. I just thought that we should meet sooner rather than later." With that, he and his man exited the house leaving Josh and his helper a little mystified.

"I don't think it was the house he was checking out," the foreman said. "I think it was you. You seem to have passed the test. Who was he anyway?"

"One of our investors," Josh said. He, too, felt like he had been the one examined. Like the victim of an alien abduction – he was probed, documented and released.

CHAPTER 38

BACK IN SERGEANT Jim Mcdonald's office, Corporal Scott Bowen was pouring the coffee. The two cops and Robin West, the forensic expert, were crammed into the small cubicle. Robin had given the shell casing found at the target range to one of his staff to compare to the casing found at the site of Cliff Lawrence's shooting. The wad of compacted lead extracted from the target tree had gone to another technician for analysis. They were awaiting the results.

"Even if these shells match, it doesn't make this a homicide case," Robin said. "People target-practise all the time before hunting season. It's not even remotely out of the ordinary."

"That's true," Scott said, "except most people I know shoot at level targets, not uphill. The exception was when I was in sniper training with the army. We practised shooting up, down, around corners." He laughed. "Well not quite, but just about any conceivable way of making a shot we could think of. Shooting uphill could be one small link in a circumstantial case."

"The problem is," Jim said while stroking his chin in a contemplative manner, "did the shooter intentionally leave the casing at the site of the killing or was that an oversight on his part? If he left it on purpose, we will probably never find a rifle to link it up to."

"Leaving it on purpose makes sense," Scott said, picking up Jim's thought. "Who would suspect a .30 calibre as a weapon of choice for a killing shot of that distance? Despite all his testing, he couldn't be guaranteed that the shell wouldn't pass through the body and be lost forever. In part, the unlikely choice of weapon led to our conclusion of accidental shooting."

"Only in a minor role," Robin said. "We had lots of blood and deer hair evidence that led to that conclusion. But," and here he smiled, " we should have similar evidence found in that tree at the target range. His practice shots were through the deer hide as well if we can believe

Chris Ritchey. My staff are examining the wad of metal retrieved from the tree even as we speak."

"Right, Chris Ritchey," Jim said. "He handed us this can of worms but didn't supply us with a person to actually investigate, only a vague description of both the man and his vehicle. Robin, we need more."

Scott hit the desk with the flat of his hand causing the coffee cups to jump. His dark eyes sparkled with the germ of a new idea. "What was it Merrill Eisenhauer told us about his son and his friends? They are out plinking at cans all the time. I wonder where?"

Jim brightened at the suggestion. "Are we that lucky that they might have seen our shooter? We've got nothing to lose. Let's have them picked up and interviewed again. If nothing else, it will keep them on their toes out there. They deserve to be hassled a little bit, at least."

"I'll give Detective Hennigar a call and fill him in," Scott said. "He said he would keep track of the boys in case we found evidence to link them to the murder."

The phone on Jim's desk interrupted the conversation. Jim picked up the receiver, listened for a few seconds and passed it over to Robin. "Our lab results."

Robin took the phone, nodded a couple of times, made a few grunts and thanked the caller. He hung up and looked at Scott and Jim's expectant faces. "Same gun at both sites," he said.

"I'll call the Crown prosecutor and tell him what we've got," Jim said. "He won't be thrilled about reopening a case already declared accidental. We're going to need to come up with some good evidence before we can proceed to court."

"Court?" Scott said. "We don't even have a suspect."

"Right, I guess we've got our work cut out for us. Let's get at it."

CHAPTER 39

THE CALL TO Detective Bob Hennigar was one of those classic good-news bad-news situations. Darrin Eisenhauer and his friends had spent one day in Calgary before moving north to Fort McMurray. Jobs abounded thoughout the province but the big money came from working on the oilsands. This was where the boys had been recruited to work, along with several thousand other Maritimers. That was the bad news.

The good news outweighed the bad. Part of the contract these Maritime boys worked under had them flying home every three weeks. They worked 20 straight days and then had a full week off. The company paid for their return flight to Nova Scotia. If they were willing to wait, Detective Sergeant Mcdonald and Corporal Bowen could conduct their own interview with the boys. In this way, they would not only get the answers to their questions, but could study the boys' reactions during the interrogation. It would be worth waiting a couple of weeks. Their having any useful information was a long shot anyway.

There was no shortage of other things to do in the meantime. Reopening an investigation was no simple task, especially one that had been ruled accidental before being closed. All the evidence would have to be re-examined with fresh eyes. Eyes that were focussed on a homicide.

Jim thought back a couple of months to his first investigation. He had to admit that he had come to the conclusion of an accidental death pretty early. That decision had probably influenced some of the investigation from that point on. It was small consolation that other members of the investigative squad had made the same error. This time around, things would be different. Small details that had no significance in an accident suddenly took on new importance.

Now, there was also an extra burden of proof required when they reached court. Any defence lawyer worth his salt would be pushing the element of reasonable doubt that even the police believed the death had been accidental. If they were wrong then in their conclusions, were they any more correct in what they now were asking the jury to believe? Reasonable doubt.

A return trip to the crime scene was in the cards. The area had been pounded by heavy rains and a covering of snow was always an option at this time of year. They had taken accurate measurements at the target range. Generally, they appeared to be the same as the situation at the site of the shooting. Once they proceeded to the courtroom, generally would not be good enough. They needed accurate comparisons. They needed comparisons that showed the practice and the actual event were beyond similar. Exact would be preferred, but they would settle for very, very close.

Then, there was the suspect pool. Cliff Lawrence was reputedly the nicest guy in the world. He had no enemies, anywhere. But his hunting trip was not just with a few of his many, many friends. It featured his closest co-workers: his builder, salesman and money-raiser. Conflict with any or all of these men was a definite possibility. Close proximity in the workplace had a way of generating resentments and often these resentments developed, over time, into serious acrimony. Throw in the fact that a financial interest existed between all the parties and all three men would require a closer look. Again, with those same homicide-searching eyes. Unlike the last time, the detectives would not be just going through the motions. They would be digging, digging deep and hard.

The month's delay in the investigation could in no way be construed as a good thing, except for one possible exception. If one, or indeed all, of these men were involved in the murder, they had spent a month thinking they had gotten away with it. Now to be suddenly interviewed again, this time with a harder edge to the questions, their guards might be down. It would be up to Jim Mcdonald to be watching for that opening and to jump into it with both feet if it indeed developed. He had worked homicide for over 15 years. He was up to that task.

Jim reached for the phone. His first call would be to his girlfriend, Stella Martin. She had been working the night shift for a week. This was her crossover day. Traditionally they met for lunch on this day. Stella would stay up until mid-afternoon and then sleep right through until morning and be ready to resume day shifts. Lunch wouldn't be happening. Their little celebration on the end of this case had come a little too early. Stella would understand the need to get up to speed again.

The next call would be to Kevin Barnhill, the apparent leader of the group. Jim would try to arrange a meeting at Kevin's camp. It would be nice if they could get permission to inspect the premises without the necessity of a search warrant. There were very few loopholes in the law which favoured the police. Jim could think of none that would come anywhere near to allowing them to search without the owner's permission. They had no probable cause. Jim would keep that piece of information to himself.

Jim listened to the phone ring in his ear. "Come on, come on. Answer." The reinvestigation was getting off to a shaky start. The last thing he wanted to do was to open it by talking to an answering machine.

Jim counted eight rings and was about to hang up when a voice came on the line.

"Kevin Barnhill."

"Mr. Barnhill, Detective-Sergeant Jim Mcdonald. We talked when Clifford Lawrence was shot."

Jim listened to the silence on the line for several seconds. Then the voice said: "I remember. It turned out to be an unfortunate accident, as I recall."

Jim decided to approach this subject head on. "So we all believed, but new evidence has surfaced. We've reopened the investigation."

"New evidence? What does that mean?"

"We are now considering this to be a homicide. We believe Mr. Lawrence was deliberately murdered."

Again there was a period of silence on the phone.

"Murdered? Cliff? I don't believe that, Sergeant. Cliff was one of those rare individuals who got along with everyone. He was like a brother to me. We had no secrets. I would have known if he had any enemies, especially enemies who would stoop to murder. This just can't be true."

Kevin's voice was taking on the confidence that Jim remembered from the previous interviews. Once he had gotten over the initial shock of Cliff's death, Kevin had taken charge of the others. Of the three, Kevin was the lowest on Jim's suspect list. He appeared to have the least to gain from the death of his partner. Everyone else stood to move up the food chain. Kevin was already in the dominant position. Cliff, from all reports, was a competent second-in-command.

"New evidence suggests that it is true. I wonder if we could meet at your cabin."

"My cabin? Sure, why not? It's always a pleasure to find an excuse to go out there."

Step one complete. "Would it be all right if we brought along a forensic team with us?"

Silence, and then: "I can't imagine why you want to, but ..." Kevin paused before continuing. This may not slip by as easily as Jim had hoped. "... I see no reason to object. I do have one condition though."

Jim smiled. Step two seemed to be in place. "Okay. What would that be?"

"Any mess you make, you clean up."

Jim tried to hide the confusion in his voice. "I don't understand."

"I want you to be like the Boy Scouts. I want you to leave the place cleaner than you found it. No fingerprint powder on any surfaces. No drawers with the contents dumped out. No bags, papers or vials left on the floor. All domestic duties are my responsibility. Keeping the place clean is challenging enough without a bunch of cops blowing through like a hurricane. This is not a crime scene. If you're going to come in and make a mess, you need some legal papers to get you in the door. Otherwise, the place is yours."

Jim couldn't help but let out a little laugh of relief. "No problem. Robin doesn't leave a mess behind. If he does, I'll have Corporal Bowen clean it up."

Kevin understood this was an attempt at levity. "The power of an extra stripe." He shared the laugh.

The sergeant turned serious again. "Let's set up a time. Are you free today?"

CHAPTER 40

WHILE SERGEANT MCDONALD discussed the possibilities of meeting Kevin Barnhill at his hunting camp, Corporal Scott Bowen was parking a four-wheel drive police vehicle behind Josh Daniels' truck at the construction site. Josh was the only one of the three without an alibi. He had been alone at the time of the shooting, supposedly sleeping, but still, alone.

The two cops had decided they would like to chat with Josh before he had a chance to discuss the reopened case with anyone else. They would have to act quickly. Scott was assigned the task of persuading Josh to drive to the cabin in the police vehicle. They hoped to accomplish this feat without any hassle from lawyers or the like. Scott wore blue jeans, work boots, a plaid shirt and a short, blue nylon jacket with POLICE printed across the back in gold letters. It would be just two working-class guys getting together for an outing in the woods.

As he walked up to the door, he could hear a phone ringing. It sounded like the two sharp rings of a British phone. Scott knocked and walked in through the unlocked door.

An expression of surprise registered on Josh's face at the sight of the Mountie. Despite Scott's casual dress, Josh recognized him right away. He held up one finger as he flipped open his phone.

"Hello." He paused. "Hi, Kevin. Guess who just walked in the door? What's up?"

His initial look of surprise transformed into one of shock. "Murdered? I don't believe it. What changed?"

Scott stepped forward and reached for the cellphone. "Excuse me sir, but I wonder if we could talk."

Josh gave him a defiant look and held on to the phone. "Sorry, Kevin, I'll call you back." He snapped the phone shut before putting it into his shirt pocket.

"That was Kevin Barnhill?" Scott asked. "Interesting."

"Interesting isn't how I would describe it. You're here to tell me that a very dear friend of mine was intentionally murdered. How did you come to that conclusion?"

"New evidence has surfaced. I can understand your shock, but I wonder if you would mind answering a few new questions for us?"

Josh seemed to mentally shake himself and relax a little. "As I told you before, anything I can do to help, I'm more than willing to do." He gestured for the Mountie to come to the kitchen where there were some stools to sit on.

Scott shook his head. "We were hoping to ask these questions out at Mr. Barnhill's cabin. I will drive you out."

Josh balked. "Kevin's camp? Why?" He dismissed the questions with a wave of his hand. "My truck can make it to the cabin with no problem."

The Mountie smiled. "Of course it can but we all have to do our share to combat global warming. Why take two gas-guzzlers out there when one will suffice?"

Josh studied the man. He wasn't sure if he was being serious or not. He decided to play along. "That's true. We'll take my truck."

Scott maintained his smile. "That presents a problem. As we speak, Sergeant Mcdonald is making arrangements with Kevin Barnhill that he, Kevin and Victor Boyd all go out in Kevin's Jeep Commander. Kevin will bring you back here. I will drive the sergeant back to our headquarters." The smile stayed on Scott's lips but his dark eyes hardened. This was not up for discussion.

"A reunion at the scene of the crime. That's a little melodramatic. Do you get us all together and one of you says, 'This is what happened' like an episode of Monk? Then one of us is expected to break down in a fit of remorse and proclaim 'I did it!' I don't think so."

Scott chuckled at the suggestion. "That would make it easier on everybody, but that's not the plan. We want to go over who was where, what they heard, when they heard it. You guys were in a state of emotional shock the last time we talked. Now that some time has passed to distance you from the initial impact, you may remember some things that can aid in the investigation. We want your help. Have you been back there since the shooting?"

Josh turned serious. "No, none of us have. We were all running around in the woods with guns like school kids, but you don't expect anyone to get killed. Now you tell me it was murder. Are you sure this time?"

Scott didn't answer. They had been sure it was an accident. The new evidence wasn't any more compelling than the old. Shell casings from both scenes matched. Microscopic traces of blood and hair were found on the spent shells. That only proved it was the same rifle. It gave no iron-clad, this could be the only way it happened, proof of intent. However, any reasonable thinking person would conclude that a cover-up of the crime had taken place. Not a simple cover-up, but a complex, well-thought-out cover-up.

"Yes, this time we are sure," he said.

Josh shrugged. "Let's get it over with. I've got work to do." He turned to his foreman who had been quietly taking in the discussion. "Call Barry to come over and help you. We've got to get this place finished today."

CHAPTER 41

DETECTIVE-SERGEANT JIM MCDONALD leaned forward in the front seat of the Jeep Commander. "Do you mind if I change stations on your radio?" He looked over at Kevin Barnhill for confirmation as his hand hovered over the dials.

Kevin gave him a surprised look. This was an unexpected request. "Go for it. All the local stations are tuned in on the push buttons."

The radio was on a country music station. Jim changed it to a classic rock. He then adjusted the balance button to put most of the sounds on the back speakers. He looked back at Victor Boyd. "Not too loud, is it?"

"I can live with it," Victor said.

They drove in silence for a few minutes before *It's Still Rock and Roll To Me* came on the radio. "Billy Joel," Jim said. "Gotta be played loud." He touched up the volume a little more. He glanced at the back-seat passenger. Victor was caught up in the solid beat of the music.

"Tell me about that morning again," Jim said to Kevin. "Why was Cliff hunting by himself? Was it his idea or yours?"

Kevin slowly turned and looked at the cop. There was a sad look on his face. His eyes probed those of the policeman, trying to discern the real meaning of the question. He turned his attention back to his driving. "I've spent hours thinking about that morning, Sergeant. The suggestion was mine. Cliff wanted so badly to get himself a deer. That site was the most promising place in the area. I insisted he take the blind while I walked the roads with Victor."

He looked back at the back-seat passenger for confirmation. Victor was oblivious to the front-seat conversation. The music drowned out any words being spoken in front of him.

Kevin checked the road again before looking back at the Sergeant. The road unfolding in front of them, Veterans Memorial Highway, was part of the 100-series highways, four lanes and straight for miles. "Do you know what thought is most prominent in my mind?" He didn't wait for an answer. "That could have been me sitting in that tree."

Jim nodded. "It could have." He briefly looked forward, then recaptured Kevin's eyes. "Would it be more accurate to say: It should have been you?"

Kevin reacted like he had taken a George Foreman punch in the chest. He studied the road for a few seconds before answering. In a low voice, he said: "You're right. It should have been me." This was the first time he had made the leap from "could have" to "should have." He looked back at Jim. "If Cliff was murdered as you claim, I was the intended target." His hands started to shake on the steering wheel. The Commander's speed bled down from 110 km/h to 80, 70, 60.

"My God, someone was trying to kill me."

Jim glanced in the side-view mirror at the traffic quickly building up behind them. He watched the front end of the trailing car dip as the driver quickly applied the brakes. No one was going to rear-end them. "That's a definite possibility. Any thoughts on who?"

A horn shattered the air in a long, drawn-out blast as cars started to speed by them in the passing lane. The first driver by shot them a finger. The sudden decrease in speed had caught him off guard. He was blaming his inattention on Kevin instead of himself.

The blaring horn brought Kevin back to the present. He got a grip on himself and pushed down on the accelerator. "Hell, no. I build houses. I build them well. No one shoots you for that."

Jim looked at the soft hands on the steering wheel, the extra 50 pounds padding the body. He tried to visualize those hands wielding a hammer, the flabby arms carrying a load of wood to the second floor of a house under construction. The image wouldn't come to him. "Would it be safe to say you're more involved in the financial end of the construction than the actual building?"

"You can't build houses without money up front. Not the way we build them."

Jim nodded. "True, but my experience has money right up there with unrequited love as one of the top reasons for murder. Is there anybody out there who might think you've ripped them off, scammed them?"

Kevin didn't hesitate in his answer. "No. We're in this for the long haul. We build quality houses. We keep our investors happy."

"And your partners all think they are getting their fair share? Cliff didn't have any disputes with you about money?"

"Cliff? You think I killed Cliff?" He looked back at Victor once more. Now Victor was trying to pay attention. The sudden slowing and the blowing horns had made him realize he was being left out of something. Still, the radio was too loud for him to follow the conversation. The sergeant's words were all aimed straight ahead. None of them carried back to Victor. He could only catch part of what Kevin was saying. He gave Kevin a confused look.

"We have to look at all possibilities," Jim said. "How about your other partners? Are they all happy?"

Kevin rallied to get control of his answers. He smiled. "I know what you're trying to do, Sergeant. I've used this ambush approach myself on occasion. You're trying to shock me into giving unguarded responses to your questions. To answer without thinking." He reached out and turned down the radio.

"My partners are all happy. We are a small company. We're not top heavy with management and we all make money. Ask Victor."

"Is Victor part of the management team?"

"He is now. He has taken over Cliff's spot. Ask him if he was unhappy with how much he was making before he moved up the ladder. It's not just management who makes money with our company. It filters all the way down to the lowest worker. We exemplify the Reaganomics trickle-down theory. We like to think we are one big, happy family."

"At the risk of stating the obvious," Jim said in a patronizing voice, "someone wasn't happy. The question we have to answer now is: With whom were they unhappy? You or Cliff?" He paused to let this sink in before continuing. "Did Josh Daniels know who was hunting where that morning? I understand he was still lodged in the sack when you set out?"

Kevin flipped on his signal light and eased onto the Exit 9 ramp. The side road leading to his camp was a few miles up Highway 14 in the community of Hardwood Lands. A few snowflakes started whisking by the windshield.

"Cliff and I had discussed it the night before. He didn't want to be skunked again. I don't know who was paying attention. Everyone was drinking but Victor. He's been recently abstaining. Josh, a little more than the rest of us. He slept late. I hope this snow doesn't amount to anything."

"Just a few flurries, according to the radio," Jim said. "Josh had been up before you and Victor returned to the cabin at noon."

"There were dirty dishes on the table, yeah."

"When we examined your rifles, none of you were using a .30 calibre carbine. Were there other rifles at the camp that we didn't see? Did Josh have another weapon in his car?"

"Not that I know of. Didn't your guys look?"

Jim grimaced. Everyone was so sure the killing was accidental that a few procedures were missed. The investigation could only be described as shoddy. He was the detective in charge. The quality of work was his responsibility. Despite his words that they would investigate the matter like a homicide, he had allowed it to be less than it should have been. This burden had been grating on him ever since the case was reopened.

Today they were going to get to look around the cabin. Kevin had given them permission to do that.

While Josh was driving out to the cabin with Scott, another officer would take a superficial look at his truck. It was abandoned at a construction site. Even if there had been another rifle, it was highly unlikely it would still be in the truck. But, who knows? It was worth a quick look.

"We didn't see anything," Jim said. "Thought maybe you might've noticed something after we left."

"We left soon after you did. You took our rifles, remember? Not that we wanted to continue hunting, but we were weaponless. If anyone had another gun, they didn't mention it. All we wanted to do was get away from that place. Josh and Victor haven't been back. I've only been out once to make sure we shut everything off that we should have."

By now, Billy Joel had been replaced on the radio by Bruce Springsteen. Bruce was lamenting the changes that had taken place in his hometown. All three men appeared to be listening to the sad tale of woe. Kevin interrupted the Boss. "Shooting Cliff from that distance was quite a shot, I understand?"

Jim nodded. "With an M1 it was. That distance is at the outer range of their effectiveness."

Kevin kept his eyes on the road ahead. There were more twists and turns to negotiate than on the highway. He stole a quick glance at the sergeant. "Not to speak unkindly of my fellow hunters, but barn doors are pretty safe with most of their shooting."

Jim suppressed a smile. "Robin West alluded to that when he examined your rifles. Cleaning seemed to be haphazard and none of your sights were properly aligned."

Kevin let that statement sink in. "I'm not surprised. None of us were hunters before I acquired the lodge. We agreed not to get carried away buying expensive gear. We tend to be a competitive bunch and the spending could have escalated out of control." Once again, Kevin took his eyes off the road and looked over at the sergeant. "So, you don't actually suspect any of us?"

"I suspect all of you. This case has been overloaded with red herrings. We are assuming that nothing is as it seems. Josh Daniels came to that hunting trip on his own, I understand. You, Victor and Cliff all came in your Commander."

"He came up early. He likes to cook his steaks on a charcoal barbecue. No gas. He had the steaks marinating and the coals glowing when the rest of us arrived."

"So he was here for a couple of hours alone?"

"He always prepares the first meal on these trips. He's meticulous about his cooking."

"After you discovered Cliff's body, you and Victor set out to find a cellular signal to call the police. Josh ended up babysitting the remains alone?"

Kevin didn't answer. He looked back at Victor who was now leaning forward to listen to the front-seat conversation. "The sergeant is interrogating me about Josh's movements on the day Cliff was murdered. I'm willing to bet Josh is getting the third degree from the corporal about our movements. Isn't that right, Sergeant? Divide and conquer?"

Jim studied Kevin's steel-blue eyes. Kevin's face had taken on a defiant set with the question but the eyes betrayed a flash of concern. Did Josh know something that had Kevin worried? Originally, Kevin had been Jim's least likely suspect. It seemed to Jim that Cliff was more valuable to Kevin alive than dead. Jim hadn't known Cliff, but he had talked to a lot of people who had. He sounded like an asset to any company. Victor moving up in the organization to take Cliff's place seemed to be a step backward.

Victor appeared to be a super salesman. Jim didn't doubt that for a minute. He had seen Victor's earnings statements. But as Dr. Lawrence Peters put it, Victor had reached his level of competence. Another promotion would make him a victim of the Peter Principle – everyone rises until they reach their level of incompetence. Jim couldn't see Kevin knowingly letting that happen. But, nothing in this investigation was as it seemed.

Jim saw this as an extra burden he had to carry. The murderer had almost succeeded in convincing everyone that the death was an accident. Only a fluke had the case being reopened. Everything had to be examined from several different angles before it was accepted as real. Suspects who were obviously innocent became more suspicious instead of less. No one was being eliminated.

As they turned off Highway 14 and onto the road to Kevin's camp, the snow became more intense. Kevin turned on the windshield wipers.

"You do have snow tires on this thing, don't you?" Jim asked.

"All seasons," Kevin said. "More comfortable ride."

"Great," Jim said under his breath.

CHAPTER 42

CORPORAL SCOTT BOWEN appeared to be in deep concentration as he made his way from the newly developed subdivision, along the service streets, towards the Veterans Memorial Highway. He wasn't. His plan was simple. Let Josh Daniels meditate on the questions he thought the Mountie would ask him. Let him work over the answers in his own mind. Let him initiate the conversation when his patience had been pushed to the limit.

Scott had deployed this method on numerous occasions in the past with various degrees of success. He used it when there was no real link between the suspect and the crime, no opening for Scott to exploit. Scott may not have known of any connection but the suspect, if he was involved, knew exactly which questions should be being asked. Those answers would be playing on his mind.

The suspect seldom broached the subject directly, but given time and enough leeway, he or she would eventually find the path leading to the crux of the investigation. It was human nature. They wanted to know what the cops knew. If they were being questioned, the cops must know something.

Josh Daniels was not playing the game. His current role in the company was either administrative, where he worked alone, or on site as a finish carpenter. Again, a task that was usually a solitary pursuit. Most of his building instructions were passed on through his foremen. Most of his foremen did not need Josh to tell them what had to be done. As a team, they had built hundreds of houses together. Josh obviously did not feel the need to break the silence.

As Scott ascended the entrance ramp to the limited-access highway, he looked over at his passenger. "You're quiet."

Josh started. He was not as relaxed as he had seemed. "How about those Maple Leafs? They almost won a game the other night."

The statement surprised Scott. "Who cares? I'm a Bruins fan myself," he said.

Josh slowly shook his head. "I've never liked them since they wrecked Bobby Orr's knees. Overplayed him way too much. Forty-five, fifty minutes a game."

Scott laughed. "You're not that old, but you are right."

"That's what my dad always said about Boston. Thinks Orr was the greatest player ever. Even better than Gretzky."

"Can't compare them," Scott said. "Not the same game now as it was then. Too many expansion teams."

"So they say. I don't really have the time or the interest to follow it." Josh made a dismissive motion with his hands.

Scott focused on the road for a few beats, then said: "I thought this case was wrapped up a month ago."

Josh nodded. He, too, stared straight ahead.

Scott pulled into traffic and accelerated to the speed limit. "You must have been surprised when I showed up at your work site."

Josh glanced his way. "More curious than surprised. What changed your minds?"

Scott smiled inwardly. He at least had the man talking.

"New evidence surfaced while we were working on another case."

Interest sparked in Josh's face. "What kind of a case?"

"Sorry, can't say."

"What was the new evidence?"

"Can't answer that one either."

"Why not? You're looking for my help aren't you?"

"We do have some additional questions for you, but I can't share what we already know."

"Don't want to influence my answers?"

Scott pulled out into the passing lane. The cars immediately in front of him had realized they were being followed by a police vehicle and had slowed down to less than the speed limit. Behind him the cars were piling up. In his rear-view mirror he could see vehicles coming up quickly in the passing lane, spotting the red and blue bar of lights on his roof and forcing their way into line behind him. An accident was in the making. He shot ahead of the pack before looking back at Josh.

"You do realize that you are a suspect?" Scott was going to try a new approach. The laissez faire approach was not yielding results.

"A suspect? I hadn't thought of it that way. What qualifies me as a suspect?"

"Think about it," Scott said. "You were the closest person to the victim when the crime took place." He paused. "Other than the killer, of course." He shrugged. "But, if you two are one and the same –" He let the thought hang in the air.

Josh looked thoughtful. "I never looked at it that way. Do I need a lawyer?"

Scott felt a chill go up his back. That was his least favourite question. He had to be careful how he answered it. "That is definitely your right." He let that information sink in. "But only you know if you need an attorney present."

The implication was that if he was guilty or wanted to risk looking guilty, he would call a lawyer. Otherwise, why bother? It was just a couple of working guys driving along the highway talking. Talking about murder, mind you, but just talking.

Josh smiled. The implication was not lost on him. "Tell me about the other case," he said. "What kind of investigation was it? Murder? Drugs? Fraud?"

"I told you I can't give you that information."

"What if I have additional information? How will I know what to tell you?"

"The two investigations aren't linked. We were charging a suspect about an entirely unrelated case when out of the blue, he offered us new information about this one. It was an attempt to plea bargain his other sentence."

Josh sat quietly for a few more minutes. Scott could see he was mulling something over in his mind. Did he have some bombshell to drop in the same way Chris Ritchey had? Were they going to be off on another tangent?

Without looking at the policeman, Josh asked: "How many of Cliff's friends and associates did you talk to? How far back did you go?"

Not many, Scott thought. The investigation came to a halt before it had seriously got started. It took less than a week for it to be definitely declared an accident.

"We talked to you guys, as you know. We talked to people in his real estate office, people in his neighbourhood. We were trying to get a feel for what kind of guy, Cliff was who might want to kill him. Would you like to suggest some new names?"

Again, Josh remained silent.

"If you know something relevant." Scott's voice took on a firmer tone.

Josh shook his head. "I don't. I'm not sure."

In the distance, Scott spotted a Jeep Commander. He also noticed a few snowflakes blowing along the road bed. He eased back on the gas pedal a little. This was not the time to catch up to the rest of the party. Some new evidence might be about to come out. He had to give it time to develop.

"Why don't you let me decide what might or what might not be relevant? That is what I do." Scott glanced at his passenger, then straight ahead again. The interrogation was at a critical point. He had to apply just the right amount of pressure.

Josh remained silent. Scott could see the internal debate taking place in the way the man held himself. He was no longer relaxed. His hands clasped and unclasped in his lap. Something was gnawing at his sense of right and wrong.

Scott could see Exit 9 coming up quickly. He was running out of time. They would soon be at the cabin. Once they were in the presence of the others, Scott knew the opportunity presented here would be lost. "Let's grab a coffee and discuss this," he said. "How do you like yours?"

Josh chewed on his upper lip, deciding whether he wanted to drop the subject completely or share his concerns with this policeman. "We missed the Tim Hortons' at the last exit and I don't think you'll find a Starbucks out here anywhere."

"They do sell coffee in other places. There's a little pizza joint at the next exit. We can go there." He flipped on his signal light and eased into the right-hand lane.

"No, let's get to the cabin. There's not a whole lot to tell. I don't actually know anything definite. It's more a feeling. I'll fill you in on the way."

Scott slowed at the top of the exit lane as he approached the round-about. Right took them to the pizza place. Left took them to Kevin's cabin. He stole a glance at the resolute look on Josh's face. He was prepared to talk but only on his own terms. It would be best to abide by them. Scott turned left. He slowly let the vehicle come up to speed. The snow was getting heavy enough that he now needed the wipers on. He took advantage of that situation to drive more cautiously than he normally would have. He waited expectantly for Josh to continue.

CHAPTER 43

ROBIN WEST FELT a sense of déjà vu. He again found himself perched in the last place that Cliff Lawrence had been a functioning, breathing human being. Unlike Cliff, he did not find the seat restraining. Robin weighed in at 167 pounds. Unlike Cliff, he had a partially unrestricted view of the surrounding woods for miles. All the deciduous trees–the maples, the oaks, the birches–had deposited their leaves onto the surrounding forest floor. The spidery frames that remained allowed Robin to see the surrounding network of woods roads through their web of interlocking branches.

His assistant technician, Lorne Dauphinee, from the crime lab stood in plain sight 250 metres away. Through his binoculars, Robin could see an orange ribbon tied to a small bush. The ribbon indicated the site where the initial blood droplets were found. The site where the murderer tried to make it appear that a deer had been wounded.

Robin conceded that it had been a clever plan. The killer had found his ejected shell casing, moved it 50 yards up the path, and made the whole thing seem like an impossible shot. The path he took to drop off the casing left a trail for the dog to follow. The killer had put a great deal of trust in the police department's investigative abilities. The police, unfortunately, had grossly underestimated the shooter.

Robin consulted his notes. One of the target sights at the practice range had been 249.08 metres. That was close enough. If Lorne were to lay prone on the frozen forest surface, his head and shoulders would probably be closer to the desired 249 metres.

"Lie down and pretend to be holding a rifle," Robin said into his two-way radio.

The field man complied. Robin focused the laser point from the binoculars on a spot below the man's right eye. Two hundred forty-nine point zero eight. The precision was uncanny. The suspect had to be a compulsive obsessive. Let a defence attorney try to argue those measurements were coincidental.

Robin flipped back the pages in his own notebook to the previous investigation. His notes indicated 249 metres. A small smile formed on his wind-chilled face. Parts of this investigation may not have been up to par, but they weren't his parts. He and his crew had done everything by the book. In fact, as far as he could see, they had only made one mistake. They had reached the wrong conclusion. They had declared the death was accidental.

Robin did not view this as a total negative. This spoke more to the diligence of the murderer than to the lack of diligence of his forensic crew. The man, or woman, anything was possible, had almost carried out the perfect crime. They were up against a formidable enemy. Robin looked around the scene. He wondered how many misleading clues the killer had left for them that they had missed.

He had spent most of the last hour confirming everything the crew had done the previous month. From a straight scientific point of view, coming to a different determination this time around would not be based on anything they found at this crime scene. Everything still pointed to accidental. The change of opinion would be based almost completely on the testimony of Chris Ritchey. That prospect made Robin a little nervous. The other cops involved in this case thought Ritchey was a kook. Robin sure as hell didn't want to be wrong again.

Flakes of snow started drifting down around him. He slipped the hi-tech binoculars back into their case and signalled his partner to come back up the hill. They had been lucky. A month-old crime scene was bad enough. Burying it under an inch or two of snow would be more than a pain in the ass. He worked his way over to the tree trunk and lowered himself to the ground and waited.

"The squibs are in place?" he asked Lorne as Lorne was scrambling up the hill. The dusting of snow on the dead leaves made for a slippery combination.

"Four of them, just like you said."

Robin nodded. "We'll wait for the others to arrive before we set them off. We need people at the cabin, down the road where two of the hunters were and inside the cabin with all the doors closed."

"That's three."

"The fourth is a special surprise we've prepared for our guests. That's the super-charged one of the three."

"What is all this supposed to prove? The man in the cabin was supposed to be asleep. We know that people take various degrees of noise to wake them. Some hear a pin drop. Some can ignore a bomb blast. The Daniels guy was drinking heavily the night before. Unless you plan on getting him drunk, then letting him sleep it off, the tests are meaningless."

"Sergeant Mcdonald understands that. He is applying the highly regarded 'Bullshit Baffles Brains' investigative technique. We have a highly intelligent killer here. Intelligent enough to fool all of us. The sergeant wants this dog-and-pony show to look like an extremely scientific experiment. Something the killer will suspect he might have overlooked. While the sergeant is studying the suspects for any twinge of doubt, we have to be making an Academy Award performance with out metres and recorders. Just don't overact."

"*I don't know nothing about birthing babies ... Luke, Luke. I am your father ... Tell me, do you feel lucky punk, do you?*" He had all the accents and voices down perfectly. "I've studied the masters. Don't worry about my acting."

Robin pointed a warning finger at him before he, too, broke into laughter. "It's a long shot, but man, I want to catch this killer. He made us look like idiots."

This thought sobered up both men. Robin looked at his watch. "They should be here soon. I hope this snow doesn't affect our results. If it gets any heavier, it might absorb a lot of the sound from the crackers." He stuck out his tongue and tried to catch a flake. "First of the season snow is the best."

Ten minutes later, as the two men sat in their van going over the new material they had collected, they saw the Jeep Commander come into view. Robin stepped out of the van. The ground was by now totally white. His boot made a crunching sound in the slight buildup of crisp, newly fallen snow. He pulled his dark blue, nylon jacket tighter around his neck and reached back into the van for his blue ball cap. "Forensics" was jammed along the front of the cap in a yellow, condensed Franklin Gothic type. Similar, but uncondensed versions of the same typeface extended the word across the width of his back.

He had been doing this for nearly fifteen years, the first ten in relative obscurity. Now, thanks to the magic of television, his team had become superstars in the eyes of the public. This only increased the pressure on them to perform. In cases like this one, it would take all the tricks of the trade to track down the killer. That person had been a student of the CSI TV shows. He had covered his tracks well.

Robin's eyes searched the road leading to the cabin. It was like looking into a Norman Rockwell painting. Snowflakes appeared to hang silently in the air. A layer of white covered all the sharp edges of the surrounding terrain. The various greens of the pines and the firs were being dusted with a shadow of white on their branches. A shiny, new vehicle climbed the hill towards them.

But that was wrong. There were supposed to be two vehicles, the Jeep Commander and the RCMP SUV. Where were Corporal Bowen and his man? The plan called for all the suspects to be arriving at the same time. This was the problem with police work. Nothing ever worked out as it was planned. He shrugged and waited for the Commander to stop in the driveway beside them.

As the three men disembarked, Robin thumbed a small switch held in his hand. A sharp crack split the air, shattering the calm. Everyone instinctively ducked. Sergeant Mcdonald's hand involuntarily grasped the butt of his pistol before he managed to relax it. Kevin Barnhill and Victor Boyd cowered behind the open doors of their vehicle. Sergeant Mcdonald stood up straight. He gave Robin a thumbs up.

"That," he said, "is what would have been heard if you were standing here a month ago. That sound came from the location of the shot that killed Cliff Lawrence."

Kevin and Victor sheepishly got to their feet. Kevin tried to laugh off his actions. "First you tell me someone is out there trying to kill me. Then you almost succeed in doing it yourself. My heart is racing a mile a minute. Sergeant, you scared the shit out of me with that little demonstration."

"Sorry, that wasn't the intention. We were just showing you how loud the shot would have sounded that morning. Unfortunately, Josh Daniels isn't here yet. Do you think he could have slept through that?"

"Apparently," Kevin said. "I'm still not buying the idea that Josh was involved in this murder. It's not in his nature."

Robin came around to the front of the Jeep. "That sounded a lot louder than I thought it would." He looked in the direction the sound came from. "The contour of the land must be different than we think. There must be a natural alley between here and the base of that hill. If sound can travel up through there, so can a person."

CHAPTER 44

JOSH DANIELS STUDIED his hands loosely folded in his lap. They were badly scarred from years of physical labour. Hammer smacks, chisel nicks, splintery wood had all taken their toll. None of these things were on his mind.

His thoughts were focused on Tony Dellapinna. What did he really know about the man? He claimed to be Cliff's friend, a long-time friend. Josh believed he was laundering money through their company. Kevin insisted that it was of no concern to the partners. They should forget about it. The company was not at risk. It was only in the last few weeks that Josh had become aware of Tony and his shady money practices. Now he was becoming obsessed. Did Cliff know that his friend, his long-time friend, had been using the company for more than an investment vehicle? Was that fatal knowledge? Could this knowledge be fatal to himself? Josh was confused.

Corporal Bowen kept stealing furtive glances in his direction. Josh avoided direct eye contact. He had suggested to the policeman that he knew something more. The corporal was expecting Josh to give him some additional information. And he would. The question was: How much?

"Have you ever heard of a man called Tony Dellapinna?" Josh finally asked.

Scott Bowen did not answer right away. There was a look of heavy concentration on his face. "Tony Dellapinna? Tony Dellapinna? He's a local businessman, isn't he? Owns a couple of the office towers downtown. Sits on a bunch of charitable boards. Maybe involved in building supplies."

Other than the last one, Josh was unaware of the ventures Tony was connected with. "Right, building supplies. He's our main supplier."

Scott waited. They were getting closer to the road leading to Kevin's cabin.

"He and Cliff were long time-friends. Go back to the same neighbourhood when they were kids."

Scott nodded.

"He also invested in our company. Was one of the original investors."

Scott signalled to turn onto the dirt road. It was now completely covered with snow. He was running out of time.

"So, what? He supplied you with inferior building products? He was unhappy with his return? Tony and Cliff dated the same girl in high school? What are you suggesting to me?"

Josh was back to studying his hands. What was he suggesting? "Tony Dellapinna," he said. His voice tried to convey that the name should have some meaning. The corporal failed to react. "He's Italian. Have you ever met him? He travels with two thugs, probably bodyguards." Josh gave Scott a meaningful look.

"Bodyguards? Are you sure? Most of these guys travel with personal assistants. People ready to do their bidding at the drop of a hat. Find a report, hold his coat. Fetch a coffee. Give a financial analysis of an investment opportunity."

"They were built like brick shit houses."

"Deter would-be thieves. Prevent kidnappings. These men are rich beyond our understanding."

"What about the name? Dellapinna?"

Scott couldn't believe the implication. Josh did not look like a racist, but what did racists look like? Everyone else in the neighbourhood. "You're a contractor. You must have lots of foreigners working for you. There must be a few Italians."

Josh nodded. Some of his best workers. They installed marble and granite in the kitchens and bathrooms. He was being unrealistic in his thinking. "You're right. I do."

"If I had drawn the same conclusions you came to from that name, I would have been accused of racial profiling. People would be demanding my resignation. You've got to give me something more."

Outside the vehicle there was a distinctive crack. It sounded like a rifle shot. Scott hit the brakes. The heavily lugged winter tires bit through the light snow covering into the underlying gravel. Scott's pistol appeared in his hand. His eyes scoped out the surrounding terrain. "Isn't hunting season over?"

Josh slouched down in his seat and shook his head. The sight of the policeman's gun unnerved him. "Sorry, I'm not much of a hunter. Can't you hunt rabbits all winter?"

"Not with a high-powered rifle." Scott lay the pistol in his lap and started up the road again. He cautiously looked around through the trees before looking back over at Josh. He noticed Josh's face was drained of all colour. "We'll check out Mr. Dellapinna. He has enough connections to Cliff Lawrence to make him a person of interest. Thanks for the lead."

Josh nodded, but he could see the look of disappointment on the corporal's face.

"I'm not a racist," Josh said.

Scott gave him a weak smile. Right now he was more interested in who was shooting in their vicinity. He knew that his partner and the crime lab crew were up ahead. Who else knew they would be out here on this day?

Josh looked away. Maybe he should have mentioned the money-laundering. That was what really concerned him. Would somebody resort to murder to protect their criminal empire? Criminal empire. He had to get control of his thoughts. He was letting his imagination blow everything out of proportion.

CHAPTER 45

IN LESS THAN two minutes, both parties were united. Scott jumped down from his cab. The pistol was still in his hand. He looked around to assess the situation. No one else seemed concerned.

"I heard a shot," he said.

Detective-Sergeant Jim Mcdonald looked at the unholstered gun in Scott's hand. He smiled. "Did I forget to mention we are running some tests? It was only a squib. How far away were you?"

Scott holstered his pistol. "A little more than a kilometre down the road. It sounded loud."

"That's the lay of the land," Kevin Barnhill said. "You were probably as close to the firing point as we were. The road takes a big swing as you approach the camp. It follows the ridge around the valley."

Robin West stepped forward. "We tracked the shooter back to that road last month. The ground was too hard for tire impressions. There were no cigarette butts. We called for a car to come and pick us up. Are you saying it would have been just as easy to walk back?"

Kevin patted his vast stomach with both hands. "Walking easier than driving? I don't think you'll ever hear those words come out of my mouth."

"As I remember," Jim said, "we followed that trail for quite a distance. The road wasn't as close as this cabin."

"That's true," Robin said. "Our path stayed down in the valley. Scott was up on the ridge. The valley must meet the road farther down."

"Right," Scott said. "The shooter was trying to create the illusion we were following a wounded deer. A deer would not have climbed a hill if he had an easier choice. This guy left nothing to chance. He may have given us credit for knowing more about hunting than we really do. You almost have to admire his dedication to producing this myth."

Jim looked back to Kevin and Victor. "Just exactly where were you on this road when you heard the shot?"

Kevin pointed up the road further along the trail. "We had gone this way. There's a little side road that turns off this main drag. Lots of tracks. No deer."

"We'll get you to show us. I want to test-fire another squib and get some readings of how loud the shot was at your location." Jim studied both men closely. They showed no reaction to the mention of the test.

He looked back at Robin. "Get out your gear. We'll run a couple of tests here and in the cabin first." He noticed no reaction from Josh, either.

Robin set a meter on the engine bonnet of his van. "The human ear can detect sounds with a frequency between 20 and 20,000 cycles per second. This machine will capture the sound from the squib in decibels. From that we can get a scientific plot of the noise and not just the subjective one from standing here listening. We may have different ideas about what is a loud sound. The machine attaches no emotional value. It gives us a straight, not open to interpretation, reading. It allows us to assign probability values to the readings. From there we can come up with a reasonable certitude as to whether someone in the area would hear the sound."

Lorne looked away. He was struggling to keep a straight face. The others nodded as if all the bafflegab made some sort of sense.

Robin once again thumbed the hand switch. Once again the sound of a rifle being fired echoed around them. Everyone winced. The dial on the gauge jumped into a red field and the top of the scope and then settled back to the lowest setting.

Robin pushed a button on the side of the machine and a narrow strip of paper fed out covered in squigly lines. Lorne leaned over it with intense interest. He pulled a notebook from his pocket and started making notations. He flipped to the back of the book where he found preprinted charts. His finger followed along a line. His head nodded a couple of times and then he looked at Robin.

Robin held up his hand. "We'll discuss the results later, in private," he said.

The others leaned in to look at the printout still lying on the engine bonnet. "Neat," said Victor. "Just like CSI."

"Exactly," Robin said. Victor missed the irony in his voice. Jim didn't. He scowled at the forensics man. Robin smiled back. Jim knew Robin's view of the TV show. The made-for-TV miracles they performed every week made it harder on the men who actually did it for a living. The producers of that show were experts at making the viewing public suspend all sense of reality. Robin could only dream that his equipment would work the way it did in the imaginary world of CSI.

"That didn't sound as loud as it did the first time," Kevin said.

Robin picked up his machine. "We were expecting it. That's why we use a machine. It has no subjective opinions. It simply tells it like it is."

"I think that was loud enough to have awoken me," Jim said. He looked at Josh. Josh said nothing.

Robin turned to Kevin. "If you would unlock the door, we'll run the same test inside."

Kevin fished into his pocket and produced a ring of keys. There were different coloured plastic tops on them. He selected the blue one and inserted it into the lock. Everyone banged the snow off their feet and followed him inside where they stood in a group looking at Robin.

"I like that painting," Robin said. On the south wall hung an oil painting of a winter scene. An old Model-T Ford had just exited a covered bridge. The trees were hanging with snow. Mountains in the background took on a bluish-gray hue. The others looked in the same direction. Robin thumbed the switch.

This time the sound was muffled.

"Takes a lot more than that to wake me," Josh said.

The dial on Robin's gauge only went halfway up. It stayed well within the green.

The two technicians eyes met. This test might prove to be more important than they had expected. Robin pushed the button releasing the paper feedout. The squiggles rose no higher than the ones Robin indicated were caused by their speaking voices. On the bottom, he wrote in a fine hand, "inside cabin."

"Derrick Watts didn't scrimp on the insulation," Kevin said. "He built this place to be used year-round. He had no intention of heating the outside air."

Scott looked around the place with new respect. "Even with no heat on, it's not that cold in here."

"It has passive solar heating," Kevin said. "That's why it's built at the top of the hill and not in one of the valleys. Catches more sun up here."

"We have one more squib planted, Jim," Robin said. "Do you want to go up the road to where Mr. Barnhill and Mr. Boyd heard the shot?"

Again, Jim studied the two men instead of answering Robin. Victor looked more interested than worried. He was getting caught up in this CSI stuff.

"I'm not sure we can lead you to the exact spot," Kevin said. "At the time, the shot didn't have the same significance as it does now."

"A ballpark location will give us accurate enough results," Robin said. He produced a piece of paper from his pack, drew an x in one spot and a straight line about two inches away.

"This is the road." He pointed to the line. "This is where the shooter was." He pointed to the x. He made a triangle from the x to the road with a three-inch base. "Anywhere along here is pretty much the same distance apart. At least close enough for this test. You can find the spot within a couple of hundred yards, can you?"

"I guess so." Kevin looked at Victor. "What do you think?"

Victor looked at the drawing. "We can come that close."

Lorne turned the drawing to face him. He lettered the three points as A, B and C. Then he wrote AB<BC. "No problem," he said. "We can apply McCartney's Theorem to alleviate any variations." He winked at Robin. He was thinking of the song *Paper Back Writer*. Lorne could write it any way Robin wanted it.

No one questioned that this would indeed improve the calculation.

"What do you hope to accomplish by this?" Kevin asked. "Neither Victor nor I are really dressed for tromping through the woods, especially in all this snow. We both admit that we heard the shot."

Jim looked down at the feet of the two men. Both were wearing shiny black dress shoes. "We hope to verify two things. That you heard the shot and that the shot was indeed the one that killed Cliff Lawrence. Our whole time line is based on anecdotal evidence from you two. If you heard some other hunter shooting, then we are basing our whole investigation on an incorrect foundation. Cliff may have been shot an hour earlier or two or three hours later."

"The shot came from that direction," Kevin said.

"Sounds do funny things," Robin said. "They bounce off hills. They get absorbed. They echo. We'd like to record the evidence for ourselves."

"In that case, let's take the Commander. Do we need everyone along?" Kevin's eyes went from one cop to the other. His forehead was raised in a questioning gesture.

"No," Jim said. "The corporal and I will stay and look around here. See if we missed anything the last time around."

"Be my guest. All I ask is that if you move it, put it back. That's our deal."

"There's no reason for me to go along," Josh said. "Do you mind if I stay here?"

"That would be a good idea," Scott quickly said.

Jim looked at his partner. "Be my guest," he said to Josh.

Scott stood in the doorway and watched the other four men drive up the road. He then turned back into the room.

"Josh has another name for us to throw into the suspect pool. Tony Dellapinna."

"Tony Dellapinna?" Jim looked surprised.

"Do you know of him?" Scott asked.

"Small-time hood in his younger days. Seems to have gone straight and turned his life around. Quite successfully, I might add." Jim pulled out a kitchen chair and sat down. "I arrested him once for petty theft or something like that when I was a beat cop. Served his time and never caused any problems after that. What's his connection to all this?"

"He and Cliff grew up in the same neighbourhood," Josh said. He was disappointed at the sergeant's summation of Tony. That did not jive with his suspicions.

"And he provides the building supplies for the company?" Scott said.

"As well as being an investor," Josh added.

Jim looked from one to the other to see if there was more coming from this new information team. When the show appeared to be over, he focused his attention on Josh. "How well did he get along with Cliff? Did they fight, argue?"

Josh shook his head. "I don't know. I had never heard of him until after Cliff's death."

"You're the builder and you don't even know your own supplier?" Jim's words were heavily layered in skepticism.

"He owns the company. He's not the person we dealt with day to day."

"And his products?"

"A-1 quality. Competitively priced."

"That sounds like grounds for murder." He pointed to another chair and indicated that Josh should sit down. "Don't hold back on us. Why do you suspect Mr. Dellapinna?"

"I have my reasons," Josh said in a low voice. His eyes studied the pattern of the maple on the table.

"He thinks with a name like Tony Dellapinna that he's connected to the mob," Scott said.

Josh looked up. "No I don't. Not anymore. That's stupid."

"He did rise through the financial community in a hurry," Jim said. "Somebody must have been backing him in the beginning. There may be some old family ties that might bear looking into." He wrote the name in his notebook. He studied it for a few long minutes. After the time spent with Josh, Kevin and Victor, they were losing their appeal as suspects. He needed some new leads.

CHAPTER 46

BACK AT POLICE headquarters, Scott and Jim sat sipping black coffee. The snow had continued falling all through their fruitless search of the cabin the previous day. They decided there was nothing there important enough to risk getting stranded six miles back in the woods.

The decision to vacate the premises proved to be unanimous. Robin West's forensic van was not a four-wheel drive. The firing of the last squib changed nothing in his investigation file. The sound carried to their location with enough punch to put the dial back into the red area. They did not even have to apply McCartney's Theorem to adjust their results. He was convinced enough of the truth of Kevin's and Victor's stories that he abandoned the charade that the test could lead to some major breakthrough in the case.

On the trip out, Jim and Scott had also concluded that their original assessments of the three hunters were correct. They were not involved in the murder. Jim still reserved the option of keeping an ear to the ground about anything they might be up to. The killer was no fool. Jim did not intend for the killer to make a fool of him either, not a second time.

Both men opted for going home instead of back to the office. Later, radio traffic reports vindicated that decision. It didn't take much of a snowfall to screw up rush-hour traffic. The two cops had done their duty by not being a part of it.

Now they sat in Jim's office. It was approaching two o'clock on the following afternoon. The storm had passed. The roads were back to normal and the entire landscape had taken on a sparkling white hue. It was as if the two officers were starting with a clean slate.

"Do you think this Tony Dellapinna is worth a deeper look?" Scott asked.

"I've been running some preliminaries," Jim said. "I pulled his rap sheet. His last arrest was 15 years ago when I pulled him in. Was sentenced to two months. Served three weeks. Hasn't been a person of interest since. Makes me think I may have been a good influence in his life."

Scott laughed. "Gotta happen sometimes."

"A month or two later I was promoted to detective. The arrest worked out for both of us."

He held up a handful of photos. "I called the boys over in vice. They know who Tony is but only by association. It seems his family is still involved in drugs, petty theft, stuff like that. He still shows up at family functions. Gets in their surveillance pictures. Gets ruled out."

"We can choose our friends, but our family is thrust upon us."

"That's probably what he thinks. They see him giving money to various cousins, nieces and nephews, but the man is a multimillionaire. Why wouldn't he help out now and then? He's turned his life around. Maybe he's hoping that with a little help some of these guys can too."

"Do we know who gave him his initial break?"

Jim had a pile of photographs on his desk. He was looking through them as he talked. "No, not yet. I'm going to have the commercial crime guys give him a quick look. He got into the construction business at the same time of the big building boom of the '90s. It may have simply been lucky timing combined with hard work."

"Typical success story? Started with twenty bucks in his pocket and a smile on his face."

"Not quite. As I recall he started with two gravel trucks and a back hoe. I doubt the seed money came from a bank, at least not through regular channels. In those days the banks were throwing money at people like us with a regular income. As long as you could sign your name and say '16% interest, that doesn't sound too bad spread out over five years,' they'd cut you a cheque. A high school dropout whose top item on his resume was a stint in jail for petty theft might not excite a loans officer quite as much. While he was running his fledgling company, he found time to go back to school and get his degree. He has the Protestant work ethic, but someone must have been helping out."

"So he started out beholding to somebody?"

"Yeah. Now the big question is have they ever allowed him to repay that debt."

"Sometimes those early markers have no expiry date."

Jim sat there quietly for a few moments. He was looking through the pictures for someone who might hold power over Dellapinna. He threw them on the table and looked up at Scott. "I think I'll get them to look at the books of Kevin Barnhill's company as well. Somewhere, somebody wanted either Cliff Lawrence or Kevin Barnhill dead. It would be nice to know which one and why."

Scott reached down and picked up one of the photos. "These two dudes here at the barbecue." He pointed to two men standing out from the crowd in dark suits while everyone else wore casual clothes, shorts, T-shirts, golf shirts, definitely no ties.

"Checked them out too," Jim said. "Both played college football for SMU. Bigger of the two, a defensive lineman, tried out for Ottawa back when they were the Rough Riders. Unfortunately for him, that was the year the team folded. He got lost in the glut of seasoned players that were suddenly on the market. Came back home to Nova Scotia. Never got his degree."

"He's the chauffeur?" Jim asked. The man fit Josh Daniel's description of the man who stayed in the car.

Jim nodded. "The other guy had better luck. He was a second string running back. Got some field time, but not a lot. Knew that his career plans lay elsewhere. He's got his masters in business administration. Works as Dellapinna's personal assistant. They all went to school together at some point. Dellapinna's got his commerce degree."

"So we're not ruling Dellapinna out?"

"Not yet. At this point, anyone who ever spoke to Cliff Lawrence is worth a second look. Dellapinna seems to have pretty strong ties to the company."

Scott raised his eyes.

"The company has seven investors. Six of them meet at the end of each building season and commit x number of dollars for the next year. Pay that money, collect their dividends. Rejoice in their business brilliance. Meet again at the end of the next year. Repeat the process. If you have money to invest, Kevin Barnhill has never failed to pay his investors. It's a really good deal. Quality product, properly marketed."

"Dellapinna is the seventh?"

"Dellapinna is the seventh. He appears to make no year-end commitment but puts a steady stream of money into the company all season long. If Kevin needs funds, he makes a phone call. The payouts are harder to trace, but they must be there. That's why I am getting Commercial involved. This is all beyond me."

"Sounds more like a partner than an investor. When Josh Daniels brought up Dellapinna's name, he was elusive about his suspicions. I tried to push him, but had no success. I wonder what he knows."

"He's a carpenter. I wonder if he knows anything or just has suspicions. You'd think he would know all the partners. It's not that big of a company. Let's let Commercial have a look before we bring him in again."

Scott shrugged. "Okay. Where do we go in the meantime?"

CHAPTER 47

"**I** DON'T KNOW HOW it happened, but your name came up in the conversation."

"My name?" Tony Dellapinna gave Kevin Barnhill a long, hard look. "Why would my name come up?"

Kevin squirmed in his chair. They were sitting in a back corner of the Seahorse Tavern, a now half-empty pitcher of beer between them. The patrons at the nearby tables were fully engaged in the TV hockey game. The Leafs were leading the Canadiens by one goal with less than five minutes to go. Kevin had been reluctant to broach this topic with Tony. This was why. Tony would ask questions Kevin couldn't answer.

"They're the cops, man. They know things."

Tony leaned forward, closer to Kevin. His voice dropped to a mere whisper. "Not if everyone keeps their mouths shut."

Perspiration beaded across Kevin's forehead. "I sure as hell didn't say anything. They are the ones who brought your name up."

Tony reached out and patted Kevin's upper arm. A broad smile formed on his face showing his perfectly even, gleaming white, dentistry-enhanced teeth. "Relax, man." Tony leaned back in his chair. "Tell me exactly how the interrogation went."

Kevin tried to relax. Outwardly he succeeded. Inwardly he was scared.

"It wasn't an interrogation. The official police business had ended. We were chatting over coffee and debating if we wanted to get out of there before the storm got any worse. We kept trying to convince ourselves that this was a fluke snow squall. That we'd drive out of it as soon as we hit the main road. I don't know what more they had to do anyway. It seemed like they had done everything to me."

"Right. You were chatting about the weather. How did my name get into it?"

"The sergeant finally decided it was time to get out of Dodge. The snow wasn't letting up and the sergeant was worried about my tires. I don't know why. They've never let me down. I got up to clean out the coffee maker. But instead of leaving, he stayed seated at the table sipping the last of his coffee. Then he pulled out his notebook and started flipping casually through pages. Offhandedly, he asks 'Anybody know a Tony Dellapinna?' The question surprised me. I guess I reacted because he looked right at me."

"And you said, 'Never heard of him.' Right?"

Kevin could feel his guts tightening again. That was far from what he had said.

"He knew I knew the name. What could I say?"

"You tell me."

"Have I ever told you I'm a firm believer in telling the truth? That way you don't have to keep track of your lies. I said you were an investor with the company."

"So far, so good."

"Then he asked if you had any reason to want to kill me. Me. Not Cliff. Me." There was a tremble in Kevin's voice. "I told him the whole idea was preposterous."

"That might have been a little hasty," Tony said. He watched Kevin react. Tony laughed. He reached across the table and slapped Kevin on the shoulder. "I'm kidding. Why would I want to hurt a nice guy like you?"

Kevin took a short gulp of his beer.

"That's what I asked the cops. Why would they suggest you would kill anyone?"

"Where was everyone else during this…" Tony paused, "chat?"

"The two lab techs had left. The rest of us were there at the kitchen table."

"Did anyone else have anything to say?"

"Josh mentioned that we bought our building supplies from your company. He told me later, on the way home, that he figured the cops knew that already. They had to know something about you to link your name to the investigation. He didn't want to appear to be hiding anything. That would only arouse their suspicions. That made sense to me."

Tony topped up his beer glass and took a swig. "No harm done. My connections to you are all legitimate I'm wondering how my name came up in the first place."

"They're digging deep. Whoever the killer is made them look bad. First, they declared the death was an accident; then they have to reopen it as a homicide. They really want to catch this guy."

"Why did they open the case again? Did they say?"

"New information as the result of a different investigation. That's all they'd tell me."

A roar went up from the surrounding tables intermixed with exasperated groans from the few Leafs' fans in the bar. Montreal had just scored to tie the game with seconds left to play. Tony watched the replay before turning back to Kevin.

"I didn't have anything to do with Cliff's death so I shouldn't be worried. You either. It's just that I hate to have cops messing around in my business." He slid back his chair. "I'm going to go home and catch the overtime. Love to watch those Leafs get beat. Keep me informed of what the cops are doing."

CHAPTER 48

"WE HAVE A photo array we want you to look at."

Four men, Detective-Sergeant Jim Mcdonald, Corporal Scott Bowen, confessed killer Chris Ritchey and defence attorney Leon Goldstein were crowded into one of the small interrogation rooms at the Regional Corrections Facility in Dartmouth.

Chris was awaiting sentencing after confessing to the murder of Gerald Booth. Goldstein and the Crown attorney were still hammering out a sentencing agreement. Information presented to the Mounties about the murder of Cliff Lawrence had earned Chris a reduced sentence. The charge had been negotiated down to manslaughter. Now the dispute was over how many years of incarceration Chris would actually serve.

Chris had told his pastor that he was in no hurry to go before the judge. Every day served now would reduce his eventual sentence by two days. Chris was doing what most people only wished they could do. Putting time in the bank.

Pastor Dave visited Chris on a regular basis. He would not be met by St. Peter at the pearly gates and told: 'I was in prison and ye visited me not.' Pastor Dave took his obligations seriously, even to the least deserving in his parish, even to the murderers among them.

"Remember," Goldstein said, "Chris is doing this on his own accord. He is cooperating in this matter in any way he can."

Scott was still standing while the others sat at the small, cigarette-scarred table. "Yeah, yeah. We know. He's a great guy and we'll put in a good word with the judge."

Goldstein put on his best courtroom smile. In this small room, you could see that the eyes did not get in on the act. "One hand washes the other. What have you got?"

Jim tapped the two sheets of eight and a half by fourteen paper on the table. Underneath were six pictures. Victor Boyd, Kevin Barnhill,

Josh Daniels and Tony Dellapinna were joined by two plainclothes detectives who worked with Jim.

"I want you to study these photos and tell us if you recognize any of them as being the man you saw target practising that day in the woods. Take your time. There's no rush. They will be dressed in a different style of clothing than what you saw that day. Don't let that deter you." He looked up at Chris. "Any questions?"

Jim thought he could detect a look of doubt in Chris's eyes. After a moment, Chris shook his head.

Jim noticed lawyer Goldstein lean closer. A positive identification would strengthen his bargaining position. Jim wondered if Chris understood how much was at stake with this exercise. Jim removed the two sheets of legal paper. He saw an immediate flicker of recognition in Chris's eyes. One of these men was familiar to him.

Seconds ticked by as Chris looked at first one picture and then another. Jim noticed two things. Chris was consciously ignoring one picture and he had smiled slightly at another one. Jim wasn't sure if it was the middle picture in the top row or the middle picture in the bottom row that Chris was avoiding. The evasion was not because Chris had discounted the picture. It was because the image had some meaning to him.

Victor Boyd's picture had caused the glint of a smile. After that first glance, Chris had not paid any special attention to it. However, the avoidance was not of the same intensity as the avoidance of the other picture.

"Can I touch the pictures?" Chris asked.

Victor, Kevin and Tony all had on shirts and ties.

Lorne Dauphinee had secretly taken the pictures of Victor and Kevin that day at Kevin's cabin. They had both been whisked away from their offices and wore their usual business attire, blue pin-stripped suits and power ties. Josh's picture had also been snapped that day. He wore a dark blue work shirt under a quilted red vest. Tony's picture had come from a newspaper clipping when he was addressing city hall over a building code change. He had dressed up for the occasion. The two detectives had posed for their pictures. Over posed, Jim thought. The hard stares and fierce scowls on their faces made Charles Manson look like a choirboy.

"Go ahead," Jim said. "Anything that helps. Which of these men look familiar?"

Chris placed his fingers over the lower parts of the pictures cutting off the dress suits. "They look different dressed like this."

Scott reached forward and picked up one of the sheets of paper. He folded it once lengthwise, looked at it and then folded it again. He picked up the other sheet and repeated the actions. Then he lay them across the pictures leaving only the faces revealed. "Does that help?"

Chris made a minor adjustment to the top row and nodded in agreement. "Much better," he said. Again he studied each individual picture.

Scott took a chair beside Jim. He lowered his head so that he could see into Chris's eyes and Chris into his. "I've done this many times," Scott said. "I know when someone is stalling for time. Which man is the one you suspect?"

"I'm not sure. I wasn't that close to the man in the woods. He was acting strangely. I didn't want him to see me so I kept my distance. At the time, I didn't know he was practising to murder someone. I didn't know I would be interrogated about his appearance."

Goldstein leaned back in his chair, a look of disappointment on his face. Chris looked over at him. "I can't be absolutely positive."

"Come on, Chris," Scott said, "as soon as the sergeant removed that paper, I could see a look of recognition in your eyes. Which man caused that?"

Chris shook his head. He remained silent.

Jim let out a deep breath. "We'll settle for someone who looks close, maybe not close enough to testify about in court but close enough to give us a lead as to whom we might want to be concentrating on."

Jim waited for some sort of reaction from Chris. "I'm going to be honest with you," Jim said. "What you have given us is useless. If you don't want your deal to fall through, you'd better try a little harder."

"You can't renege now," Goldstein said. "The deal has been struck."

"We'll see," Jim said. He didn't believe Chris was having any trouble with the identification. There was some other factor coming into play. "Are you afraid of someone in one of these pictures? We're not going to announce to the man that you picked him out of a lineup. He's not going to come after you."

Chris thought about that for a few seconds. "What if we end up in the same prison? How will you protect me then?"

"I won't let that happen," Goldstein said. His hopes had been raised again. "We'll make it part of our agreement. He'll end up in a penitentiary somewhere doing hard time. We'll get you in a medium-security facility or less. He'll never get near you."

Chris's attention turned back to Goldstein. A smile formed on the lower part of his face. The eyes remained worried. "Unless he gets a lawyer as brilliant as you."

Jim couldn't argue with that logic. Simply being guilty, even for murder, didn't guarantee you would get your deserved punishment. The proof of that sat across the table from him. "You point out the man you saw. We'll protect your identity."

"Okay," Chris said. "I'll hold you to that, but I think I'll put my faith in my Lord for my safety. His will will be done."

Scott groaned.

Chris reached out his hand.

Jim concentrated on the two middle pictures. He knew one of these would be the choice and he figured he knew which one. The top photo was Kevin Barnhill; the bottom was Tony Dellapinna. Chris hesitated slightly then touched the top picture.

Scott slid back his chair and stood up. "You've got to be kidding. This man weighs at least 220 pounds, probably more." He pulled his notebook from his pocket, searched through some pages, then glared at Chris. "You described your man as weighing between 160 and 170 pounds, walks with a limp. This is bullshit."

"Sit down, Scott," Jim said. He looked back at Chris. There was no hiding the contempt in his look. "What the corporal says is true. You're either lying to us now or you were lying when you gave us the other description. The two stories don't go together."

Chris's face instantly bled red up from the collar of his shirt. He looked surprised at the policemen's reaction.

"You're blushing," Scott said. "You've been caught in a red-faced lie. Pun intended."

"No. No." Chris was stammering. "I told you I wasn't sure. The man was too far away to see clearly. And as to being wrong about the weight, I'm a farmer. I guess the weight of cows, not men. Anything under 400 pounds and I get a little shaky in my accuracy." Confidence was returning to Chris's voice. He tapped Kevin's picture twice. "This looks like the man I saw. If it's not him, I'm sorry. That's the best I can do."

"What about the limp?" Scott asked. "I can assure you this man does not limp."

"Who the hell knows?" Chris's religious veneer was slipping. "He may have twisted his ankle that day on his way in. It might have been better in a week, even the same day. I don't know."

Jim held up his hands. "Everyone settle down." He had come into this room not expecting much. Proper procedure told him to show pictures of his suspects to his only witness. The flicker of knowledge in Chris's eyes when he first looked at the photos had raised his hopes. Scott's as well, it seemed. There was one thing Jim was sure of. Chris recognized someone in that photo array. Maybe it was Kevin, maybe not. The two men looked at him, glared once more at each other and remained silent.

"You're sure this is the man you recognize?" Jim asked once more.

Chris shook his head. "I'm not sure of anything. He looks familiar for some reason or other. If you say he can't be the man in the woods, then maybe I saw him somewhere else. Who is he anyway?"

"That's not important. I want to thank you for being cooperative." Jim looked over at the lawyer. "We'll be sure to mention that to the Crown."

Leon Goldstein gave a slight shrug. The message was clear. Goldstein had no control over anything Chris might say or do.

Jim signalled towards the door and two guards came in to take Chris back to his cell. Goldstein followed him down the hall. The two were whispering together.

"I'm sorry, Jim," Scott said. "There's something about that guy that pushes my buttons. I don't like him. I don't believe him."

Jim made a dismissive gesture with his hand. "He's not the kind of guy you want for a neighbour. Gerald Booth is testimony to that fact."

"Right. What about his ID of Barnhill? Think there's anything to that?"

"Like he said, he must have seen him somewhere else. Barnhill can't be that good of a shooter without someone knowing something about it. We'll check him out, again. Let's get out of this place. It gives me the creeps."

CHAPTER 49

CLIFFORD OICKLE LOOKED like an accountant. His complexion nearly matched the white, starched shirt showing through the opening of his dark gray suit. His thick, dark-rimmed glasses suggested that Clifford's days of 20-20 vision were a distant memory, maybe even beyond memory. The large, green eyes with brown specks that were magnified through the lenses declared someone whose attention to detail would approach that of a compulsive-obsessive. He had piano player fingers. Jim imagined they would dance over the keys of an adding machine.

"You realize that without probable cause and warrants, I can't do a thorough analysis of Anthony Dellapinna's holdings."

The timbre of Clifford's voice and his slow, meticulous way of speaking told Jim that most people probably didn't understand what they were being told when Clifford started rattling off numbers. He sounded like a kindergarten teacher. He most likely had to rephrase and explain himself so often that he overcompensated and tried too hard to simplify things.

"I understand that," Jim said. "I also understand that you are the best in the business. If anyone can sneak in through a back door, it's you."

These words created a flicker of a smile on Clifford's face. Even with his computer-like mind, he wasn't above a bit of flattery.

"My understanding was that you wanted to know two things. Where did Dellapinna get his startup cash and what is his current connection to Kevin Barnhill's development company."

He looked at Jim for confirmation. Jim gave him a subtle nod.

"The first part was easy. He walked into a truck dealership, told them what he wanted and negotiated a repayment program based solely on his signature. Then he put the trucks up as collateral for the back hoe."

Jim was astounded. This was exactly what he had told Scott could not happen. "GMAC financed his trucks?"

"On the recommendation of the dealership loans officer, yes."

"I don't believe it."

"It's true. The dealership has changed hands a couple of times since then, but there is one salesman still there. I talked with him. He didn't really remember any of the specifics but vaguely recalls the event. Mostly he recalls that he didn't get the sale. It was up for grabs to the first salesman who stepped forward. Easy money. Most of them ignored the young Dellapinna.

"According to rumour, a couple of muscle men in black suits had visited the dealership earlier in the day. They apparently made an offer the loans officer couldn't refuse. The salesman's words. When Dellapinna walked in, all the preliminary work was done. All any salesman had to do was shake his hand and put in the call to the loans guy. The paperwork may have been a little sketchy but it went through without a hitch."

Oickle shrugged. "I guess these things happen."

"Here's the thing. Dellapinna never missed a payment. Both loans were fully repaid and on time. The rest is history, as they say."

Jim shrugged. "Once you have a good credit rating and rolling stock to back it up, there's no end to how much you can borrow. Did I tell you I saved him from a life of crime?"

Clifford stared at Jim for a few seconds. Then the corners of his mouth came up slightly to nearly form a smile. "That's a joke, right?" he asked.

"Apparently not, but it was an attempt."

The near smile disappeared. Clifford shuffled the papers in front of him and brought another one to the top. "The second part of your request proved a little more difficult. No one at Dellapinna's company, bank or any of his business associates wanted to discuss anything to do with the company with me. That's not entirely unusual. That's why we have warrants. But, as I said, I had no grounds to get a warrant."

Jim's face must have shown his disappointment.

"Then I realized that we are investigating a murder. I should have access to Cliff Lawrence's financial dealings. His family had no objections when I told them I was trying to track down Cliff's killer.

"What you wanted was the relationship between Dellapinna and the development company. Cliff Lawrence was a principle partner in the development company. Voilà. I was in."

"Great. I knew if anyone could do it, you could."

"Not so fast. I didn't give these books a full fledged audit. There doesn't appear to be any need for that. Dellapinna has a unique relationship with the development company. His interests are tied up with his building supply business. He is the principal supplier. It's in his best interest to keep Kevin Barnhill and his boys in the black.

"You told me that he and Cliff Lawrence were boyhood friends. Dellapinna has been along for the ride since the beginning. If it were not for these two facts, I would raise a few red flags about his involvement with the company. He is making emotional investment decisions instead of strictly logical ones. He doesn't appear to always be getting the return that he should on his money. I see that happen time and time again in family concerns.

"Mr. Dellapinna seems to have a vested interest in keeping this small development company profitable. Early friendships sometimes lead to bad business decisions."

"Kevin Barnhill told me they are like one big family. So Dellapinna is losing money with them."

"Heavens no. No one is losing money there. He just could be making more somewhere else. But, it's not like he needs any more." Clifford made a dismissive gesture as if money were of no concern. "Is he involved with the murder of Cliff Lawrence? I can't say one way or the other. I can only say with a reasonable certainty that if he is, it has nothing to do with money."

Jim's shoulders sagged. It was not that Tony Dellapinna looked like a good candidate for the murder. It was simply that no one else did either. He was back to square one.

He looked at the calendar on his desk. How many more days before those kids got back from Alberta? Had Darrin Eisenhauer and his friends seen some stranger in the woods? Even that was a long shot. They may have been nowhere near the target range behind their houses. They may have done their shooting in their own backyards. There was plenty of room.

CHAPTER 50

STELLA MARTIN STACKED the empty supper plates into a pile and slid them to one end of the table. She held the wine bottle, a red Bordeaux, up to the light and then poured an even amount into each of their glasses.

"It amazes me how you can do that every time," Jim said. "I bet there's not a millilitre difference in the contents of those glasses."

Stella gave an indifferent shrug. "Old family tradition. One divides, the other chooses. You learn to make sure the results are close to perfect."

"I guess you would. Someone did that to the case I'm working on."

"Split it in two?"

"Sort of. I'm not sure the victim was the intended target. I think the wrong man got killed."

"There's a lot of that going on. Isn't that what happened to the old farmer? It's just like everything. The world's going to hell in a hand basket. No one works as hard as they used to. Nothing's made as good. Murderers aren't as competent as they once were." She laughed. The effects of more than a half bottle of red wine were being felt. Jim had not kept pace with her. The first few times, she simply topped up the glasses. She had the lion's share of the wine. "If they got the wrong guy the first time, you would think the killer would try again."

Jim was toying with his wine glass, obviously lost in thought. He looked at Stella. "We got the man who shot the old farmer the same day. He didn't get another kick at the can. But the other case, we declared that an accident for almost a month. It should have been open season on Kevin Barnhill."

"I remember. We had a celebratory dinner when the case was initially closed. Maybe you're wrong about the intended victim."

"If that's true, I know who the killer is. Josh Daniels. He's the only one who knew Cliff Lawrence would be in that tree. On every other occasion when these men hunted together, Kevin Barnhill sat in that tree stand. He owned the hunting lodge. The change was a last-minute thing."

Stella raised her glass in a toast-like gesture. "Well, there you go. We can celebrate again. Case closed."

Jim couldn't suppress his smile. Stella was not a frequent drinker. It did not take much to set her off. When it happened, she was a friendly drunk. He liked that.

"Knowing and proving are two different things. To add to the confusion, he keeps throwing red herrings into the mix. New suspects that look good enough to actually cause us to investigate them.

"And our witness is not a lot of help. He can't keep his story straight. First the killer weighed in at 160, then he shot up to 220. The guilt must have caused his weight to balloon in a month, I guess. I'm thinking accidental looked like a better conclusion."

Stella giggled. "Well you know what they say. Three wrongs make a right."

Jim looked perplexed. "What?"

Stella finished off her wine. "Oh no, that's three lefts make a right." She laughed again.

She set her glass on the table. The sparkle drained from her eyes. "Do you have protection around Kevin Barnhill? His life could be at risk."

"I'm not sure enough that he's in danger to justify the expense. I have advised him what I think. Hopefully he's taking precautions on his own."

"Why wouldn't the killer have tried again? He must know he got the wrong man."

Jim took a sip of his wine before answering. "The first murder took a great deal of planning. We were fooled into thinking it was an accident. Either he's working on a new plan or he realizes that a second attempt too soon wouldn't fool us again. He could be out there simply biding his time. It all depends on why he wants Kevin Barnhill dead."

"Or he got hit by a car, or arrested for something else, or had a heart attack. These things happen to people every day. If some act of nature intervened, you may never solve this case."

"Thanks. That makes me feel so much better."

"I'm only telling you not to get lost in this case like you tend to do. Life goes on. Somewhere out there, you might find a semi-intoxicated young lady who wants to get into your pants. And if you have your head buried in your work during your off-duty hours, you might miss a great opportunity."

Jim's eyes came alive. "If only I could be that lucky." He downed the rest of his wine. "These dishes can wait. That's what dish washers are for, anyway." He reached across the table and took her hand, helping her to her feet.

"At your service, Madame."

CHAPTER 51

"**Y**OU LOOK TO be in particularly fine form this morning," Scott Bowen said as he walked into Jim Mcdonald's cubicle at the Halifax headquarters of the RCMP.

Jim had his feet resting on the extended, second drawer of his desk and was leaning back in his desk chair. Balanced on his thighs was a steaming cup of coffee, held in place by his right hand. Some sort of report filled his left hand. A smile stretched across his face. He appeared to be watching the dwindling rush-hour traffic outside his window, but his eyes were not capturing any of the moving images.

He allowed his chair to rotate slightly towards the door and lifted his mug to acknowledge Scott's presence. "Looking at the world with a new perspective," he said. "There's more to life than solving murder cases."

Scott hesitated in the doorway. Then he reached out and picked up the nameplate on the sergeant's desk. He brought it up to his eyes and studied it closely. "Yep, right office. Let me guess. You're talking about robberies, drug dealing, frauds. There is a whole other world out there besides murders."

"I'm talking about people you love, reading books, watching television."

"Television? You mean Law and Order 1, 2, 3 and 4; CSI 1, 2 and 3?"

Jim laughed. "Stella was over last night and…"

Scott held up both hands. "Say no more, say no more. I don't want the gory details."

Jim dropped his feet to the floor. "She says that sometimes you have to step back from these complicated cases. Look at them with a new perspective."

"That's the phrase of the day?"

Jim's eyebrows went up.

"New perspective?"

"What she says makes sense. This is a sophisticated killer. He's put a lot of work into this job. We both agree on that. Now that we're looking so hard for him, Stella says he'll just hunker down. Keep a low profile or maybe leave the jurisdiction for a while."

"No arguments here."

"Assuming that his beef was with Kevin Barnhill or possibly even with Cliff Lawrence, although I don't believe that, then he's not an immediate threat to anyone else. We'll keep an eye on Barnhill. Try to keep him safe and observe any strange goings-on around him."

"Has he agreed to this?"

"We're not going to tell him. I've assigned the task to a couple of other detectives. You and I are going to work on other things." He gave the sheaf of papers in his hand a little wave. "The killer will think we've stepped the case down."

"So we're using Barnhill as bait?"

"If Kevin Barnhill was the intended target, his life is at risk anyway. We are not adding to that risk. If the rest of the team is alert, we will save his life. The team knows what's at stake. This is Barnhill's best chance and our best chance of catching the killer."

Scott sat down in the other chair across from Jim's desk. His lips twitched as if he was searching for the proper words. "I know we can't make these cases personal. I do know that. But, I would really like to be in on catching this guy."

Jim held up his hands. "I understand that. That's where the new perspective comes in. You and I have to be willing to step back for the good of the case. We don't know who the killer is. We've run out of leads, but the killer knows who we are. He's able to track our every move. He may even see to it that we are being fed false information." Jim's eyes brightened. "In fact, if he thinks we've lost interest, he may even contact us."

"Why would he do that?"

"He put a lot of work into this. He may be enjoying his moment in the sun."

Scott shook his head. "I think he's smarter than that. This whole thing was put together to look like an accident. I don't think he wants any investigation. I think he'll be happy if we just go away."

"And that's what we're going to make him think. If the undercover boys discover anything that needs immediate action, we'll be brought back in. We will still be the face of the police investigation. I'll still get regular reports."

"And me? What will my role be?"

Jim smirked. "There's always an opening here in this office for you." He threw the report on the table in Scott's direction. "There are no shortages of cases to work on."

Scott stood up and went over to the window. The snow on the lawns was becoming a memory. Along the sides of the road, it was looking dingy and dirty. "You know my feelings about that. You can have the boredom of this office and its paper shuffling. The Lawrence case is something else altogether. I've been involved from the beginning. I want to be in at the end."

He turned and faced Jim. "In fact, I was thinking about this last night. How drunk was Josh Daniels? Did he really know that Cliff Lawrence and Kevin Barnhill had decided to change hunting locations? He may have thought that Barnhill was in that blind.

"We've been giving him a pass because we can't find a motive for killing Cliff Lawrence. Kevin Barnhill was the money man. We both know that money matters trump logic. If Barnhill was the intended victim, as we believe, then Josh Daniels may have thought that was who he was shooting. He may have been as surprised as hell when his good buddy, Kevin, stepped through that cabin door at noon."

Jim's face showed he was caught up in the story that Scott was spinning. He was about to respond, then he hesitated. "Stop, Scott. Don't you see? That's exactly what I'm talking about. We have been letting this dominate our lives. We spend as much time thinking about it when we're off duty as we do when we're on duty. Both of us agreed Josh is innocent. Now we're bending the facts to fit the outcome we're hoping for. " He pointed a finger at his sometime partner. "We're moving on to other things. At least for now."

Scott covered the distance from the window to the desk in two strides. He leaned towards the sergeant. "No I don't see. This is how cases get solved. You plug away at them every waking hour. Then you go to bed and let your subconscious take over. You keep doing this until you get a breakthrough. That's known as police work."

Jim sat, slowly shaking his head. He understood Scott's frustration. This killer, whoever he was, had made the department look bad. "I understand what you're saying, but we're stepping back from this case. I've already discussed this with the Inspector. He agrees."

Again, he picked up the papers from the desk and waved them in Scott's face. "This is my new case. You're welcome to join me. I can always use your help."

"Not friggin' likely." Scott walked to the doorway, then turned back to face Jim. "You must have had one hell of a fun evening."

"Wait, Scott. We're not off the case. This is a different tactic. When something new comes up, we're right back in the middle of it. In the meantime," Jim shrugged his shoulders, "let's see what shakes out when it looks like we've let it go cold."

Scott eyes studied the floor in front of the desk. "I know. I just want to catch this guy bad, really bad." He looked up at Jim. "Relax. We're still good."

Jim only smiled. Then he said. "Last night? It was good. It gave me a new perspective."

CHAPTER 52

"**H**AVE YOU HEARD from the cops since the day we were out at your cabin?"

Josh Daniels, Kevin Barnhill and Victor Boyd sat in the dimly lit corner of a small neighbourhood pub built in one of their own subdivisions. The area catered to the middle-aged blue-collar crowd. Their kids were growing up but still hadn't left home. Next door was the community centre which provided activities for people in their teens all the way up to people looking forward to that first old age pension cheque.

It was a place where you could have a beer after work and still make it home in time for supper. Or, you could walk down after supper, have a few ales, watch the game and not have to worry about driving back home. In time, it would become a place where everyone knew your name. That was the hope of the owners who were the three men sitting in the corner. It was part of their extended empire. So far, they were not losing money on any of the pubs in the older subdivisions. Those in the new ones would eventually establish themselves. Until that time, they would be carried by the owners.

Kevin looked at Josh. "Not a word. It's like we've been given a clean bill of health and they've moved on to search in other directions."

"What about those questions they were asking about Tony Dellapinna? Do you think Tony is involved?"

Kevin thought about that before answering. He remembered his conversation with Tony the other night. "You don't give up, do you? I honestly don't think he had anything to do with it. I think Tony's as baffled as we are by the whole thing."

"What about the upcoming building season? Is he still in?"

That was the big question. Even though Kevin figured they could get by without an investment from Tony Dellapinna, his money certainly gave them a lot more options. But, Tony was involved in money-laundering through their company, this would be a good time to break the bonds. Unfortunately, that was a decision Tony would make. Not Kevin. Not Josh.

Kevin, personally, wanted the investment. What he didn't want was to have dissension among the members of the executive team. He, Josh and now Victor worked too well together to break up the unit.

"The last time I was talking to him, he was. Tony is a businessman. Supplying materials for the number of houses we are putting up every year makes good business sense. Investing in our company, even more. Let's face it, gentlemen," and here he smiled at the other two, "we are a hot commodity."

Josh returned the smile. "I hope so. Things go more smoothly with his company than any I've ever worked with. Ronald Sutherland runs the outfit like the operating system on a Mac. There are no bugs."

Kevin raised his glass. "To keeping out the bugs."

The other two men followed suit, Josh with a beer, Victor with a glass of orange juice.

"Still swilling that OJ?" Kevin asked. "Too much vitamin C gives you yellow pee."

Victor responded by raising his glass again. "To yellow pee and a healthy lifestyle."

"Why not?" Josh said and joined in the toast. Kevin complied.

"I know who Tony Dellapinna is," Victor said, "but who is Ronald Sutherland?"

Josh reached out a hand and patted Victor on the shoulder. "Just another worker bee like you and me. Like we do all the scutwork for Kevin, Ron does it for Tony. He's our building supplies agent."

Victor nodded as if he understood. He was only used to working with the finished product. He knew the houses were well built. He knew they sold quickly. As far as he was concerned, that information gave him a complete education. There was nothing else he needed to know.

Kevin gave him a searching look, wishing he could find more depth in the man. Cliff, he thought, you don't know how much you are missed.

CHAPTER 53

S COTT BOWEN WALKED into the airport Tim Hortons and looked around. Jim Mcdonald was sitting in the far corner away from the windows. His hand was raised as if he wanted permission from the teacher to leave the room. When he realized Scott had seen him, he gave a little come-hither flick with his fingers.

"Is there a breakthrough in the case?" Scott asked. Jim had been sending him daily updates on the progress of the undercover detectives, but they could hardly be called progress reports. This was their first face-to-face meeting in two weeks.

Scott had been back on highway patrol, a job he much preferred over playing detective and Jim had enough outstanding cases to keep a squadroom of detectives busy. Major crimes was not a division for someone who didn't want to work hard.

Jim pointed to a medium-sized cup of coffee on the table across from him. "Black, just the way you like it."

Scott sat down. He looked over at the line from the counter, snaking through the coffee shop and out onto the concourse. Thanks," he said. "Flights delayed?"

Jim shook his head. "No, just the menfolk coming home from Alberta for a week of R&R. Everyone on the plane will have someone excited to see them again after their three-week absence."

"Ah, that explains why we're here. The prodigal sons return."

"The Eisenhauer family is waiting at the arrival gate. They were here when I pulled in 30 minutes ago. Mrs. Eisenhauer had tears flowing down her face then."

"Oh great." A disgusted look formed on Scott's face. He turned and faced in the direction of the soon-to-be-arriving passengers. From this vantage point, he was unable to see the waiting relatives. He didn't need to. He had made airport pickups before. He knew the confrontation with the parents would be greater than the confrontation with Darrin Eisenhauer.

He remembered Mrs. Eisenhauer's surly attitude when they first met three weeks previously. She was not the kind of person who listened to reason. She was not the kind of person who listened at all.

"Have you alerted the entire airport contingent to be standing by?"

Jim's smile lit up his face. His eyes twinkled. "Better," he said. "We're going to meet the boys on the other side of the security barrier. I've arranged a room on the second floor for a quick interview. It shouldn't take long. Either they saw someone target practising in an unorthodox manner or they didn't. If they did, we'll see how their description lines up with that of Chris Ritchey. If not, their parents will not even know they were delayed."

"You think we can do it that quickly?"

"I've arranged for an officer to follow the last passenger down the steps into the arrival lounge. If the boys don't show up a couple of minutes behind them, he'll tell the parents they've been delayed on the upper floor and will be along shortly."

Scott snorted. "Is he being punished for some indiscretion? Mrs. Eisenhauer will tear him a new one if the boys are delayed more than 20 seconds."

"If there's any trouble, he'll move the families into one of the interview rooms on the first floor." Jim winked. "Then lock the door and leave them in there."

Scott looked up at the overhead television announcing the status of departures and arrivals. Flight 807 from Calgary was not due for another 20 minutes. He sipped his coffee. Jim had a blue folder lying on the little table. "What's in the folder? Pictures?"

"I keep telling you it's time for you to get out of your cruiser and into the detective branch. You're a natural at it." Jim flipped the cover open and turned the contents so that Scott could get a better look.

"These are new pictures the undercover boys took. No suits. No ties."

Scott looked closer. "No camouflage either."

Casual shots of Kevin Barnhill, Tony Dellapinna and Victor Boyd had been added to the portfolio. The two detectives in the mug shots still looked like serial killers. Josh Daniels still wore his red vest and blue shirt.

"I thought of that," Jim said. "A few minutes with photo shop and we could have had them all looking like they were doing a stint in Afghanistan." He gave a short grunt and turned his palms upwards. "But you know those damn defence attorneys. They frown on doctored photos."

"So we're going to show them a photo array and see if anyone looks familiar? You think the boys may have seen some stranger in the area? Nobody I talked to remembers seeing a big, black SUV anywhere in Raymond's River. No one but Chris Ritchey."

"We'll see if they saw anyone in the woods first. Both Tony Dellapinna and Josh Daniels match the description given by Chris Ritchey, even if Ritchey didn't pick them out of our little lineup. His choice of Kevin Barnhill baffles me."

"Well, you know what I think of Chris Ritchey."

"I know, but these boys might remember seeing the SUV. The fact that the local farmers and housewives don't remember seeing it doesn't mean it wasn't there. It means it didn't register on their subconscious. It's not something they would realistically have an interest in. Now boys in their late teens, early twenties, they could visualize themselves driving something like that. Even more so if they had a job lined up in the oil fields and had prospects of making big money."

Jim took a sip of his coffee. "They would have their dreams; we must have ours."

"And ours involve new witnesses and new leads?"

"You got it."

Scott looked at his watch. "We'd better get moving if we want to get through security and come out on the other side still armed with our pistols. My uniform will help me, but you, are you one of the guys in that photo array?" He laughed.

"All the palms have been greased. I didn't spend that first half-hour sitting here drinking coffee. Aim for that door over there." Jim pointed towards a steel door marked security.

CHAPTER 54

JIM AND SCOTT stood at the end of the disembarkment passageway attached to the 737 that had just flown in from Alberta. They had asked airport officials to deplane Darrin Eisenhauer and his friends ahead of everyone else. Jim was sure that caused some unrest among the other passengers, especially those who liked to be standing in the aisle digging their carry-on luggage from the overhead compartment while the plane was still taxiing down the runway.

At first the officials had been reluctant to cooperate. They had to prepare the plane for a quick turnaround and wanted as few hassles as possible. When Jim told them it was part of a murder investigation, they quickly changed their minds. Jim did not elaborate. He simply let the imaginations of the airline personnel take them wherever they wanted to go. Even Jim didn't know of the extreme influence the upcoming interview was going to have on the case.

A small office was made available behind the check-in counter. Two uniformed Mounties herded the boys into it amid vocal protests. These were not the same kids who left Nova Scotia three weeks ago. These were oilsands workers. They had money to burn and attitude to go with it. The Mounties remained unimpressed.

"Look man, you can't be hassling us anymore. We don't even live here now. We live in the Big Mac."

Jim looked up at Darrin Eisenhauer. He gave him a world-weary smile. The kid had the world by the tail. His wallet was crammed full of cash, folding money Jim's father used to call it, probably for the first time in Darrin's short life. Jim had seen it all before. Sudden apparent wealth, followed by real-life massive spending. Jim wondered if the new truck was ordered yet back in the "Big Mac". He smiled at the misnomer. "Fort Mac" was the generally accepted nickname for Fort McMurray, Canada's oilsands capital.

He looked the boys up and down. He wondered what a search for drugs would yield.

He dismissed these thoughts. What he really wanted to know was if Darrin had seen the mysterious shooter target-practising out behind Darrin's house. Another quirk of geography put the Eisenhauer homestead less than half a mile from the target range. The hills protected the house from the bullets but the sounds carried to the upper windows. Scott had seen the complaints filed with the department, although he had never responded personally.

Little had been done to alleviate the problem. While it was the women worried about their kids who made the complaints, it was the men who answered the doors and thought the Mounties should mind their own business about a normal rural practice. Go catch some real criminals, they were told.

"Sit down Mr. Eisenhauer. This won't take long. We just have a couple of quick questions for you."

Darrin slumped into the chair. "It had better not. My mother is waiting for me downstairs and she told me not to linger when I got off the plane. I thought she was the one who got us off first."

There would be a can of worms, Jim thought. Let the waiting mothers determine the order the passengers got off the plane. There wouldn't be enough Mounties in the county to handle those riots.

"Your Momma was partly responsible," Jim said. "We knew she was waiting and we didn't want to hold you up any longer than necessary. Your cooperation will speed this along."

Darrin said nothing. He gave Jim an expectant look. It was good to see that he still feared his mother. Maybe she would have some influence on how he handled his newfound wealth.

"You and your friends target shoot at that range behind your house?"

"Used to, when we still lived here. It's not against the law." Darrin was an Albertan now.

"Did you ever see anything unusual back there? Other people shooting targets?" Jim wanted to get to the crux of the matter without putting words into Darrin's mouth. The boy was liable to tell them anything just to get out of there.

Darrin looked at his friends. They all nodded. "There was one time a couple of months before we left."

Scott Bowen, who had been standing in one corner of the room came closer. "What did you see?" he asked.

One of the other boys spoke up first. "The dude was shooting through a piece of deer hide. Had it on a roll and kept moving it with every shot."

Scott slid into a chair beside the desk. Jim could see that Scott shared his own thought. This was more than they could have hoped for.

"Don't know what the big deal is," Darrin said. "You've already arrested the guy. My Dad told me last week when I called home. Said he murdered Gerald Booth."

Jim's hopes sagged. He could hear Scott sliding back his chair again. Scott got to his feet and reached out and touched Darrin's shoulder. "I think you have two separate incidences confused. Who do you think you saw?

Darrin shrugged off Scott's hand. His voice took on a sullen tone. "I'm not confused. It was Chris Ritchey, farmer from up the road. Best shooter in the whole country. I've seen his trophies."

"Let's everyone relax here," Jim said. "Chill out."

Scott looked at him and smiled. He mouthed the words "Chill out?"

"Did you ever see anyone but Mr. Ritchey back there target-practising?"

"Sure, lots of times, but it was Chris that was shooting through the deer hide."

"Chris? You knew him well enough to call him Chris?"

Again Darrin looked at his friends for support. "We used to go shooting with him all the time. He's a Canadian champion, you know. He taught us how to use a rifle." He held up his hand and smiled. "Don't tell my dad that. He thinks he taught me. But it was Chris who really showed me how to shoot, how to hold the rifle, how to breathe, when to breathe. 'Caress the trigger, don't pull it' he would say. Those were the good, old days."

Jim suppressed a smile. "The good, old days? When you saw him that day in the woods shooting, did you talk to him?"

"No way, José. We don't hang with him anymore. Not since he got religion."

The others nodded. The taller of the three spoke up. "Every time you see him now, he has one thing on his mind. 'Have you found Jesus in your life? Have you been saved?' The guy turned into a real nut case."

"I like Chris," Darrin said. "I really do. But this religion thing is like a sickness with him. It's all he talks about now. I was surprised to see him back there shooting. He had told me that firing a gun was contrary to the teachings of Jesus. I told him: 'Whatever,' but that didn't stop him from trying to convert me. So now, anytime we see him anywhere, we hightail it the other way."

Darrin was silent for a few seconds. His voice seemed a little older when he resumed speaking. "I have nothing against church. I go every Christmas, Easter and on my mother's birthday. Chris wanted me to go two or three times a week. That wasn't going to happen."

"But, you're sure it was Chris that was shooting through the deer hide?" Scott still wanted reassurance.

"Positive. He used to practise all the time, but he was so good he had to do things to make it more challenging. He would try to graze a full can of pop without making it leak or shoot through a hole in a board at something behind it. He learned to shoot in the army, you know. He was a commando or something. It was a big secret. I wasn't supposed to tell anyone about it."

Darrin looked over at his two friends. "I couldn't even tell you guys."

He shrugged. "We thought this was some new challenge he had dreamed up."

Scott turned to the sergeant. "JTF2. I checked I out."

Jim simply raised his eyebrows before turning his attention back to Darrin.

"What kind of weapon was he using?"

"Bigger than a .22 but smaller than a hunting rifle. You know, like one of those army rifles they use in the movies."

Both officers nodded at this infomration. Jim flipped open the folder on the desk. "Do any of these people look familiar to any of you?"

The boys crowded around the table. The tall one pointed to one of the detectives. "I think I saw him on America's Most Wanted."

CHAPTER 55

ONCE AGAIN JIM and Scott were drinking dark, bitter, instant coffee in Jim's small crowded office. They were still reeling from the information given to them by Darrin Eisenhauer.

"Why would Ritchey tip us off about the murder if he did it?" Scott asked. "I know he's crazy, but that doesn't make any sense at all."

Jim slowly sipped from his stained coffee mug. "He had nothing to lose. He was looking at 25 years to life for killing Gerald Booth. He must have figured it was worth the gamble. Two murders don't give you any extra jail time if the sentences run concurrently."

Scott shook his head. "The arrogant son of a bitch thought he would get away with it. He thought his scheme was so clever that we would never catch him. I knew right from the start there was something wrong."

"What about him being a member of JTF2? That doesn't seem to jive with his actions. You served a hitch with them, didn't you?"

A smirk of a smile crept onto Scott's face. "Can't tell you that. If I did, I would have to kill you." Then, his serious demeanour returned. "Serving with an elite unit doesn't necessarily make you one of the good guys. Everyone leaves a changed person from that experience. Chris found religion. Maybe his time in the unit had some bearing on that. You see and do things that most people never see or do. The effects don't always become immediately apparent as soon as you get out.

"And wearing the same shoulder flash doesn't necessarily make you buddies for life. Some of those guys become pretty cocky about their abilities. Chris seems to be one of them. I didn't care for those clowns then, and I sure as hell don't care for them in civilian life. This is just one more reason to put him away for the rest of his life."

"Well, we haven't nailed him yet. We only have the word of those three boys. They are not exactly what you would call model citizens of Raymond's River. I think most everybody was glad to see them head out west." Jim paused. "Except for their mothers, of course. They're cocky. They're arrogant. Leon Goldstein will make mincemeat of them on the stand."

Scott suddenly stood up. He slapped his fist into the palm of his other hand. "Ritchey admitted to owning an M1 rifle just like the killer used. Bragged about how well he could use it. Did you ever check to see if he actually turned it in for destruction?"

Jim shook his head. "Didn't feel the need at the time. He wasn't even being remotely considered as a suspect."

Jim stood and grabbed his coat from the hook in the nearby corner of the room. "Now I think we do. I'll call records and get them looking. You find the paperwork on that last search warrant we filled out. Change the date and refile. Then, we're going for a ride in the country."

Both men hustled from the office to carry out their respective tasks.

An hour later, they were standing on the doorstep of Chris Ritchey's farm house. The fact that the intended subject of the search was already in jail for another murder greased the wheels with this warrant application.

Linda Ritchey was shaking her head. She vaguely remembered the rifle they were describing, the short one, but she hadn't seen it in years. Jim and Scott were welcome to come in and look around the house if they wanted to. Chris had a locked gun case in an upstairs room.

Just then, another police car pulled into the driveway. A friendly barking sound caught their attention. The door opened and a big police dog jumped out. "Hey, Roscoe," Scott said. The dog came bounding up the driveway, pulling his handler behind him. Scott had previously been in the K-9 unit. Roscoe's father, Roscoe I, still lived with Scott. He had been injured in the line of duty and forced into retirement.

"We've had a quiet couple of days," the dog handler, Eric Parks, said. "Roscoe is anxious to get to work. I understand we're looking for another rifle." He looked around the familiar property. "That shed proved productive the last time. Let's start there."

"Good idea," Jim said. "Scott, you go with them; I'll check the gun case inside."

Scott nodded and set out after Roscoe. The dog sniffed unsuccessfully around the shed. He then headed for the barn. A few late-season calves were chained in the walkway. They skittered to one side to avoid the dog. The older cows turned their big, brown eyes on

Roscoe and let out a low, mooing sound. Roscoe was indifferent to all these animals. He was searching for metal and oil combined together. The smell was imprinted on his brain.

Scott opened the door leading to the haymow. Roscoe lowered his head and shot through the door. He ran the full length of the room and then he abruptly sat down and gave two sharp barks.

"That's it," Eric said. "He's found something."

"Oh shit," Scott said. "There go my sinuses if I have to go pawing through all that hay."

"Not with Roscoe," the handler said. "The rifle should be no more than a couple of feet away from him." He kicked at the loose hay on the floor, raising a cloud of dust.

Scott involuntarily sneezed. He pulled a small packet of Kleenex from his pocket and struggled to get one free from the wrappings. His nose ran visibly, forming a drip. He blew into the tissue, completely soaking it. Now, his eyes had turned red and were watering.

"I can conduct this search on my own if you want to wait outside." Eric gave Scott a sympathetic look.

Scott pulled another tissue from the packet. "I'm okay. I just want to catch this bastard."

He reached down and nuzzled Roscoe's head. "Where's the gun, fella? Show us the gun."

Roscoe barked and scratched at the floor in front of him.

"The shed contained a false floor, as I recall." The handler got down on his hands and knees and moved an armload of hay aside. The floor boards looked solid and extended for several feet away from the wall."

"There could be another opening underneath," Scott said. He braced his hand against the wall and leaned down for a closer look. The wall board tipped, almost dumping him onto the floor.

Eric grabbed Scott's arm and kept him from falling.

"Good work, Corporal. I think you've found it."

Roscoe let out a couple of enthusiastic barks.

Both men moved closer to the pivoting board. The barn had six-inch studs forming the walls. This four-foot section of board moved in to allow something to be placed in the hollow created in that space beside it.

Eric's hand disappeared into the darkness and then reappeared with a green leather gun case. He struggled to get it through the small angular opening.

"This what you're looking for, Corporal?"

Scott smiled. He gave the dog an affectionate pat on the head. "Nice work, Roscoe. Another criminal is about to bite the dust." With that he let out another sneeze. "Our work is done. Let's get out of this barn."

Jim was coming down the steps of the house when the two men and dog popped back out into the sunlight. He immediately spotted the rifle case. The disappointed look that had been occupying his face disappeared.

"I can tell by the length of the case that that is what we came looking for."

Scott gave the rifle a shake in the air. "All we need are a couple of tests and we've got ourselves a killer. Guns are a weakness with the man. He can't bring himself to throw them away even after they've served their purpose."

By now Jim and Scott were face to face. Jim looked into Scott's eyes. They were red and watery. Jim pulled a handkerchief from his pocket. "I knew you wanted to solve this case, but I didn't think you would get this emotional about it."

Scott took a wipe at his eyes with the back of his hand. "Damned hay fever. One more reason that I'll be glad to see the end of this case. Let's go make the arrest and get this over with. From now on, I only go after urban criminals."

Jim laughed. "No rush on this one. Our suspect is not going anywhere. We'll have to get him out of jail so we can put him back in."

Now Scott smiled. "Let's do it."

CHAPTER 56

JIM MCDONALD STOOD looking through the two-way glass at Chris Ritchey. Leaning against the wall in front of him was the rifle found in the Ritchey barn. Ritchey sat passively in the hard, wooden chair. There was a look of serenity on his face. Why not? He had gotten away with one murder and was going to serve an extremely reduced sentence for a second. Or so Chris thought.

Jim turned to Scott Bowen, standing beside him. "Look at the bastard. Butter wouldn't melt in his mouth. He thinks he has the world by the balls."

"You know what I sa–"

Jim held up a hand. "I know. I know. You never liked the look of the guy. Full points for intuition. You're a natural detective."

"We've been waiting for 20 minutes for Goldstein. Should we go in and chat with Chris while we're waiting for the lawyer to arrive? You know how Chris likes to talk once we get him started."

"No way," Jim said, shaking his head. "We had all the evidence we needed to close this case except for one thing: the actual killer. We're not going to rush into it now. I want Goldstein in that room when we lay this out to Chris. I want someone looking out for Chris's rights." Jim slowly turned to face Scott again. "Because this time, he's going down for 25 years or more. There'll be no more plea-bargaining."

"Do you think Goldstein will resurrect the insanity plea?"

"Not a chance. Cliff Lawrence's death was meticulously planned. The guy may be nuts. Hell, he is nuts, but not in the eyes of the law."

"There's no link between the two men that we could find. No link between Chris and Kevin Barnhill, either. What would possess him to go to all that trouble to kill someone?"

"Maybe he'll tell us. As you said, once we get him talking, it's hard to shut him up again. I intend to get him talking."

Just then, the door to the room opened behind them. Leon Goldstein stepped in. "What's going on now? Chris has already confessed to murder. The deal is in place. What more do you want?"

Scott was the first to speak. "Are we cutting into your busy schedule, Mr. Goldstein. These pro bono cases are a real bitch when they just won't go away."

"I don't begrudge my time to Chris Ritchey. It's you who is wasting my time with trivialities. What is it now?"

Jim took one last glance through the glass at Chris Ritchey. He then started towards the door. He paused in front of Goldstein.

"Oh, Mr. Goldstein, you're going to enjoy this. Let's go inside."

"Not until I know what this is about. I may want to talk to my client alone."

Jim reached out and double tapped the lawyer on the chest with two extended fingers. "Murder, Mr. Goldstein. Murder."

Jim did not wait for a reaction. He opened the door and walked into the interview room. He was not going to enjoy this as much as Scott. The corporal had been at odds with the two men from the opening gun. This was the vindication of Scott's gut instincts. But Jim would enjoy it. He was curious, however. He wanted to know what Chris Ritchey's motives were.

Whatever Chris was thinking would not change anything about his guilt. Knowing might help Jim in another case. Every case was different, but only to a point. At some stage the motives all came from the same pool: pride, lust, envy, anger or covetousness. Five of the seven deadly sins. Who knows, maybe even gluttony and sloth worked their way in as well. Which one would this be?

Chris stood up. A look of genuine peace enveloped his face. "Thank you, Sergeant, for getting me out of my cell for awhile. Jail is a good place to meditate and read my Bible, but it is nice to get out every so often." He offered his hand.

Jim couldn't tell if the smile was sincere or if Chris was being a smart ass. He no longer trusted his instincts around the man. He did know that he wasn't going to shake hands with a double murderer.

Leon Goldstein was still spitting and sputtering as Corporal Bowen crowded him into the interview room. "In the name of God, Chris, what have you done now?"

Chris gave the lawyer a blank stare. "Why are you here?"

Before Goldstein could answer, the sergeant stepped forward. "Chris Ritchey, you are under arrest for the murder of Clifford Lawrence. You have the right to remain silent. If you give…"

"What are you talking about?" Leon Goldstein's face was so red, it looked like he might burst a blood vessel. "You had given that death up as an accident. Chris is the one who tipped you off to the fact that it was a murder."

Jim faced the lawyer. "Are you waiving the reading of Mr. Ritchey's rights and declaring yourself as his legal representative? If so, sign here." He pushed a piece of paper into Goldstein's hands.

Goldstein turned towards Scott Bowen. "This is some kind of a sick joke, isn't it? Well, let me tell you it's not funny."

"You're damn right it's not funny." Scott leaned down and into the lawyer's face. "Murder is never funny."

Jim turned back to Chris. The muscles of Chris's face had slackened like a battery draining of its charge. He let himself plop back into his chair.

"I don't know what you're talking about. I don't even know Cliff Lawrence." The words were of denial but the body language screamed of his guilt.

"More lies," Scott said. "You call yourself a Christian, but every time you open your mouth it's to tell more lies."

"I'm not lying. I don't know Cliff Lawrence." As usual, Scott managed to bring out more life in Chris's responses.

"And you never will," Jim said. "You killed him in cold blood." He turned towards the two-way glass and made a hand signal. Seconds later the interview room door opened and a uniformed policeman appeared with the murder weapon in his hands.

"Does this look familiar? We found it in your barn."

Chris's face ebbed of colour. His eyes opened wide as he stared at the rifle in the policeman's hands. "Why would someone's rifle be in my barn?"

"Not someone's rifle," Scott said. "Your rifle. You wiped the gun clean of fingerprints but you forgot to clean up the case. Perfect thumb print on the zipper tab; each finger tip, as clear as the fingerprint card itself, on the handle. What did you think was in the case you were hiding in the haymow, a really skinny fiddle?" Sarcasm dripped from every word of the last question.

Chris's eyes flashed back to life as his mind sought a retort to the question. None came. The lights in his eyes then flickered out. His head dropped.

"How did you know?" The words were barely audible.

Silence enveloped the room.

"Everything was perfect. How did you know to look for the rifle?" A little more volume.

Chris's eyes went from one policeman to the other searching for answers. Then he lowered his head to the table and started to cry.

Goldstein tried to push Scott out of the way so he could get around the table. Scott stood back and let him go.

"That was not a confession," the lawyer said. "That was not a confession."

He fell into the chair beside his client. "I want to talk to Chris alone." He was trying to get a grasp on the situation. "Please, get out and let me talk to Chris alone."

Jim started towards the door. He gave Scott a little jerk of his head. Scott smiled. "Sounded like a confession to me," he said and followed Jim through the door.

CHAPTER 57

J IM TAPPED LIGHTLY on the interview room door before letting himself in. "Time's up. We want to talk to your client."

"He has nothing to say. He's invoking his right to remain silent."

"No problem. His rights only extend to his not talking. They don't cover his not listening and I have some things to say."

Scott eased into the room behind the sergeant. He carried a tray with four cups of coffee, some packets of sugar and a couple of coffee creamers. "Might as well get comfortable."

The two policemen sat on the opposite side of the table from the lawyer and client. Jim took one of the coffees and took a sip. "This stuff isn't the best coffee in the world, but it gets a heck of a lot worse when it's cold." He made a serving gesture towards the two men.

"I don't drink coffee," Chris said. "My religion frowns on it."

"What can we get you? Tea? Water? Fruit juice?" Jim looked back towards the door. A minute later, the same uniformed policeman who arrived earlier with the rifle brought in a can of orange juice.

"It's interesting that you mention your religion," Jim said. "What number commandment is it, Scott?"

"The ninth?"

This was obviously orchestrated while they were outside the room waiting for Goldstein to finish talking with his client.

"Right. The ninth. 'Thou shalt not bear false witness against thy neighbour.' Is that the translation your religion uses?"

Chris looked up, surprised at the tactic the cops had chosen.

"Or do you use the New English Bible? It puts it more to the point. 'You shall not give false evidence against your neighbour.' Those words leave no room for interpretation, Chris. If you are giving false evidence, you are breaking one of the tenets of your religion. Kevin

Barnhill might think he has been the victim of you breaking this commandment."

Chris started to make a reply, then remained silent.

There was another knock on the door. Scott got up and answered it. Pastor Dave stepped into the room. Scott brought in another chair.

Chris jumped up. His entire body lost all its rigidity. "Pastor Dave? Oh God, what have I done?"

Goldstein pulled Chris back into his chair before he collapsed. "Chris. Don't say anything." He looked over at the policemen. "This interview is over."

"No," Jim said. "It's not. We are not asking your client any questions. Chris can sit there as quietly as he wants. We are merely letting him know what kind of a hole he has dug for himself. Chris can decide if Pastor Dave stays or leaves. You, Mr. Goldstein, can give Chris legal advice. The good pastor is here to look after Chris's immortal soul. We feel this may be more important to Chris at the moment."

"Chris, these men are saying you did terrible things." Pastor Dave reached out and took Chris's hand. "I had to come and hear it for myself. I can't believe it's true."

"No, no gentlemen. That's a nice try. Invite the lawyer to sit in while a priest browbeats a confession out of my client. I'm not going to allow this charade either. Pastor Dave, I want you to leave."

Chris looked over at his lawyer. "Shut up, Mr. Goldstein. It's over. I want to confess."

Goldstein started to protest but Pastor Dave stopped him. "Leon, sometimes we have to let nature take its course. Let's save the fight for the sentencing hearing." He turned to Chris. "Tell me son, why did you do it?"

Chris's whole body was sagging into his chair like a Raggedy Ann doll. His face had lost all its features. Tears were welling in the bottoms of his eyes.

Goldstein was not giving up. "If you want to take a confession, do it in private. Confessions are between a man and his God. The priest only acts as an intermediary. He has to respect the confidentiality."

"Not in our church, Leon. You know we don't do that. We declare our sins in front of the entire congregation. Praise Jesus." He turned back to Chris. "Speak son. Bare your soul."

"I did it for you," Chris said. "For you and your church."

Now it was Pastor Dave's turn to be taken aback. Despite his effort to remain neutral, shock registered on his face.

"Here we go again," said Scott. "Voices in my head told me to do it for the glory of God."

Chris perked up again. A new intensity came into his eyes. He looked at Jim. "Does he have to be here?" He jerked his thumb in Scott's direction.

Jim sat silent for a few seconds. There was a natural animosity between the two men. Would this work in his favour or work against a full confession? "No," he said. "Please leave, Corporal."

Scott gave Jim a critical look. He slid back his chair and stood up. "Gladly. I don't want to listen to any more of this crap anyway."

But that turned out not to be true. He left the interview room and immediately went into an adjoining room where the Crown prosecutor sat staring through a one-way window.

"Good to have some company," the Crown said.

"Good to get out here where I don't have to pretend to be interested in every golden mot that pours from that lying mouth. We've got him cold. A confession is just a bonus."

The Crown nodded. "But surely you're curious as to what motivated him to kill Cliff Lawrence? I can hardly wait to hear what he says."

"Not really," Scott said as he leaned in closer to the window. His actions belied his words.

Back in the interview room, Pastor Dave was struggling to get himself back in control. "I don't understand that, Chris. How could you ever think that murdering a man would be something I would want? I don't even know who Cliff Lawrence is."

"No, that was a mistake. Cliff Lawrence was not the intended target. It was Kevin Barnhill. I don't know what went wrong."

Pastor Dave sighed. He gave his head a "not again" shake and thoughtfully stroked his chin. "That name is vaguely familiar, but I don't remember from where."

"He's the crook that cheated Derrick Watts out of his forest property in Hardwood Lands. The property Derrick was trying to buy back to donate to the church as a retreat. Don't you remember?"

Recognition flashed in the pastor's eyes. "Derrick did mention owning a cabin that would serve as a perfect retreat. He lost it in a card game during his other life. Losing that piece of property helped him to realize what a waste his life was becoming. It helped to lead him to the path of taking Jesus as his saviour. He has his lawyer looking into reacquiring the property."

"I know but Barnhill wouldn't sell."

"Negotiations take time. Why did you think shooting Barnhill would make any difference?"

"Because his wife would sell. You know Victor Boyd? He's a friend of Kevin Barnhill's."

"Yes, I know Victor. He's a new member of the congregation. He's still learning the ways of the Lord."

"You might like to think so, Pastor. I think he's just mining the faithful for real estate leads. A lot of the congregation are selling off their big houses and moving into small accommodations so they can donate more money to the church. Victor Boyd has brokered a lot of those sales. I've tried to get him to spend more time studying the Bible, but to no avail."

"I'm sure you're wrong. Victor is working at becoming a true believer." Pastor Dave shrugged his shoulders. "And even if he isn't, he's donating a tenth of all those commissions back to the church, a sizable donation each month. What has Victor got to do with anything?"

"Victor had heard that Kevin's wife never set foot on the property after the first weekend there. She hated it. Victor believed she would sell it in a heartbeat.

"He also told me that he and Barnhill were going to be hunting at the cabin for two or three days. Barnhill, Cliff Lawrence and their contractor had done it every year since Barnhill stole the cabin away from Derrick. They always went during the second week of November. This year, Victor was invited to join them. I tried to talk him out of it. I told him that killing innocent animals was not God's way. Victor had laughed at me and told me that God's animals were probably safe. In the three years since they had been going there, only one deer had been killed. That was by Kevin Barnhill the previous year.

"When I mentioned that to Derrick Watts, he became very upset. Told me all about the blind where he used to always get his deer every season. Now, he told me, Kevin Barnhill would be sitting in that tree. Kevin Barnhill would be trying to snuff out the life of one of God's four-legged creatures from a contraption that Derrick had built. He felt bad.

"It was then that I saw the light. I could see this as a way for the church to gain possession of the cabin and punish a sinner at the same time. The Lord was showing me what had to be done. He had given me a talent. I wouldn't hide that talent under a stone. I would assist Derrick in regaining his building and donating it to the service of the Lord. God was sending all this information my way. There had to be a reason for that."

"Oh Chris, Chris, Chris. You poor, deluded man. Jesus teaches us to love one another, not to kill one another. If you thought God was giving you directions, you should have discussed it with me. That's why I am here. To help you understand God's teachings."

"But everything was falling into place. With God's help, I pulled off the perfect crime."

"Chris. You murdered the wrong man. Would God allow you to do that?"

Jim Mcdonald and Leon Goldstein were going from face to face like spectators at a tennis match. Now they both waited for Chris to return the serve Pastor Dave had delivered him. For a minute, it looked as if it had been an ace.

Chris started again slowly. "I was confused about that at first. Then I realized the real purpose God had for me. I was to put the adulterer Ralph Foley to death just like it says in the Bible. Your Bible. In Leviticus it instructs us. '*And the man that committeth adultery with another man's wife, even he that committeth adultery with his neighbour's wife, the adulterer and the adulteress shall surely be put to death.*' That was God's will. This first death was only a warm-up to make sure I was worthy of the task. It was to help me prepare the way."

Leon Goldstein raised a hand to object to the turn of direction. Then he waved his protest away. To Jim it appeared that Goldstein had given up on the case. "Not in a million years could you get an insanity plea out of this," Jim said. "There was too much advanced planning and deception to even suggest he didn't know what he was doing was wrong. Way too much."

Pastor Dave ignored this by-play. "Chris, you poor misguided fool. Not only that, but you killed the wrong man again. Please tell me your plans didn't also include killing your wife."

Jim remembered the black eye that Mrs. Ritchey was sporting. Had she been lucky or was the job incomplete? "When you killed Gerald Booth," Jim said, "you didn't even try to make it look like an accident."

Chris turned on the cop. "That shows what you know. I could have convinced anyone that Ralph Foley died accidentally. It's just that when I saw Gerald lying there, my mind collapsed. I couldn't believe I had failed again. I was a disappointment in God's eyes. He had given me this talent and I had let Him down on two occasions."

"We caught you within hours of the killing. How could you have convinced us it was an accident?" Jim found it hard to reconcile that the two murders were carried out by the same mind.

"I had captured two coyotes alive. I fed them live chickens and then shot them both, twice. One shot just grazed the skin like a near miss. The other was fatal. When you discovered that Ralph Foley had been shot, I, as a concerned neighbour, would be there. I was going to tell you about hearing shooting coming from up the road. You would have found the dead coyotes, assumed someone had shot Ralph accidentally while killing these varmints, and ceased your investigation. If you continued to investigate, you would be searching in the wrong spot. You would never find anything. Simplicity in itself."

Jim shuddered to think how close that plan had come to working. Both he and Scott and he and Robin had discussed the fox in the hen house theory of the murder. The investigation would have continued to find the actual shooter, but when no one turned up, the case would have gone cold. He looked back over his shoulder through the two-way mirror. He bet Scott was sharing his thoughts.

"I still don't understand why you persuaded us to open up the Cliff Lawrence case again. You had gotten away with that."

Chris's face took on a new light. "That was part of the Lord's plan. By giving you that information, Mr. Goldstein, a very capable lawyer and a member of the church, was able to bargain the charge down to manslaughter. We figured I'd probably spend no more than two or three years at most in prison. I would spend the time in Bible study and meditation and when I got out, I would be able to become an ordained minister. I could help Pastor Dave with his duties."

Jim observed a shiver pass over Pastor Dave.

"Well," Jim said, "all I can say is thank God for the way things worked out. By the way, did you and God discuss these things in prayer? Did you reveal exactly how *you* figured everything should work out?"

Chris nodded enthusiastically "Every step of the way."

"There's an old saying," Jim said. "If you want to make God laugh, just tell Him *your* plans. It appears you gave the Lord a real belly buster."

CHAPTER 58

"SORRY, MAN, FOR turfing you out of the interview room."

Sergeant Mcdonald had joined the Crown attorney and Scott Bowen in the adjoining room. Pastor Dave and Leon Goldstein were still talking to Chris Ritchey in the interview room. The intercom was turned off.

"No problem. It was a hell of an idea to bring in Pastor Dave. Despite being a cold-blooded murderer, Chris still thought he was on the side of the angels. Did I say it before that the man was dumb?"

"No, I don't think you did. I think you just said you didn't like him."

"Check the transcripts. At one point, I must have called him a dumb son-of-a-bitch. The man is the most abysmal excuse for a murderer I've ever come up against. Two for two in killing the wrong guy."

Jim glanced through the one-way window. Chris was writing on a yellow legal pad. Pastor Dave was obviously coaching every word. The reputation of his church was also on the line. He had as much at stake here as the police. Leon Goldstein was sitting back in his chair and ignoring the whole procedure. He had washed his hands of anything to do with the confession.

"You're right. No points for execution but you have to admit, his planning was diabolical. He thought God was leading his crusade. I think God was the one who stuck out His foot and tripped Chris up."

The smile danced in Scott's eyes. He gave a dismissive wave of his hand. "Whatever, as the kids say today."

The resolution of the case couldn't have been better for Scott. He had been right all along in his assessments, even though he was as surprised as anyone when Darrin Eisenhauer fingered Chris Ritchey as the killer of Cliff Lawrence. He slapped Jim on the back.

"You playing good cop and Pastor Dave playing divinely good cop left no room for your typical bad cop like me. I was glad to get out of there." He waved his thumb in the direction of the interview room. "And that's what the whole game is about. Getting the bad guys to confess to their evil doing and getting them off the street."

Now Jim was catching Scott's excitement. "Right on, brother. Right on."

"Now the fun begins."

Both men turned towards the Crown attorney. Jim put a hand on his shoulder. "Good luck, pal. You've got your work cut out for you on this one. It should be a cut-and-dried prosecution with the evidence we have given you." The smile disappeared from Jim's face. "I think you're in for more twists and turns than we can imagine. There's no telling what a mind like his will come up with as he bargains in exchange for a guilty plea. He still thinks God is guiding his every move."

The Crown attorney nodded in agreement. "I think you're right, Sergeant. You're more than welcome to testify at the sentencing. It could be interesting."

Jim flipped open his notebook and pretended to check some dates. "Sorry. Can't make it. I'm busy that day. An open murder case. The corporal will be helping me with it."

The two lawmen laughed and headed for the door.

CPSIA information can be obtained at www.ICGtesting.com
Printed in the USA
LVOW091807221111

255972LV00001BA/1/P

9 781426 971372